TRADWIFE

TRADWIFE

A Novel

Michelle Brandon

An Imprint of HarperCollins*Publishers*

 For information, address HarperCollins Publishers, 195 Broadway, New York, NY 10007. In Europe, HarperCollins Publishers, Macken House, 39/40 Mayor Street Upper, Dublin 1, D01 C9W8, Ireland.

HarperCollins books may be purchased for educational, business, or sales promotional use. For information, please email the Special Markets Department at SPsales@harpercollins.com.

hc.com

FIRST EDITION

Interior text design by Diahann Sturge-Campbell

Broken glass illustration © Tartila/Stock.Adobe.com

Library of Congress Cataloging-in-Publication Data has been applied for.

ISBN 978-0-06-347053-8

Printed and bound in the UK using 100% Renewable
Electricity at CPI Group (UK) Ltd

2 CPI 26

MIX
Paper | Supporting responsible forestry
FSC™ C013604

To my husband, who never blinks when I ask very weird questions. Don't worry, babe, it's just for research.

Part One

Smokescreens . . .

Chapter One

There's a body on Crystal Harbor Beach.

But not just anywhere on the beach.

The body lies between the muted beige of the dunes, hidden by thick, lush, green sea grape hedges. Forty feet from where the hushed waves lap against the sand. On the other side of the dunes are beachside homes, cafés and shops that line the inlet road, and beyond that, quaint neighborhoods that surround Echo Lake on three sides.

Above the still form on the sand, early-morning beach walkers cross over the wooden planks of the dune bridge, completely unaware of who lies just a few feet away, shielded by the sea hedges' thick round leaves and twisted trunks.

The sun is starting to rise. Orange slashes bleed into the purple horizon. But the body has been there for hours, first arriving in the dead of night underneath a full moon and star-dotted sky. The body's party shirt is ripped near the collarbone, exposing skin. Golden, toned skin. The linen pants are loose around a trim waist, the belt missing, the top tortoise-shell button undone. There are no shoes on the body, but they might be found on the beach. A pair of black leather sandals. The belt is probably there too. Lying where it was discarded.

If the early beach walkers lean over the wooden rail, and the wind gusts hard enough, they'll catch a glimpse. Toes. Legs. Then the whole thing. They'll squint their eyes, trying to see into the dim light, through the thick vegetation, wanting to decipher if what they see is real or a figment of the imagination. But the plants will hide their bounty.

And no one leans. No one looks. No one suspects.

Why would they? In all the years that have gone by, no one has ever found a body in these dunes. Other dunes, sure, but not here. Not this quiet little beach town where nothing bad ever happens.

Well, nothing bad that anyone knows about.

Secrets and maliciousness have a way of happening just underneath the noses of those who want the world to remain benign.

The body could be there for days. Maybe even consumed and disposed of by nature itself. A few heavy gusts could bury it with sand. A few hungry creatures could take it to the bone. A high tide could wash it out to sea.

The possibilities for the body are endless.

The unmoving lips used to say, *The night is endless, and we make the rules.*

But someone broke the rules.

A black skimmer bird lands on the body's forehead, feet shifting, beak half open, ready to peck. Another black skimmer lands on the chest, the desire to feast great. A squirrel plucks a sea grape, biting into the sweet, slightly acidic fruit as it studies the body, the birds.

But a sound comes from beneath the body. A ringing, musical

tone that sends the birds flying and the squirrel scurrying. A cell phone.

The call goes unanswered.

A ding from the device indicates a message has been received. Voicemail or text, it doesn't matter. There won't be a reply.

The body could lie undiscovered there for hours. Days. Maybe forever.

Except, someone knows the body lies in the dunes. Someone knows because they were there.

The question is, will they tell, or will this be another secret buried in the sand?

Another rule broken . . .

Chapter Two

Ariel

Two months earlier . . .

Chopin's Nocturne in C Sharp Minor filtered through the lavish house's sound system. Tinkled from white speakers in her white ceilings. Stroked its soft musical fingers over creamy shiplap walls, the muted tones of her modern farmhouse aesthetic. White couches. Beige pillows. Coffee table made of reclaimed wood. Stone hearth. Wrought iron accents.

The house was perfect. Orderly. Calm.

Just like her life was supposed to be.

What more could Ariel Olsen, a former Tony Award–winning Broadway star, ask for? A handsome, sexy husband. Five gorgeous children. Hardly a wrinkle on her smooth forehead. Not a single gray on her blond head. A body that turned every eye. A house that overlooked the cerulean Gulf from panoramic sliding paneled-glass doors.

She never imagined she'd come back to this town after leaving at eighteen. Not much had changed, and yet everything had.

The house was still quiet. Upstairs, Shane was in the glass and marble shower, washing the sleep from his eyes, the sex from his body. Morning was the only time they ever had sex. With five little kids, nighttime was out of the question. Exhaustion too deep. But mornings, just before sunrise, when Shane's body was still warm with sleep, not a sound in the house except for the tick of the old grandfather clock, Ariel opened for him. Luxuriated in his strong, muscled body. In the way he could make her soar, almost crest.

This morning, it ended with the cry of a baby down the hall, and her disappointed sigh. She'd been so close. Maybe only a minute longer. Shane finished in two strokes, and then it was over.

Down the hall, she stared too long at her daughter. Nine months old, she reminded Ariel of a ghost—pale in the morning light, her features a whisper of her namesake's. Shane's twin, Tara. Gone, but still here. And every time Ariel looked into those eyes, she felt the weight of the things she hadn't said all those years ago, pressing like fingers at the back of her neck.

Downstairs, with the baby nestled against her, Ariel slipped into her rubber work boots, then pushed outside into the sunrise. Dew slickened her boots as she walked across the lawn toward the chicken coop for her first outdoor chore of the morning. The salty sea air was unusually cool as it filtered off from the ocean, which sprawled in front of the house. Feeding the chickens and gathering the eggs. An uninteresting metaphor for what her life had become.

The gate opened as silent as the morning she was about to shatter with her voice.

Once a Broadway musical star, always, right?

Ariel licked her lips, drew in a deep breath, her throat opening. "Pop. Six. Squish. Uh-uh. Cicero. Lipschitz." She sang out her six chickens' names in the same notes as "Cell Block Tango," which she'd belted out when she'd played Velma in the musical *Chicago*. As she sprinkled seed, she sang. Danced. Performed for the only creatures who'd watch her now, on the only stage she claimed—an earthen, shit-littered wood-shavings platform.

The chickens wriggled forward out of their nest boxes. Rich red, salmon and white feathers fluttering, buttery feet scurrying, claws clicking on wooden planks, beaks pecking at seeds.

The oldest of her hens, Lipschitz, clucked in a way that reminded Ariel of one of the older performers she'd worked with on *Mamma Mia!* The jerky bobble of her head was similar too. With every flutter of Ariel's jazz hands, seed went flying and her chickens gobbled up the offered gifts.

Even with baby Tara secured in a designer carrier to her chest, Ariel managed to execute Fosse's jazz moves, rolling and thrusting her hips, doing a high kick and using the fence around the perimeter of the chicken coop as a makeshift cell block as she dropped down in a hip swivel and stared through the chain link.

For every chore, Ariel chose a song she'd performed onstage, keeping her voice honed, her dance moves sharp. Every line from every musical was still embedded in her mind. *Chicago, Mamma Mia!, Wicked, Les Misérables* . . . The list went on. But this role, of mother, wife, caretaker, oceanside dweller, was the most challenging and the most rewarding.

A giggle sounded from behind her as she shuffled to the right then the left, and she twirled in the rubber boots she'd traded in her character dance shoes for. Four tiny blond heads peered from behind the coop, wiggling their fingers with the same jazzy enthusiasm as their mother.

She pointed at her children and kicked a leg. "They had it coming," she belted out.

"They had it coming all along," her children answered in song, down to tiny Noah, whose words were more garbled baby talk than anything else.

"Who wants breakfast?" Ariel hung up the now-empty chicken feed bucket and wrangled her brood, each child brought into the world each year since the anniversary of the day she and Shane had said "I do."

The house smelled of the fresh puff pastry breakfast rolls that she'd whipped up this morning before dawn. Before she'd woken her husband. Before they'd made love in the warmth of their cotton sheets. Before she'd left unsatisfied.

Puff pastry didn't take as long as sourdough, which was Ariel's true love. There was something about kneading the dough, her fingers sinking into the thick gluten, that reminded her of flesh.

The breakfast pastries were filled with eggs, sausage and cheese and sure to fill the bellies of her babies. They kicked off their boots, and she poured them all the fresh milk she'd milked from her cows while serenading them with "Super Trouper." She put enough milk aside for her protein shake, hoping it would be the energy kick she needed to make her promotional videos today for the goat cheese she was selling.

Shane's shoes thudded on the wooden stairs, and he clapped then rubbed his hands together as he marched into the kitchen, a hungry grin on his face. Hungry for both the breakfast pastry and her, no doubt. Just another thing for her to be grateful for, her husband's insatiable desire. What woman after birthing five kids wouldn't be grateful for that?

He bent to kiss her, the thrill of his lips on hers still just as strong as it had been the second time they'd kissed. The first time had been too swift, too hard, both of them too nervous. A super-adorable story their grandkids might think was funny fifty years from now.

Dressed in a golf polo and stylish linen shorts, his brown hair purposefully tousled, he was ready for the course, where he'd spend most of his day training for the next tournament. She straightened the champion pin on his collar. Shane wanted to be the next Phil Mickelson.

With the kids fed, Shane off to play golf and her mommy's helper—she didn't like to use the word *nanny*—arrived, Ariel slipped up to her bedroom, locking herself in the bathroom. She stared into the mirror at the dark circles beneath her eyes. The blond hair that had once shined in the sunlight but now looked as dull as the fur of a mouse locked behind a wall. Eyes that seemed to lose their sparkle with each passing day. Cheeks that were a little more sunken than the day before. Freckles that had faded as if the sun had taken back its kiss.

The coolness of the metal handle beneath her fingertips was a promise of another mommy's helper. Ariel slid open her makeup drawer, reaching for the back, where she removed a small wooden partition, a false end to the drawer. The orange plastic bottle, as unnatural and false as her cheerful smile, was heavy in her palm.

The lid opened with an audible pop, and she half expected Shane to come charging through the door, demanding to know what the hell she was doing. Except he would say "heck." Cheery yellow pills tumbled into her hands. She counted out three—today felt like a three kind of day—and tossed them back, swallowing them dry.

As dry as she felt on the inside. As lost as she felt in the dream she thought her life would be. Weathering a storm that was not there.

"What do you have to be so miserable about?" she asked the woman staring back at her in the smudge-free mirror. "Your life is perfect."

But the woman in the mirror didn't answer.

Chapter Three

Miranda

Anyone who claims to love cleaning toilets is a lying motherfucker.

Miranda Peterson slammed the porcelain toilet lid down and flung the scrubbing brush back into the white apparatus that held it, watching and daring it to fall over like it did half the time, which only meant more mess to clean.

She wasn't a damned maid.

And yet, in Crystal Harbor, a wife who didn't keep house, didn't present the most perfect, pristine, white and glossy home, probably didn't love her husband and was definitely a sinner. And had a messy house.

Frustrated, she ripped off her rubber cleaning gloves and tossed them under the bathroom sink. Then, imagining Benjamin's face at seeing them there, her future self castigating her past self, she wrenched open the cabinet and folded them neatly into the bathroom cleaning organization bin.

The three-carat marquise diamond on her wedding band winked at her as if it were reminding her why she was here, what she'd vowed to do. She straightened the gold and diamond watch on her wrist to cover the small burn underneath, courtesy of an ironing mishap.

Benjamin was taking care of her. They were rich. They had the biggest house on this side of Echo Lake. When she opened her front door, there was the Gulf just across Ocean Boulevard. From the back, the lake and the tiny cottages that dotted its opposite side, the pier and the old boathouse at the far end.

Benjamin said she'd never have to work another day in her life.

What the fuck did he think this was, then?

Ben's irritating little dog yipped at her. Miranda rolled her eyes and opened the slider, letting the filthy mutt out into the yard, hoping that an alligator had scaled the fence so she could be rid of the damn thing.

At one point in her life, Miranda had been all about the rich men. Men who supported her extravagant lifestyle. A little nose and chin job. Breast augmentation. Highlighted hair, manicured fingernails and toenails, tanned, hairless skin. She hardly recognized herself sometimes. Thankfully, no one else did either. Her affinity for rich men meant she had all the right ensembles. The right shoes. The right purse. The best seat at a show. The best seat in a restaurant. The best seat on a plane.

The best for the best.

And she was the best.

But then she'd gone and done the one thing every young hot woman knew was a cardinal sin in that world—she'd agreed to marry the man who'd been putting clothes on her back just as often as he'd been ripping them off.

But a girl had to do what a girl had to do, didn't she?

Worse, she should have hated him. And yet, she felt something that most people would probably describe as love. That was why she'd just cleaned the goddamn toilet in a pink midi wrap dress, hair done, makeup done and Chloé wedges strapped on.

Miranda sighed as she trudged down the stairs like a good tradwife, checking on the butter she'd basically churned this morning—with the help of her stand mixer. Not quite ready for toast, although she'd not had a slice of bread in years.

Mondays were bathroom cleaning days. And thank God she was done. It was her least favorite of all the chore days.

She clicked her long, acrylic nails on the counter, the contrast between the white marble and the hot pink nail polish at least giving some life to their house. Benjamin had said if they were going to live in this community, and if he was going to maintain the respect of people in town, their house had to be demure. Which meant a lot of white and beige. A designer had come in to redecorate. So now their house looked like everyone else's, and Miranda wasn't even sure where to sit. Everything felt like a forbidden room. The type of fancy living room that children entered only on holidays.

Miranda had been trying her best in Crystal Harbor. Bringing Crock-Pots of meatballs to the neighborhood cookouts and wearing dresses to church that didn't show even a hint of cleavage. She'd even joined the neighborhood book club, walking club, mahjong club, cooking club. Most of them were boring. The books were always dull. She didn't know how to play mahjong, so she was always lost. The food tasted like lies. The only club she was in the vicinity of liking was the walking club. Steps were important, and everyone always gossiped; even if they tried to keep their chatter quiet, she heard it all.

Gossip, a sin as their bishop liked to remind them, was one of

Miranda's favorite pastimes. The juicier the better. But despite those four miles, three days a week, she was shrouded in blah.

There was also the little matter of her womb still being empty. Not for lack of trying. Her husband was at least being patient about the shortage of results, but Miranda knew the clock was ticking on that front. And if she failed to provide, then he, too, would fail to provide—for her. At least that's what the prenup she'd signed made pretty clear. Not that she dwelled on it too much. All the talk of babies and wifely duties was boring as fuck.

All the blandness of this tradwife existence was making her start to itch. And at church this past Sunday, Bishop Wilder said that boredom breeds contempt, and anyone who was feeling the idle hands of boredom creep in should shun the hands of the devil and find something they were passionate about and do it with all their might.

Funny, because when she'd looked around, the number of people who appeared uncomfortable edged toward more than half the audience—aka the congregation. Religion had never been her strong suit. Seemed like she wasn't the only person bored out of their mind, though, in this small, idyllic town. The type of town that was painted on a postcard, and when someone visited on vacation they thought, *Oh, how I'd love to live here*, until they actually lived there and felt their soul slowly depart from their body from lack of amusement.

Miranda needed the *fun* to start. Something she loved.

The only problem was, what she loved to do, in addition to gossip, had gotten her into trouble more times than she could count and was definitely considered wicked. Had to be, because thinking about it now in her sunny, bleached kitchen took away the itch and instead made her heart race with need.

With Benjamin at his office for several more hours and Miranda having agreed at the altar to be faithful to her husband—appearances were important—she'd have to scratch this itch herself. No time like the present. Besides, if cleanliness was next to godliness, then she deserved an indulgence.

Miranda raced up the stairs to her bedroom, yanked open her nightstand drawer and pulled out Mr. Pinkie—her favorite vibrator. If she couldn't have sex with her husband, or anyone else, Mr. Pinkie would do just fine.

Chapter Four

Jennifer

The Fifteen Commandments of a Tradwife

> **One:** Thou shalt submit—but make it pretty for the socials. Smile sweetly while handing over your autonomy, but make sure there's a filter and preferably something floral involved. Obedience is cute when it's curated.

Everything is not what it seems. Unless you lean in a little, stare harder; then, more often than not, it's exactly what you seem to think.

Jennifer Davis wished she'd spent more time in her life ripping off layers than she had pretending everything was smooth and flat. More time with her eyes open than making sure surfaces were dust-free, and her kids had sandwiches in the shape of ducks packed in their lunches. More time paying attention than ironing, vacuuming, putting on makeup, memorizing Bible passages. More time in school learning something useful and less time learning exactly the way her husband liked his underwear folded.

More time telling the truth. And less time being the perfect tradwife.

The list of "mores" outweighed everything and tipped the scales of her regrets past equalization.

Instead, here she was coming close to her thirtieth birthday with a bank account near zero, four kids who thought Daddy's house was more fun, no husband, not even the family dog, and the number of friends she could count made up less than one hand. As soon as Jamie had left, most of her so-called friends couldn't look at her.

Because looking at her, hearing what happened, only broke the fantasy of the life they had built around themselves in their insular community. Made the idea of what could happen a reality. Who would want to abandon perfection for sorrow?

This community had a way of burying things no one wanted to talk about.

She missed Snow the most—her sweet and slightly psychotic Jack Russell. Jamie had taken Snow from her, too, saying it would be cruel to make her leave the only home she'd ever known. She'd asked what about their kids and he'd offered to take them, too, which she had protested.

Snow had loved her unconditionally. Everything else in life had come with stipulations.

Perhaps the shittiest thing of all was that she'd loved the restrictions of her marriage. Fresh-pressed juice in her husband's hand at exactly six o'clock. Twelve hours later, dinner on the table at exactly six o'clock. Clean house. Clean kids. Dresses not jeans. Heels not flip-flops. Beds made. Dishes done. Serve her husband. Serve her church. Serve her community. Serve missionaries dinner on Sundays. Always smile for pictures.

Do as she was told and be safe.

And now she didn't have any of those rules, and she felt like she was simply falling through the cracks, like sand swept away on her front porch.

The fan overhead stuttered, and she jerked her gaze up. "Don't die on me now, fucking fan. I need you." Florida heat was no joke, but worse was the humidity. And as she clawed at her blankets in the night, tossing them aside, she wished she could claw Jamie's eyes out. At least she'd bought the cottage by the lake with her divorce settlement, and the sea breeze helped with the heat, but with her limited funds, the AC was kept at 76 degrees at all times.

The fan picked up its pace once more, and Jennifer breathed a sigh of relief. Already her hair was a mess and up in a not-neat-enough bun that Jamie would have frowned at, maybe even yanked out. She was also in shorts and a tank top. In the last year she'd worn more shorts, tanks and flip-flops than she had in a decade. Small acts of rebellion. Begrudgingly she admitted they were way more comfortable. And not having her hair on the back of her neck when she was sweating like a pig left on the beach was heaven.

Hate-scrolling through her phone, she swiped on pic after pic of Jamie and his new slutty wife on an extravagant vacation in Turks and Caicos. Their tanned skin in contrast to the white sandy beaches, and the blue in their eyes matching the ethereal ocean waters. Jennifer had always wanted to go to Turks and Caicos. Had asked for a trip there for her birthday but got a new Dyson vacuum instead. Now *she* was taking *her* vacations.

Bastard.

She instantly felt guilty for her hateful thoughts. But that guilt turned swiftly to anger. How *dare* he?

How much had really changed, though? Jamie was still Jamie. You could slap on a pretty vacation, but that wouldn't change the bag you packed.

The way Jamie had spun it to his friends, their friends, was that he'd met his new fuck stick *after* he asked Jennifer for a divorce. But she didn't believe him. The man had come home from work trips smelling like another woman. There'd even been a red thong in Jamie's bag that he swore he had no idea how it got in there.

When he'd finally dropped the D word, he'd declared it was Jennifer's fault. That she had changed. Jennifer had not been living up to the expectations of their marriage. Jennifer had broken the rules. But it was all bullshit. He'd found someone shinier. Less squishy around the middle.

What she hadn't known about Jamie when they met as teenagers, or perhaps she'd been too blindsided by his I'm-gonna-rock-your-world smile, was that he was a complete narcissist.

Married for ten years, and this was the thanks she got? Barely able to make ends meet, worrying about a stupid fan, while he lavished vacations and diamonds upon his new wife.

Jennifer had been so shocked on her birthday when he'd left her that she'd even agreed to give back her engagement ring. Who did that? How much had he gaslighted her into believing that was okay?

What that diamond could have changed for her now. A new overhead fan. A new life. A new view.

The small cottage she'd purchased on Echo Lake had a perfect view of the back of her old house, which overlooked the lake from the rear. From the front, her old house had bright blue views of the Gulf.

The oceanside houses on Echo Lake were for the rich, blocking the view of the sea from the quaint cottage neighborhood on this side where she lived. But really, it was the lake she could never fully tear her eyes from anyway.

The money from their marriage settlement had not gone far. Between the cost of the cottage and the divorce lawyer, what little was left she kept for a true emergency. Not nearly enough, but Jamie hid his money well. And even now, half the monthly child support he sent her went to paying the kids' private school tuition, a stipulation Jamie had insisted on in the divorce proceedings.

Upstairs, little feet were starting to thud on the floor, indicating her kids would be in the kitchen soon. They'd be *starving*, whining about the generic cereal they were going to have to eat when Stepmommy's meals were much more appetizing, made from scratch in a designer gown.

Bitterness soured her stomach. Jennifer closed her eyes, blew out a breath and reminded herself that none of this was her children's fault. Of course Homewrecker's homemade chocolate cereal tasted better than the off-brand puffs Jennifer could afford. They probably even used fresh milk squeezed from the udders of the Olsen cows. That's what Jennifer used to do too. When they were still friends. Ariel's cow milk had a sweet, buttery taste. But who named cows after characters in *Mamma Mia!*? That was just weird.

Friends all through high school and early adulthood. And then, wham. Ties severed. Though there were some things that could never be severed. Secrets that they kept well hidden.

Jennifer watched several kayakers paddle by as she dumped her Diet Coke down the drain, wondering if she should take up drinking coffee, just as a big FU to her community, who didn't drink caffeinated hot drinks but loaded up on all the soda they could find. Did God really think high-fructose corn syrup and aspartame were better than the antioxidants in coffee and tea? Jennifer wasn't bold enough to question that logic. And some habits were hard to quit—diet soda was one of them. She couldn't even afford to make it a dirty diet soda. What she wouldn't give for a little coconut syrup and thick creamer.

At least the meager amount of child and spousal support left after private school tuition paid for the on-again-off-again leaking roof over their head. And she couldn't begrudge her children an education, nor did she want them to suffer from trying to find new friends like she was trying to do, if she were to take them out of their private school.

"I need a win," she grumbled into the sink as she rinsed down the soda, which had gone flat since she'd brought it home from the diner the day before.

Having only ever worked as a hostess at a local diner in high school, and lacking a college degree, Jennifer had been waitressing at the same place to make ends meet since the divorce. But she could work just during the day when the kids were at school, and the lunch shift never paid as much as the dinner shift.

There wasn't any family she could count on to help with her kids. Most of her friends had abandoned her for the shiny new toy. The couple of acquaintances who still talked to her were willing to help with the occasional car pool, but they were too busy to babysit. And the one time she'd asked Jamie to take the kids so she could work a dinner shift, he'd told her it wasn't his job to babysit the kids.

Babysit.

As if they weren't even his own kids. As if they weren't brought into this world by the two of them. As if he had no responsibilities at all.

As if even with the death of their marriage, he still controlled her every move.

Jennifer gritted her teeth, her once manicured nails biting into the edge of the counter until one broke.

"Shit!" She winced, staring down at the jagged line of blood forming on the top of her nail. Another reason to hate Jamie.

On a whim, and needing to get herself out of the negative death spiral, Jennifer didn't set out the sawdust cereal puffs and nearly expired store-brand milk. With the few slices of bread, including two ends, that were left in the cupboard and a single egg, she made them French toast and hoped they wouldn't notice they were each only getting two-thirds of a crusty slice.

Just as she'd coated the thin egg over the slices of bread, she coated the truth of her misery with a smile as thick and sweet as the syrup she poured on their plates.

Not all truths needed to be ripped open.

For some people, deceiving appearances were a safety net.

There was one deception Jennifer still had up her sleeve. One Jamie knew nothing about. One thing she'd kept for herself. Tucked away in a secret, locked drawer—but she'd only use it if he pushed her too far. Her children deserved to have their father, and she didn't want to be the reason they didn't. Despite the rage she was trying to keep buried deep, each day brought her a little closer to the edge.

Jennifer wasn't going to go quietly into the night. Not yet.

Sometimes she narrated her own life in her head, like she was already telling it to someone else—an invisible audience who'd understand the difference between being bitter and being honest.

Chapter Five

Ariel

I'm fine. Everything's fine.

Ariel stood stiffly in the produce aisle of the grocery store. The refrigerated air smelled faintly of plastic and wax, and a hint of tangy citrus lingered, the scents blurring together like everything else lately. Like the series of abusive Instagram DMs she'd received.

Who gives up a life in theater for shit-covered boots? LOL. Fake bitch.

I tried your recipe for stew, and it was fucking disgusting.

You have a wonderful view of the ocean.

The anonymous messages weren't always so mean. Some could be nice. But the cruel ones always stamped out everything else. And that last one . . . Messages like that always creeped her out. Did they mean from the picture she'd posted, or because they'd seen it? That was a question she wasn't sure she wanted an answer to.

The sounds of ABBA's "Dancing Queen" mocked her over the intercom. The strands of music and happy lyrics laced with the rhythmic *ding-ding* of the cashier's scanner, the rolling squeal of shopping cart wheels, the click of heels on the polished, loathsome linoleum, the crinkle of packages, murmur of voices, a bump of a cart. Her cart.

She glanced down to see that she'd unwittingly wheeled herself right into the apple display. A few of them teetered from their perfect placement, but none of them fell. Thank goodness. That would have been more embarrassing than realizing she was wearing the wrong shoes. Matching shoes, but the wrong ones. Her boots still had a few flecks of mud from her morning chores.

Back in New York, apples had meant autumn festivals and perfect photo ops. Here, they just reminded her of everything she couldn't grow. Apples were her Florida failure. Every bud was eaten by a squirrel—or maybe it was the deer. People from up north were surprised to find out she had squirrel and deer, thinking her move to Florida had placed her squarely in alligator-only territory.

The polished, waxed skin of a Pink Lady caught her attention, and she picked it up, rubbing her thumb over the fake shine. She scraped her nail against the apple, wax displaced. Then her nail pierced the skin, and she stared, mesmerized, as a few droplets of juice beaded in the crevice. Then she bit hard into the apple, juice spilling over her numb lips. What if she ate this entire apple right here without paying? Swallowed every bite and tossed the core into the trash.

"What did that apple do to you?"

Ariel stopped chewing, the pulp lying dormant on her tongue as she glanced up into the smiling face of a woman she would have recognized anywhere.

The mayor's wife was perfectly made up. Blond hair styled, glossy. Ariel had tried to do her hair this morning, but the strands felt limp, so she'd done a French braid in an attempt to show she cared a little. She opened her mouth to speak, but then froze, embarrassed at being caught mutilating grocery fruit, and swallowed hard even though she'd not fully chewed.

If she choked right now, at least that would put her out of the melancholy misery she felt most mornings.

"I'm kidding, hon." Miranda's makeup looked like she'd followed the exact instructions laid out for her in a tutorial. In fact, she might have been the one giving the tutorial.

Ariel only had on lip gloss. Shane preferred an all-natural look, and she liked to keep him happy. Besides, after years of wearing stage makeup, her skin thanked her for being able to breathe.

But more than the hair and makeup, Ariel admired the other woman's dress . . . a dress that looked like it belonged fifty years in the past. Strikingly white with red cherries splashed all over. Ariel's eyes were drawn to where two of the cherries were placed directly over Miranda's hard nipples. Realizing where she was looking, she glanced up sharply into Miranda's lipsticked smile and smoky, knowing eyes. And surprisingly, there was no judgment in her features at the black leggings Ariel wore with a somewhat trendy sweater that she only just now noticed had a yogurt stain in the center. She shuddered. Florida was warm, but their grocery stores were iceboxes.

"If you put that apple back upside down, no one will know you took a bite. I won't tell." Miranda's eye dipped in a conspiratorial wink.

Ariel stared down at the apple, feeling foggy since taking more than she should have of her little "mommy's helpers."

"Oh, no, I couldn't." Ariel snatched a plastic produce bag and put the apple inside, then stared in horror at what she'd done. Plastic? She never used plastic.

"I'm Miranda, by the way," she said, clearly not recognizing that they'd met before. "Are you feeling okay? You're looking a little pale. Want me to get you a coffee or something?"

Miranda's name didn't fit her face, more like a stage name. Ariel squinted her eyes and shook her head. She didn't drink coffee. Any caffeine. But what she wouldn't give for a shot of espresso at that moment.

"Are you sure?"

She wasn't sure at all, but if Shane smelled coffee on her breath . . .

Miranda was staring at her the way Ariel sometimes stared at her toddlers when they were doing things that just weren't right. This was probably why her secret doctor had told her to be careful with the prescription. Not to operate any heavy machinery. She'd thought that meant a forklift, but currently, her brain was feeling pretty heavy, the cogs not working quite right.

Maybe an energy drink. Any one of them would do. Shane didn't like those. Too many chemicals. But sometimes the boost was exactly what Ariel needed to get through the day. Too bad her secret drawer wasn't big enough to hold a few Alani cans.

Mustering up her best stage smile, she flashed her teeth at Miranda. "I'm fine, just tired." And not wanting to get into it, she changed the subject. "We've met before."

Irritation flashed so briefly on Miranda's face, Ariel was certain she imagined it, because then Miranda pressed her hand over her heart, her chin tucking down in what was obviously a staged show of modesty. As an actress, Ariel could always tell when someone was being genuine.

"Oh, have we? As the mayor's wife, I meet so many people." Miranda's voice was as sweet as key lime pie, a little added tang on the end. The subtle show of modesty disappeared and as she stared into Ariel's eyes, there was a confidence there that was unnerving.

"At church." Ariel's smile faltered and she was also struck with the realization that Miranda didn't know who *she* was. In New York, even on TikTok, Ariel's face was recognizable. Once, strangers had stopped her in the street. Now even the people she saw every Sunday barely spared a glance. How odd that this woman she saw every Sunday didn't recognize her at all. Every day she faded a little more, blending into the background like wallpaper no one noticed—a ghost in her own life.

"I'm Ariel." Her fingers tightened on the cart handle, as if that might help her to stand taller, be more visible. Or at least, keep her grounded in this place instead of completely sinking to the floor.

"Nice to meet you, Ariel, again. I'll look for you on Sunday. Oh, wait." Miranda started to dig around in her purse, pulling out a mint. "Try this. Sometimes the spiciness of the mint wakes me up."

Ariel took the mint. "Thank you."

"Anytime."

The cart wheels squeaked as Miranda pushed away, their sound swallowed by the bright, hollow store. Ariel watched Miranda's hips swish, somehow making pushing a cart through the produce aisle look . . . sexy.

A spike of jealousy lanced through her middle. Everything about

Miranda was so . . . perfect. The contrast between the two of them couldn't have been clearer.

Absently, she unwrapped the candy, putting the mint in her mouth, surprised that yes, indeed, she did feel more awake. Something about that instant minty sting sent a jolt to her nervous system. She drew in a deep breath, the cool mint freezing her lungs. The sharp coolness reminded her of the breath mints Shane always had in his mouth when he got home from a client meeting.

Then she stared down at the filmy plastic mint wrapper in her palm. The wrapper was plain. No text. Could have been gotten anywhere. She'd just taken an unmarked candy from a practical stranger—the same thing she'd told her children not to do. Except Miranda wasn't really a stranger. They went to the same church, and her husband was the mayor of Crystal Harbor. She'd watched them, the way Benjamin Peterson looked at his wife, like she was the star of his world. The way he put his hand on the small of her back. The move both intimate and protective. Possessive. The way his wife lowered her eyes, perfectly modest. Demure. A model for all the women in the community.

A woman like that wouldn't give her poisoned candy.

Ariel was being ridiculous.

And Ariel worked hard not to be ridiculous.

There was no room in her life for ridiculousness.

The music coming through the intercom changed to an old Annie Lennox song, "Walking on Broken Glass." Sort of like how Ariel felt every morning, trying to step lightly enough the shards didn't break the skin.

She stared after Miranda, who was pinching avocados and then placing them—*sans plastic*—into her cart. There was something about her . . .

Ariel stared into her own cart, which held only the bitten apple, a bruised head of lettuce and the box of crackers her kids liked. Not nearly enough for dinner. Ariel tuned out the music. If she didn't gather up the ingredients she needed for the pot roast, they'd never eat dinner on time. Shane liked his dinner on the table at exactly five thirty.

And Ariel loved to make Shane happy. She told herself that every day. Even when it meant losing little pieces of herself.

Ariel took the bitten apple out of the bag and finished it right there in the middle of the aisle.

Chapter Six

Miranda

As another child's piercing scream ruined the ambience of ABBA, Miranda reminded herself that this was a life she'd chosen. This was a choice. Her choice. And it would be worth every irritating scream. She had a husband. He was good in bed. This small-town perfect life was exactly what she'd sought.

And though she missed her old life, this one was a hell of a lot better than puking up last night's vodka into some stranger's bathtub, which she had sadly done more than once.

Besides, she was on a mission.

A wife's duty was to provide good nutrition to her husband. Because of this, a trip to the grocery store should be something a wife looked forward to. Miranda was certainly trying—except for the fact that going to the grocery store was probably the saddest part of her day.

She picked up an English cucumber, wrapped in clear plastic, which was odd. As if customers didn't want their long English cucumbers to touch their short, fat American ones.

That's what she said.

Miranda smirked as she studied the two variations, eyeing them with contempt. Humor helped. Humor kept her from screaming. Humor kept her from revealing her true reasons for being here.

"Got plans for that cucumber?"

Miranda's pulse quickened, her stomach tightening, and as she turned to see her neighbor Brad snickering in her direction, she forced herself to retreat back into propriety. His dark brown hair had taper-faded sides, the top left longer, where waves curled with the effortlessness of someone who didn't care—or pretended not to. Timothée Chalamet energy, but more cringe.

"Nothing yet," she quipped.

Brad chuckled, only to have his laugh interrupted by a pair of mini-Chalamet toddler twins in the car cart he was pushing.

"Why Daddy laughing?" one of them asked.

"Nothing, munchkin," Brad said back in a voice so sweet she wondered if it was rehearsed.

"Kennedy working?" Miranda asked, wondering how many times late at night Brad was left lonely. She'd kept her distance, passing him as they went on their runs or brought in the mail. He waved occasionally from his backyard to hers while they grilled meals, and she reluctantly waved back. Brad was the type of man who couldn't be trusted. Did his wife notice the way he looked at other women in town? The way he spoke to them as if making a conspiratorial promise? If there was one thing Miranda was good at besides manipulation, it was reading people. And, well, Brad's actions spoke for themselves.

"A case up north."

"Oh, I didn't realize she traveled."

Brad nodded, handing out granola bars to the twins, who looked like they needed the distraction from arguing over which side of the car cart to sit in. "She's in high demand for defense. And these two are lucky to stay home with Dad."

Miranda raised a brow for a fraction of a second before she caught herself. Brad was every bit the tradwife as the rest of the women in this store. But she hadn't seen him at any of the luncheons, clubs or playdates. Maybe he found them all to be as awkward as she did. Or maybe he'd had his hair tousled one too many times by eager, manicured fingers.

Most of the time, she just felt like she was faking this life.

If they knew the real Miranda, they wouldn't eat her cucumber even if it was topped with salmon and salvation. Well, maybe Brad would.

In any case, if the wives of Crystal Harbor had shunned Brad, she couldn't risk being seen with him out in public. Couldn't risk any attention beyond being the mayor's devoted wife.

"Good to see you, Brad." She tucked the plastic-covered cucumber back in place, keeping the fat one for tonight's salad. She preferred girth over gimmicks. Plastic might make things look pretty, but it didn't fool anyone who knew what they were looking for.

"If you ever—" Brad started but was interrupted by one of his toddlers pinching the other.

Saved by the screech of a munchkin. If she could call it being saved. The sound coming out of the tiny human was decidedly inhuman and she had to resist the urge to stick her fingers in her ears.

Miranda hurried toward the packages of chicken. She was making coq au vin tonight. As she pinched the meat until she found the perfect bird, she watched the other women in the store doing the same thing. Their tight, performative smiles barely covered the way they judged each other's breasts as much as the chicken's. They could size up a woman's breast augmentation faster than they could pick a ripe bird. And God forbid you left with boneless or skinless—that was practically an admission of sexual frustration.

Most of them she recognized. They all went to the same church. Attended Ben's fundraising events. Lived in their neighborhood. But she was close to none of them. And she needed a good friend, not that she'd had one in a really long time. Her friends in New York were fun for a few things, like dancing until dawn. Shopping for the sexiest dress, the spikiest heels. Trying trendy new restaurants and counting the celebrities they saw. But none of them had been close. And in this life she wasn't sure she'd get that either.

Miranda plopped the chicken in her shopping cart and headed toward the register. The scent of artificial vanilla from the bakery aisle wafted past—sweet, fake and trying too hard. Like everything else in this place. As she passed through the store, she spotted Brad staring longingly at a bottle of wine. The rows caught the light from overhead just right, making the wine aisle look almost like stained glass. Confession: stained glass didn't impress her unless it came in a Bordeaux bottle.

Colleen, a woman Miranda recognized—not Brad's wife—sidled up beside Brad, her fingers dancing up his arm in a move too intimate for friends. Thick as thieves. The look in her eyes was both a question and a promise. Was Brad about to have an illicit meetup at the grocery store? Colleen was a mess and a half. Dirty. The secrets those two held . . .

Most people in their little community were teetotalers, sober Brad and Kennedy included. But not Colleen, though she pretended.

Even Benjamin, despite the fact that his favorite drink had been a Manhattan when she met him in New York City. And Miranda made a mean Manhattan, with her own simple syrup recipe and Amarena cherries, not the fake maraschino.

Now, she made him fake Manhattans that mocked her from the glass with their perfectly circular ice cubes rolling around in chilled tea sweetened with the same simple syrup.

Miranda paused by Brad's cart while he was facing away, immersed in whatever Colleen was saying, and handed each of his kids a small bottle of La Marca Prosecco for shits and giggles. Served him right. Then she walked away, unnoticed by Brad or Colleen.

This town needed more excitement. She'd been so patient and quiet. Waiting. But she was going to go completely stir crazy if she had to spend many more of her days cleaning, cooking, pretending to be sweet and then going to church on Sunday—which felt more like a punishment than anything else. Every time she sat in a pew, she was certain that people would see her for who she was. As if God was going to come crashing through the ceiling, a long, bony finger pointed at her while he whisper-screamed *Sinner*.

Then the jig would be up, and everyone would know that Miranda was not the sweet and innocent wife of the town's mayor. That she had sabotaged his first marriage. That his kids hated Miranda. That she used to be someone else. That she used to spend more time on her back, completely intoxicated, than she did on her feet kneading sourdough. That, in fact, she preferred a nice ultra-processed slice of white bread that she could pick up from this very grocery store to the thick, sour, yeasty-tasting bread she baked. Every. Single. Day. She missed the reckless freedom of the past, even if she didn't want to admit that out loud.

Noting how tightly she was holding on to the handle of her cart, Miranda forced herself to ease off the inanimate object and start scanning her items.

She liked the self-checkout lines best. She might be living large in Crystal Harbor, but deep down, in the very heart of her, Miranda was still a girl who had spent plenty of time scanning products for purchase—and if she was going to keep at least one part of herself real, it was going to be this.

Ariel passed by, stopping to watch Miranda scan under the fluorescent lighting that seemed to give everyone's skin a weird tinge. The obviously overmedicated woman was openly curious, or stuck in whatever loop the pills she'd taken had put her in. Miranda knew tranquilized when she saw it. One didn't get into the life she'd led before without seeing it a hundred times. Small towns weren't much different from stages, Miranda supposed. The costumes in Crystal Harbor just involved more sedation and pearls.

Miranda smiled at her as she continued to scan, tucking her items into the reusable bags she brought from home and avoiding the smelly plastic ones. Ariel shook herself out of her stupor and then moved into the checkout line, before backing up and going to the self-checkout scanner behind Miranda.

Interesting. Ariel, whom she'd lied about not recognizing, was an influencer. And now Miranda was influencing her. Or maybe Ariel wasn't as lost as she seemed.

"I've never done this before," Ariel said from behind her, a weird giddiness in her tone. "But I should have, shouldn't I?"

"There's a first time for everything." Miranda grinned, hoping it would calm some of the obvious nerves in the other woman. Guess the special mint hadn't done the trick. Though she did notice the missing apple from the cart.

Another woman spotted Ariel, stopped, stared and then got in the self-checkout line to be next. Like a bunch of robots. Perhaps Miranda was going to start a trend. God help her if they started copying anything else she did, though. There wasn't room in this town for more than one Miranda. Besides, if they did, they'd likely start burning each other at the stake.

And how fucking pathetic that the trend she was starting was checking out their own groceries. My God . . . She needed to focus on why she was here in this small town.

This town noticed everything—even the things you wished it wouldn't. And sometimes, it remembered long after you tried to forget. But Miranda planned to keep them distracted so they didn't look too hard at what lay beneath.

Chapter Seven

Jennifer

The Fifteen Commandments of a Tradwife

Two: Thou shalt not work outside the home (unless it's an Etsy store or TikTok shop selling your handcrafted items). Modern tradwives hustle, too—just never with a 401(k) or dental. A wife's labors are for fun and spiritual growth, not survival.

For the first time in a week at her new job, Jennifer wished she was back at the diner, waiting tables for customers who never tipped.

His wife had been striding up and down the aisles as if she owned the grocery store today. Women like *her*, the one who stole her life, didn't have to serve anyone. In fact, as soon as she'd seen *her*, she'd had to rush to the bathroom to splash cold water on her face. The slightly sulfury scent of Florida water still clung to her skin.

Jennifer knew *her* name, but she refused to use it.

She'd yet to run into *her*, thinking that Jamie had hired a personal shopper for *her*. A personal shopper who would pick out Jennifer's children's apples and bread to be eaten on a table that she had once set every night for dinner. A personal shopper who would deliver the bags of delicious and nutritious food to the house across Echo Lake that should have been hers—its lights shining like they didn't know she was watching.

Jennifer swiped a pack of meat over the scanner, the sharp *beep beep beep* ringing in her ears like an alarm as she moved quicker, as if her hands were trying to escape the one woman she never wanted to face. But she wasn't going anywhere. In fact, the faster she went with this current customer, the closer she was to having a shorter line that might attract *her*.

"Are you all right?"

Jennifer glanced up at the pretty blond woman standing in front of her, recognizing her almost instantly. And not for the reasons most people knew her.

"Ariel?"

The once-famous Broadway star cocked her head to the side, a nostalgic smile on her face that didn't last as long as it took her to make it. Before she'd gone on to make it big in the city, Ariel had been known for her theatrics in Crystal Harbor High School's drama club. Both onstage and offstage. They'd been friends once. But drifted apart after . . . Jennifer shook her head.

"I loved you in *Wicked*."

Jennifer didn't admit to her that it was the first and last Broadway show she'd ever seen. That Jamie had splurged on her twenty-fifth birthday and taken her to New York City. Jennifer hadn't wanted to see Ariel's show. Hadn't wanted to see Ariel. Seeing her brought back too many memories, but Jamie had forced her. It had been a whirlwind trip that ended in tears she'd rather not remember. They'd never even gotten to see Ariel after the show, even though he'd promised her an autograph.

"Thank you." Ariel glanced at the self-checkout line. "Tried and failed over there."

Jennifer nodded. "Machine is always broken anyway." Glanced back toward where she'd seen *her*, but she wasn't there anymore. Furtively, she craned her neck this way and that, stopped scanning to search. Where was she?

Ariel tapped a manicured nail against the machine to plug in her telephone number for membership rewards. Maybe the gesture was carefully designed to pull Jennifer back to the task at hand. Maybe Ariel didn't want to be in Jennifer's presence any more than Jennifer wanted to be in hers.

"Sorry about that. My mind's a maze these days." Jennifer returned to scanning, though her heart had spilled out somewhere down aisle sixteen, the last place she'd seen *her*, pumping out every ounce of blood she had onto the polished linoleum.

"I know the feeling, Jen." Ariel's voice was tired. As tired as Jennifer often felt. Even the beautiful ones got tired. Maybe especially the beautiful ones.

It was only after that Jennifer realized Ariel had referred to her by her high school nickname, even though they hadn't spoken in forever.

"Do you ever still perform?" Jennifer asked, even though she knew the answer.

Ariel smiled broadly, the peel of her lips almost macabre. She looked so mannequin-like that Jennifer nearly felt sorry for her. Until she remembered that Ariel had also shunned her.

"Every day." She issued a laugh that sounded as practiced as one in a play. "Though the only ones giving me a standing ovation are my hungry kids."

Jennifer winced. Ariel didn't know a thing about hunger. Unless she was hungry from self-imposed starvation—which, from the look of her collarbones jutting from the top of her sleek sweater, she probably was.

Ariel noticed her stare and broke eye contact to rummage in her purse.

"Maybe you could perform in town. There's a community theater—"

"No," Ariel said abruptly, startling Jennifer and the young man bagging her groceries. "But maybe one day. My kids need me now."

Jennifer bit her tongue. Her kids needed her, too, which was why she was here at the grocery store, giving a performance of her own. Every swipe of the scanner, every tight smile for customers, every dab of concealer under tired eyes—her costume, her role. Just like all the other women on this stage they called Crystal Harbor, with all their secrets and hidden agendas.

A sharp ring of laughter from somewhere in the store had her glancing up, dropping the scanner she'd been using on a large pack of seltzer water. The sound was familiar, but there was no *new wife* in sight.

"Mack, take over, will you?"

Jennifer didn't wait for her bagger to acknowledge her. All she could do was listen to her trembling body, her mind, which had about thirty thousand warning bells going off, her pulse racing until it roared in her ears. If she had to scan *her* groceries, she would walk out into traffic.

She had everything. The looks, the body, the clothes, the friends, the house, the husband, the kids, the happiness. She'd stolen Jennifer's life.

Well, to be fair, Jamie hadn't been immune, and he wasn't innocent. He'd given *her* everything.

"Jennifer!" the store manager called her name behind her. Shrill. But she couldn't stop. Wouldn't stop.

Getting a job here had been a blessing. Steady hours. An hourly wage. No more wondering if she was going to be stiffed on a tip. They even said after three months they'd give her health insurance. The job that had saved her had become a curse, the aisles closing in on her. No matter what, she'd end up serving the woman who'd stolen her life. There was no escaping that. Funny how quickly a lifeline could turn into a noose. At least at the diner, she'd had the security of knowing Jamie and his new wife would never step foot through the door. They would never be seen in such a low-bar establishment.

Women like that didn't eat at greasy spoons. They didn't drink black coffee from a pot. They didn't eat piles of pancakes or eggs over easy with a side of bacon. Women like *her* probably hadn't eaten bacon in two decades. Hadn't had a slice of pie or a burger with fries.

Women like *her* didn't have to wait on other people. Women like *her* didn't have to serve anyone.

But as soon as she thought that last one, Jennifer knew she was wrong.

Every woman shopping this morning was serving someone. Their husbands. Their children.

Fetching the ingredients for the perfect meal. Out of the house in the perfect dress that would rustle against the cart filled with organic produce. Manicured nails poking grass-fed, grain-free chicken. Styled hair swishing over a satisfied shoulder when they picked out the flour and yeast for their sourdough.

Even the way they looked served others. No one wanted to look at a woman sans makeup in yesterday's workout gear, her greasy hair pulled into a slicked-back ponytail. No one wanted to smile at a woman who didn't present herself to the world in the best light.

Jennifer knew the difference. She'd lived the difference.

Her sneakers squeaked against the waxed floor as she pushed through to the back and hurried into the bathroom *again* to splash water on her face. Her mascara ran down her cheeks from the frenzied scrub, and she winced. The mess spreading as fast as the mess in her life. Just like that, all the careful work of making herself look presentable had melted. It didn't take much these days. One surprise, one memory, one glimpse of the life that should have been hers—and suddenly Jennifer was the mess everyone expected her to be. The mess Jamie told everyone she was. She grabbed for the paper towels, attempting to clean away the mascara smears she'd just created, but they only smudged her cheeks more.

A flush sounded behind her in one of the stalls, and the door opened to a carefully manicured tradwife.

"Oh," she said. "I thought I heard someone out here."

It was a weird thing to say. Too friendly. Why acknowledge the help at all, unless it was to scold?

"You've made a bit of a mess, huh?" And there it was.

Jennifer frowned. A polite person would ignore her messy face.

But not Samantha. A friend who'd become an ex-friend the moment Jamie left.

"I've got some powder." She was rummaging through her tiny

purse, sifting things around as if she might find anything other than her keys in the small space. Miraculously, she pulled out a mini compact, holding it out like an offering. “Here. Use it.”

Jennifer wanted to protest, but really, she couldn’t go back to the register looking like she was strung out. So, she took the makeup, returned to the mirror and fixed her face.

“It’s cutthroat out there, isn’t it?”

“Cutthroat?” Was Samatha fucking with her?

Samantha laughed. “A race to get the best tomato. I sometimes wonder just how far a woman might go for the last jug of kombucha. It’s why I make my own.” She held out her hand, and Jennifer stared at it, not sure what she was supposed to do, then realized she was still holding the compact and gave it back.

“Thank you,” Jennifer muttered, completely confused by Samantha’s kindness.

Samantha laughed. “Don’t let her have your tomato. Or whatever else it was that brought you in here.” She winked and then left the bathroom while Jennifer stared at the closed door in shock. Was it pity? Or just the solidarity of women who knew the fight wasn’t over the tomatoes? Or was she referring to Jamie’s new wife?

“She already has my tomato.” Saying it out loud sounded just as crazy as it did in her mind.

If not for her precious children, she would get the hell out of Crystal Harbor, the only place she’d ever lived. But for the next decade or more, she was going to have to figure out how to live with someone having stolen her tomato. Hell, the whole damn bush . . . vine? Whatever the hell tomatoes grew from. Maybe she should warn other women about the cutthroat lifestyle in the produce aisle. But how?

People had a way of suppressing women when they didn't want them to sound the alarm. Jennifer should know.

With a groan, Jennifer peeked out of the bathroom. No sign of *her*. No sign of *her* anywhere.

Thank heavens for small favors—though favors in Crystal Harbor usually came with strings.

Chapter Eight

Ariel

This is what happiness looks like.

Despite the three Diet Cokes that Ariel had consumed today, exhaustion seeped through her bones in heavy, melodic waves. If she stood still, she would sink—maybe right through the floorboards to the earth beneath her house.

There'd been another anonymous message earlier this evening that spooked her. With a view like that, how could you not share it?

What did that even mean? Did she have a stalker? She'd been looking over her shoulder for what felt like a decade.

To distract herself, she kept moving. Cooking. Cleaning. Mothering.

She was dressed in Shane's favorite female color—a deep maroon—and her skirt swished around her legs as she placed the pot roast on the table, adjusting a sprig of rosemary and wiping a dollop of brown sauce where it had dripped over the side. She straightened the platter. Presentation mattered. In food. In family. In every piece of her life.

The aroma of the meat filtered through the fog of her brain. The potatoes were baked until the skins were perfectly crisp. The green and orange vegetables sautéed to give them just the right crunch before they'd baked in the juice of the meat. The brown sauce savory and fragrant with sage.

All of it looked delicious. Smelled divine. Punctuating perfection with the platter adorned with fresh herbs.

Freshly acquired milk, still warm from the cows who'd not protested their offering, filled her children's cups.

Ice water with sliced lemon for her and Shane. She sat down, staring at the droplets of condensation as they meandered down the sides of the glass.

"Shall we say grace?" Shane nodded toward her. This was always the way. She was the one who offered grace at their table. There were days she wondered why Shane, as the man of the house, the one who should be at the helm of their family's spiritual journey, didn't thank God but handed the task to her. Most days, however, she didn't want to think of the answer.

Ariel pressed her hands into his and the hand of her oldest son, waiting for each of their children to clasp on to each other. Dinner with her family was one of her favorite times of day. To give them sustenance, a meal worthy of them, a meal to nourish their bodies and minds. The very idea that she'd created what would help them grow was a blessing. Proof her sacrifices weren't just burdens—they were seeds.

Ariel gave the blessing, smiling at Shane, who gazed at her as if she might be the Virgin Mary Herself. Of course, she would never say something like that aloud. That was blasphemous—to even consider herself as good as His blessed mother. But Shane's expression was there all the same. Making her feel trapped. No woman on earth could ever compare to, or hope to be as pious and reverent as, the mother of Christ. And Ariel didn't want to be—which was a secret she'd never share.

And she understood the woman. How she would do anything to protect her loved one, even if it meant pushing through the censure of people who didn't believe. Like the people who didn't believe that Ariel should have quit theater. They couldn't understand why she would give up a life they thought was best for her, for a life they thought was beneath her talent. For returning to the town where she grew up, rather than remaining in the one she'd run off to and flourished in.

Truly, though, her accomplishments onstage—her acting—that was for her family, wasn't it? A life lived and learned, experiences she brought into this new era that would help to shape the children she and Shane had created.

Ariel swallowed the bitterness that rose in her throat, the little voice in the back of her head that hissed, *So you say, but you know it was all for you . . .*

"This looks fantastic." Shane clapped his hands, rubbing them together in the way most men did when they were about to dig into a delectable feast. "You've done it again, babe. You never fail to impress me."

Ariel smiled, the same giddy feeling in her chest she'd had when she'd gotten a standing ovation. Only now, the standing ovation was for the meal she'd put on the table. The roast she'd lovingly slathered, getting the spices rubbed into the skin. Massaging the flesh until it was supple.

They ate their dinner, the children sharing stories of their day, and then Shane talking about the golf game he'd had on the course. No one asked Ariel about her day. She swallowed a bite of potato that mirrored the lump in her throat. But that was okay. She didn't really want to share anyway. No one wanted to hear about grocery aisles, apples, guilty feelings or moments she wished she could undo.

The evening routine rolled forward, predictable and steady as always. The sturdiness of a balance beam they all had to cross over safely.

After the table was cleared—with the help of her little ones—and Shane checked on the animals before bed, Ariel bathed her babes, then she, too, jumped into the shower. This time of day was also one of her favorites. The kids asleep, hot water sluicing down her back.

A few moments of uninterrupted peace. Where the past slipped away.

She smiled under the water, eyes closed, washing her face in slow, gentle circles.

Hands slid around her waist. Shane. She'd not even heard him come in. Their shower was a walk-in—no door, massive. When they'd first had it done, she'd joked that they could have a party in here. Shane had been offended, not understanding she was joking. Of course she didn't want a party in the shower.

Ariel opened her eyes, the bathroom fogged with hot steam, and turned in his arms, her face tilted as he bent to kiss her. Shane loved to make love in the shower. Ariel didn't mind. The water was soothing.

He lifted one of her legs around his hip, his fingers skimming over her sensitive parts—all too brief—before he entered her. Her back pressed to the cool tile where the water had yet to warm it.

Arms around his neck. Mouth on his. Leg wrapped tight. He plunged into her, grunting against her mouth with the exertion, his pleasure.

"Was it good for you, baby?" he asked.

Ariel nodded, smiled, pressed her lips to his again, then stepped aside as he lathered soap on himself and washed his hair. They'd talked about having his and hers showerheads installed, but Shane didn't want to take away from the intimacy of only having one. And Ariel had thought that was a good idea—so romantic. Sometimes, though, when she stood to the side, chilled from the loss of warm water, waiting her turn, gooseflesh marring her skin, she thought she might have preferred to have two.

By the time she finished showering, Shane was already asleep, curled up on his side of the bed. The pillows she arranged artfully on their bed each morning were strewn about the floor. Ariel smiled at the mess. But not all smiles meant joy. Her husband was such a . . . silly man. She picked up the pillows, stacking them a little more forcefully on the cushioned bench at the end of their bed than was required.

She stared at Shane for a few minutes. Counted his even breaths, and when she was sure he was sleeping, she slipped away. She paused at the bedroom door, breath held, listening for the shift of Shane's weight. Silence.

Ariel slinked through the quiet, darkened house like a burglar on the prowl. Only she wasn't trying to steal anything other than a few minutes to herself. Carefully, she opened the back door and stepped out under a sky full of stars, the heady scent of gardenias in the garden. There she waited, listening for the sounds of anyone else, for whoever was sending her messages. Sensing she was alone, she made her way to the barn, unlatching the hinges so as not to disturb any of the animals.

Inside, she found her small speaker tucked into a cabinet and pulled it out. Using only the light from a lantern and the music app on her phone, she fired up her playlist of songs and shed the roles of wife, mother. For a moment, she hesitated. Once the music started, it would all fall away.

And she danced. Not for applause. Not for approval. For the girl she used to be. The girl before. Her bare feet slid over the wooden planks of the barn, a piece of stray straw getting stuck between her toes. Hay dust sparkled in the lantern light, like ethereal specks of gold.

She twirled, feeling the tension radiate from the ball of her foot to the arch of her ankle, up through her calf. Her torso stabilized the spin, every muscle working in concert. That familiar ache returned—the strain of holding every part of her body precisely in place. As she leapt, her limbs stretched wide, a slight sting flaring in her inner thighs as her legs hovered parallel to the floor. For a moment, she was weightless. Then gravity reclaimed her. Still, she maintained absolute control, locking her muscles in a chokehold until her body became art—her willpower, the artist.

Ariel spun until sweat dripped down her clean back, and hair stuck to her dampened temples.

This was her twilight performance. The one moment of the day that was hers and hers alone. The only time she let herself fall back into the past. Her body pulling forth memories as her arms elongated, her legs kicked out and she soared through the air. Dancing was almost like flying.

Just like living almost felt like dying.

But maybe, for these few minutes, this was what happiness looked like.

A scraping sound against the side of the barn made her footsteps falter. She stilled in the darkness, listening. Waiting for another sound. A voice. But the world was dangerously quiet, like her.

Chapter Nine

Miranda

Thirty minutes was all she had, and that was plenty of time.

Miranda rushed to her bedroom closet, pulling her shoe rack out of place, and then lifting the loosened floorboard where she kept her small locked box. If Benjamin ever found out about this, he would lose his shit.

Inside, the box was filled with photos from every moment of her life. She sifted through images of herself partying in New York City. A view from Club X, where she'd stood on the interior balcony dancing. It was from that view she'd first seen Benjamin and labeled him her mark. That had felt like serendipity.

That, however, wasn't the photo she really needed to look at. No, the photo she wanted was buried deeper.

The summer of 2013. The summer before senior year. There wasn't really much of anything distinctive about the photo that had circulated social media, which was where she'd found it. The image was dark, the only light coming from the dancing flames on the beach, surrounding a group of teenagers with red Solo cups. She'd made sure to scratch out the faces with an unbent paper clip.

But she didn't need to see their faces to remember. To remind herself of why she was here. She picked up the next photo, downloaded from the same account. The stillness in this one was almost ghostlike. White limbs against a dark, sandy backdrop of the lake's beach. Discarded black sandals.

Her heart stuttered the way it did every time she saw this image. She closed her eyes, remembering the voices. The laughter. The humiliation.

Miranda had thought of nothing all day long except the fact that she needed to shake things up. It was time to move into phase two of being Ben's wife. To gain more control of what she wanted, before she burned this whole facade down.

She could keep pretending everything was fine, but the creeping boredom, the antsy itch, was a cruel master threatening to invade their life.

The sound of the garage opening startled Miranda. How long had she been staring into the distant flames? She shoved the photo back, locked the box and carefully tucked everything back in place. Then she pulled out her sexiest bikini and walked downstairs to tempt her husband for some fun. It never took much to lure Ben.

Twenty-five minutes later, in the hot tub, beneath the moon and stars, their mocktails ignored on the lanai floor, she straddled her husband's hips, her arms resting on his shoulders, her fingers curling in his hair. His damp skin was warm beneath her thighs, the crisp and spicy bergamot scent from his bodywash wrapping around her.

"I want to have a party." She purposefully pushed her breasts closer to his face—the perfect enticement.

"What kind of a party?" He eyed her warily.

In New York, the types of parties they frequented involved liberal liquor-filled libations and bountiful bendy bodies. Those were the best parties. A little tremor started at the base of her skull—the first pulse of restless energy demanding change—one that had been happening more frequently when she thought of her old life, and what her new life had become.

"An innocent one," she answered, knowing that was exactly what Benjamin was hoping for. "I need to make some friends."

This part was partially true. She'd gone to numerous classes, joined several clubs and charity groups, and attended church every Sunday like a good wife, inserting herself into the lives of the women of this town. But those activities were so focused, so regimented. Attending fulfilled a purpose.

Well, that wasn't exactly true. Most of the women who went to all the things Miranda did had been friends for years, since high school even. They'd formed cliques she was trying to infiltrate, but her connection with the others always felt a little off. They had plenty to yammer on about. But they'd yet to include her. They'd grow quiet when she approached, shifting topics to stupid things like how to steep tea and what was on sale at the grocery store. But she always heard.

She often felt shafted—and not in the way she liked. If she didn't carve out her place soon, she'd become invisible, which would ruin everything. Miranda Peterson did not do invisible. Not anymore. She'd fought too hard to matter. To be admired. To be unforgettable.

"All right. I want you to have friends. I want you to be happy here."

Miranda squealed, bouncing on her husband's lap in delight. He liked that, just as much as she liked his answer.

Benjamin could be so generous and often said her happiness was a priority. His words, and his actions, were the reason why she was trying so hard to be the type of wife he wanted.

"Oh, thank you, lover. I'm going to start planning right now." Miranda started to move—she had lists to make, and internet searches to do, and—

Benjamin grabbed her around the hips, a little rougher than she liked, pulling her back into place. "Not so fast."

Miranda schooled her face into sultry siren. Ah, so he wanted a little reward for his agreement. Better a reward for him than a punishment for her.

"We need to establish some rules first," he said.

"Rules?" Her tone was innocent, but her mind was anything but. A thousand deliciously unholy possibilities sprang to mind.

"No alcohol."

"Of course not. I'll make sure there are plenty of mocktails. And water, of course." The same way she always made sure Benjamin's mocktails stayed virginal. Hers were another story.

"Good."

"What other rules?" She swirled her finger over his collarbone to his muscular shoulder. Benjamin wasn't a small man, working out daily in the gym. Working her out daily at night. Most women would consider themselves lucky.

"Classical music."

This one made her laugh. "So, you don't want the town to know what music their mayor really likes?"

"I don't think Rage Against the Machine is exactly mayoral music. And neither is Cardi B." There was a playful edge to his smile, but Miranda knew he was also serious.

Miranda giggled, wriggling against her husband's clearly aroused lap. "I promise. Classical only."

"No bodies."

Now she really laughed; if only he knew. "You think I was going to throw that kind of party? I want you to keep your position as mayor. Though . . ." She danced a finger down his abdomen, gripping his cock to distract him. "If the ladies in Crystal Harbor knew what you are packing below the belt, they might vote you mayor for life."

Benjamin groaned, both of them ignoring the fact that more than one woman in town did know just what they were missing, given he'd grown up there.

"We need this to be a clean party," he gasped as she slid her bathing suit bottom aside and took him in. This part was easy.

The warm water swelled around them like the secrets she kept inside, the faint light of the hot tub illuminating their writhing shadows.

"I'll make it as clean as you want, darlin'," she cooed. "Just as long as when everyone leaves, we're as dirty as I like it."

"Oh God, yes." His fingers dug into her hips, sure to leave a bruise, his head lolling back, eyes closed.

She stared at his exposed neck. At how easily he let himself be vulnerable. It would only take a split second, a hidden blade, and she could slice that neck wide open. "Don't take the Lord's name in vain, baby. I'm going to have to punish you for that."

Ben gritted his teeth. "I'll take any punishment you have."

Miranda grinned, riding her husband until they were both just on the brink of orgasm—and then she stopped. Edging was a specialty of hers, and she used it to her advantage. Taking control when she could. Even if only in this moment.

"Don't stop."

"You said any punishment," she drawled out.

"Anything but that." He lifted his head, then dipped to kiss her collarbone, his teeth biting into her flesh.

Miranda gasped at his warning but also at the power she wielded. The bedroom was the one place he often let her reign supreme. If in the daylight she had to be the perfect wife—the epitome of what was good and right, the icon for all the other ladies of Crystal Harbor to want to be—when the sun went down and the clothes came off, she shed that perfect persona and let her be herself. And one day, Ben would see her for who she really was.

After sating herself and her husband, she climbed from the hot tub, collected their mocktails and made her way into the kitchen to start planning a party that would be both tame and epic at the same time.

"I'm going to shower," Benjamin said. "Then I have a few proposals to go over."

"Perfect. I'll get started on the planning."

The music in the house was blasting, and while Benjamin wasn't looking, she put a little spike into her mocktail from the bottle she kept hidden with the cleaning supplies, ignoring the judging look from the rat dog curled by the back door. If Bennie didn't love the ball of fur so much, Miranda would have tossed her into the lake.

The liquor burned sweet and sharp as it hit her tongue. A little fire to light up the dull, dutiful life she wore by day. Freedom in a glass. Lord, whoever thought a mocktail was good had to be drinking something else. Whoever would enjoy such a thing had to be insane.

She danced around the kitchen in her partially wet bikini, chugging one shot, then two, before she got down to the real business of planning: a caterer, a string trio. Screw recorded classical when she could have live music. If this party was going to get the attention of people, she needed to make it awesome. Invite everyone.

And then when they were here, she'd chat up those she knew were worth inviting back for another party—the one she didn't want to ask Benjamin about yet. One that would be a little more fun. That party—the one where the real connections happened—would be invitation-only by a precise list she already had in her head. Real connections—the kind Crystal Harbor's pearl-clutchers would never dare speak of. Not the kind of connections forged over tea and charity luncheons. The kind whispered about behind closed doors.

The kind of party where Miranda got what she came for.

As her husband liked to say, first you do the work, and then you get to play.

The tremor at the base of her skull subsided.

That was a saying Miranda was fully embracing. She was going to work this party like no other, and then she would get her ultimate reward. Years of careful planning, and everything falling perfectly into place.

If she had to go to the grocery store one more time and face the endless lines of Stepford Wives, she might just start knocking shit off the shelves and throwing groceries at people to wake them up. It'd be the most excitement the organic produce aisle had seen in years.

There was only so much one person could contain.

Miranda liked to party.

Miranda liked to have fun.

Miranda wanted to be the life of the party. And the lifestyle she was currently living? Completely stifling.

Miranda also wanted retribution. And she wasn't going to let go of that.

Tomorrow she'd go into town to pick up the invitations she'd ordered and then have Benjamin's secretary pre-address all the envelopes. In two weeks, she was having a party. And in two weeks, maybe she'd be able to start breathing again.

After finishing with her list and research, she hand-washed her not-so-mocktail glass and then swished with her secret stash of mouthwash beneath the kitchen sink. It wasn't like Benjamin would ever look there. And he didn't know she still took a nip or two. In Crystal Harbor, even rebellion had to be rehearsed. Secrets tasted better than any mocktail anyway.

After all, appearances were meant to be deceiving, weren't they? Just like the best performances always were.

Chapter Ten

Jennifer

The Fifteen Commandments of a Tradwife

Three: Remember the kitchen and keep it holy. A true tradwife hand-rolls sourdough, jars jam and churns butter . . . all while looking like a 1950s pinup girl. Anything out of a box is blasphemy.

At the end of her shift, Jennifer—bone-tired, her feet aching—tugged her purse over her shoulder and walked out of the grocery store toward the parking lot. Today she was going by the Crystal Harbor Humane Society to get a dog. She'd decided to surprise the kids, but really, she'd missed having a dog at home.

She'd parked all the way in the back, because one: steps, and she still wanted to maintain her health, and two: because the manager said the front parking spots were for customers only.

The sun had set over Crystal Harbor, meaning it was yet another day she hadn't gotten any vitamin D, and by the end of the year, she was likely to look a bit like a vampire.

I'm doing fine. I'm better off now than ever. Even her own lies were starting to sound like strangers' voices in her head.

Parked next to her old minivan—which made her sad every time she looked at it, considering she'd always driven an Escalade around town—was a luxury SUV. A Range Rover. The brake lights were pressed, the red glowing against the asphalt. But the car wasn't moving, and the reverse lights weren't on.

Music blared from the vehicle, and Jennifer was sure she was about to interrupt a sundown teenage make-out session, only to see—rounding her own driver's side—that there was a single woman inside, sobbing over the steering wheel, slapping the circular leather as if she were trying to teach it a lesson.

On instinct, she wanted to knock on the window, as if there was anything she could do for someone mid-breakdown. But she'd been in that situation not too long ago. Someone had once asked her if she needed help when she was having a meltdown in the car. And she'd never forget that. Sometimes, the only way to cry and rage was in a grocery store parking lot. And who was she to judge?

Jennifer stuck her key in the lock of her car—this old beater didn't come with automatic locks—and turned, the key clicking in time with another slap on the wheel and then another piercing scream.

Eyebrows marching up her forehead, Jennifer stared into the luxury car, making awkward eye contact with Colleen Christensen, noting her smeared mascara and a spilled purse on the passenger seat.

They'd avoided each other since the summer before senior year after . . .

Fuck.

Colleen rolled down her window, the music quieting, but the echoes of her scream still pierced Jennifer's ears.

"I'm sorry you had to see that." Colleen smoothed her hair behind her ears, giving a long, slow blink.

"We all need a minute to ourselves sometimes." Jennifer shrugged as if the steering wheel beating she'd just witnessed was totally normal.

Colleen let out a sharp snort, eyes flashing in Jennifer's direction. "Exactly, so I'd appreciate you not staring."

Jennifer wanted to snap back and say Colleen didn't have to roll down her window and engage. She wanted to say *If you don't want people staring, then don't come to a public place to throw your tantrum.* But she didn't say any of those things. It wouldn't be the first time she'd covered something up for Colleen.

"Are you okay? Do you need me to . . . call someone? Zach, maybe?" Jennifer said instead. Because she decided she needed to pay it forward. To be kind to others in hopes that someone would be kind to her. In hopes that it would erase the guilt she'd carried for over a decade. There was a saying about what you put out into the world, you get back tenfold, and she'd gotten quite the dicking-over with Jamie, and she had an idea of what she'd done to deserve that.

Colleen frowned. "Obviously, I'm not okay. Normal people don't just scream at their cars."

Jennifer cocked her head, contemplating just how to reply. "No need to be salty. Just trying to help. Besides, I think more normal people have than you think."

Colleen rolled her eyes. "Who would you even call?"

Professional help. "Whoever you wanted me to?"

Colleen groaned, scoffing like Jennifer had just said something incredibly offensive.

"Well, there is no one to call. I've got six kids at home waiting for me and a husband who expected dinner on the table hours ago," she seethed, white-knuckling the poor steering wheel. "I ran out of pills. I want a drink. But I can't have a drink. It's forbidden. Alcohol has been canceled. And I'm going to hell for even wanting to have a fucking drink in the first place."

Jennifer's heart skittered behind her ribs. She listened, didn't comment, didn't judge. Colleen was willing to tell someone she hadn't spoken to in over a decade about her private business. She obviously needed to vent a little bit.

"You have kids, don't you?" The question came out more like an accusation.

Jennifer nodded. "Four, actually."

"And you're here without them." Colleen's lip curled, and there was so much more behind her statement: an accusation. As if Jennifer were a bad mother for being at the store without them, even though this bitch's car was also empty of her spawn.

They were at their dad's. Not that it was any of this woman's business. And what she wouldn't give to offer the excuse of needing to run so she could go home and make them something for dinner, do the whole nightly bath-time routine, inhale that sweet baby-shampoo scent while reading not three but four stories before bed so they all felt like they'd gotten equal treatment.

"And you haven't made dinner either." Again, more accusation. As if Colleen needed to make Jennifer out to be the bad guy. Red flag, much?

"Maybe I made it early." Jennifer hadn't, but she hated that Colleen was making assumptions about her. Trying to project her own misery onto an unsuspecting bystander.

"You didn't." She pointed to Jennifer's shirt, where she'd forgotten to take off her name tag.

Jennifer braced, feeling her face flush hot and her palms itch like they always did when she sensed a slap coming—even if it was only verbal.

"You work here?" There was such offense in Colleen's tone, as if by conversing with Jennifer, she now reeked of grocery store carts and sadness and the sharp scent of generic hand sanitizer.

Jennifer bit the inside of her cheek, tasting metal as she nodded, ready for whatever judgment she was about to get for having a job when this woman got to stay home all day with her six kids.

"Well, I wouldn't expect someone in a grocery store apron to understand what real stress is." And then, as if to add insult to injury, she smirked. "I've never needed a job."

"Maybe you'll be lucky enough to never need one," Jennifer couldn't help saying. Couldn't help but remind Colleen that she was lucky, for more than one reason. That she had the luxury—the privilege—of crying in a parking lot.

"Why would I?"

Jennifer bit her tongue. She shouldn't say anything. She should just open her car door, get inside and go home. There was laundry to do, dishes to put away and her own dinner to make. The kids would be home tomorrow after school, and she always liked to have something special prepared for them when they got back—especially after spending the evening in that mansion with Stepmommy dearest.

Her home wasn't as nice.

Her food not as good.

But they were loved. And she wanted them to remember that above all else.

"Well? Are you just going to stand there or tell me why?" Colleen's shrill voice yanked Jennifer out of the endless to-do list. "I'm sure you just love watching someone like me fall apart. Makes you feel better about your little job, doesn't it?"

How dare Colleen stare at her as if *she* were the one being confrontational? All she'd wanted to do was get in her car and go home.

Ignoring the barb, Jennifer offered kindness. "If you ever . . ." Jennifer paused. How to put this delicately? Well, really, there was no way to do it. "I thought I'd never need a job either. But then my husband left me for another woman. So now I have to work. I hope that never happens to you."

Colleen's hand smacked hard against the steering wheel. An obvious wish that it were Jennifer's cheek. "Ohmygosh! You are one spiteful woman, wishing ill on me like that. Why would my husband ever leave me?" But even as she said it, doubt crept over her features. "I make him very happy."

"Does he make you happy?" Jennifer could have kicked herself for even asking. It was none of her business, and she didn't want to prolong this conversation any more than she already had.

There was a pause, a flash of fear on Colleen's face, then she snorted, as if it were a joke to expect happiness. She glared when she snapped, "Does it matter?"

This time she couldn't help but reply honestly, without holding back. "Maybe that's the real problem. He doesn't. Your whole life doesn't. And that's why you're in a parking lot crying and screaming in the dark."

Jennifer didn't wait for an answer. She got into her car and locked the door. She turned up the music so as not to hear Colleen's rantings. Some people would never be grateful for other's grace. That didn't mean it shouldn't be given.

The following morning, she was in her manager's office, hearing the formal complaint written by Mrs. Colleen Christensen about how she'd been harassed in the parking lot.

Of course she'd twisted the story. People like Colleen always rewrote the endings. If Colleen cost her a job . . . Well, it wouldn't be the first thing she'd lost to a tradwife.

Probably wouldn't be the last either. But it might be the last time she stayed quiet about it.

She didn't have much left that was hers. But her kids were hers. Her dignity was hers. And if she had to smile through another parking lot accusation or worse, she would. Because this time, no one was taking those things from her.

Jennifer could write an entire novel just from the looks exchanged across the grocery store parking lot.

"If I ever wrote a book about this town," she muttered, changing out the receipt paper in the register, "I'd call it *Every Lie You Told*."

Chapter Eleven

Ariel

Ariel sometimes wondered what it would be like to sink her hands into flesh. This happened a lot when she was kneading dough. She wasn't a murderer or anything, but the doughy toughness always made her think about it. After each of her babies had been born, she'd done the same thing with her stomach that she was doing now with the sourdough.

Sinking her fists into the thickness of it. Kneading it. Rolling it. Spreading it. Pressing, pushing, stretching.

The dough was sticky today, clinging to her palms, as if trying to tether her to the counter, to the past, to the version of herself she wasn't sure she liked anymore. She dusted it with more flour, pretending that was enough to stop it from sticking. Pretending flour could fix everything.

There was supposed to be a predictability to bread baking that mirrored real life. Unless you forgot salt. Or yeast. Or the water was too warm or too cold. The oven not at the right temperature.

A fleeting thought that bread always did what it was supposed to. Children, husbands, friends and lives did not.

Ariel shook herself.

Making sourdough was one of her favorite things to do. Watching the yeast foam in the warm water. The flour fall in a powdery plunge. Mixing it took some oomph. Her arms always got in a good workout, but the best part was dumping the sticky dough out onto a floured surface and shoving her hands into the warmth.

Push. Press. Stretch.

The dough slapped softly against the counter, a wet, sticky sound that echoed louder in her mind than it should have. The cool flour clung to her forearms like powdery silk, dusting the edges of her sleeves.

If she could just have a minute. Preferably five whole minutes, without a tug on her sleeve or someone calling "Mommy." Even the bread had become less about pleasure and more about duty. About feeding. About producing something. The same way she produced snacks, homework help, laundry loads and perfectly behaved children.

As she shaped the loaf, Ariel glanced at the oven. Waiting for the rise always felt like holding her breath. Would it lift? Would it fall? She wasn't sure if she was still baking bread . . . or just waiting to see what else might collapse.

Strapped to her belly was her baby, asleep in the carrier. The carrier strap dug into her shoulder, damp with sweat where the baby's warmth radiated against her. The yeasty scent of the dough mixed with the soft, clean scent of baby shampoo, as familiar now as her own breath. On the other side of the table, her kids were playing with the flowery invitation that had arrived today in the mail.

The floral paper fluttered between Edith's small hands, too bright and cheery, the kind of bold pinks and greens that demanded attention. It crinkled loudly in the quiet kitchen, louder than it had any right to be.

Mayor Peterson was having a party. Or rather, his wife was having a party. A garden party, she'd called it. There was going to be light music, light fare and probably light conversation. Which didn't feel at all like the typical backyard barbecues they usually attended, where people dined on hot dogs, potato salad and as many brownies as they could stuff into their bellies.

Ariel hated parties. Had since high school.

Miranda Peterson had named the party the Peterson Garden Party, which sounded a lot more like a fancy soiree that might serve cocktails. Of course, drinking in Crystal Harbor was frowned upon, so it was almost a guarantee the party would be dry. Besides, cocktails weren't Ariel's thing. Nor were they Shane's, after his mother's substance abuse.

Kids were welcome, which meant that it would at least be a family-friendly get-together.

But still . . . There was something off about Miranda Peterson, and Ariel wasn't sure she wanted to see her again. Talk to her. She was afraid the other woman might say something in front of Shane about how she'd been out of it. Loopy. Obviously on something.

Ever since that day in the produce aisle, she hadn't taken a single mommy's helper. She'd also lost all of her appetite and couldn't wait for her children's midday nap so she could breathe again. And she'd had nightmares. Nightmares of a stalker. Nightmares of a dark, sandy beach, and the quiet after a storm.

The only thing that was enticing her just slightly was that Miranda hadn't judged her. She seemed to be the first person she'd run into who didn't expect anything from her. There was always someone expecting something.

Even herself.

Before Shane. Before babies. Before the perfect house with the mortgage and the good schools. She used to be onstage. Under lights. She used to have a name people knew. Now her name wasn't Ariel anymore, it was Mommy.

She could still remember the heat of the spotlight on her skin. The hush of the audience before a scene. The swell in her chest when they clapped—not for being a wife, or a mother, or a hostess, but for *her*, the new her, the one who'd left Crystal Harbor to start over. That woman was gone. Swallowed up by diapers, farm animals and sourdough starter and right back where her life started and ended.

"Mama, this is for a party." Edith held up the card stock, a toothy grin on her young face. "Can we go? There's going to be a bounce house."

"A bounce house?" Ariel said with a smile. She used to love a good bounce house. The freedom of flying in the air and knowing you'd land on something soft and bouncy like a cloud, rather than the hardness of reality.

Arthur snatched the invitation, staring at the words he couldn't yet read. "I want to play in a bounce house. Do you think the bounce house will be taller than the house?" he asked, eyes wide.

"I want to jump higher than the roof!" Noah grabbed a toy truck and started making it jump, chanting, "Bounce! Bounce! Bounce!"

Ada jumped up and down on the floor, shouting her agreement.

All the commotion had baby Tara stirring, a little whimper on her pink baby lips, which only gave Ariel a sense of panic. *Not yet. Don't wake up just yet.* If one piece of her carefully curated day wobbled, the whole act might collapse, and with it, the walls she'd built to keep the past out.

"All right. I'll talk to Daddy about it."

"Talk to me about what?" Shane marched into the kitchen, his usual smile on his face, and kissed her, his hand palming her rear with the promise of his insatiable desire. The scent of his aftershave—cedar and something faintly metallic—cut through the warmth of the bread and the baby, sharp and out of place in her domestic cocoon. She froze for a moment before smiling.

"Mayor Peterson and his wife are hosting a garden party. There's a bounce house." Ariel tried her hardest to seem excited, but even the process of kneading dough had grown tiresome, and she feared Shane would see right through her.

Fortunately, he didn't appear to be paying any attention as he tickled each of his children and then chased Ada, who gripped the invitation.

"Looks like it'll be a good time. Do we have anything else on the calendar?" Shane glanced at her with a boyish, hopeful smile.

The idea of standing in that garden, the eyes of the other wives appraising her dress, her weight, her marriage, made her stomach twist. They'd see her. And if they really looked—if they peered past the smiles and the sourdough and the seven-seat SUV—they might see the woman who almost fell apart in the grocery store.

Another performance. Another audience.

Ariel's phone dinged, and she glanced down toward the counter, the message's phrase making her heart skip a beat. What do you like better, watching or acting? I think you like to watch.

Taken out of context, the message was just weird. Completely creepy. When put together with the others, when she thought about a night over a decade ago when she did watch something, when she kept quiet, it made her want to run.

"Everything okay?" Shane looked at her expectantly.

Ariel blinked up at him. This performance, pretending everything was fine, was getting harder. The lines heavier. The audience more demanding. One day soon, she feared, she wouldn't remember the cues. She'd drop the whole act and say the wrong thing. Or worse—she'd say exactly what she was really thinking. She'd tell the truth she'd been hiding for over ten years. The reason she'd left this place.

Bread wasn't the only thing she was holding together with flour and prayer.

Ariel shook her head. "Sorry, just tired. Everything's good, we have nothing on the calendar."

"Then let's go. What harm can a little garden party cause?"

Ariel smiled and shrugged as she formed her sourdough into a ball and then used a knife to score the top. A little party in the past had caused more harm than anyone could ever want. And Shane knew that. Maybe Shane knew it more than anyone. Because Tara had died after attending a party. "I can't think of a single thing," she lied.

Except she could. She could think of a lot of reasons it was a bad idea to go. But none of them Shane, who'd buried his pain, would understand. She hardly understood them herself. Missing this could mean further isolation. Going could mean exposure. But Crystal Harbor always seemed to reveal exactly what you didn't want anyone to see.

And in Crystal Harbor, simple things always got complicated.

Chapter Twelve

Miranda

For a hot minute, Miranda was pretty sure they were going to have to cancel the *garden* part of the party.

The weather had not been cooperating all week—storm clouds rolling in over Crystal Harbor as if they'd transformed the town from its usual sunny, blue skies to the overcast, depressed state of Seattle with its constant drizzle.

She'd only been to Seattle once and once was enough. How everyone in that town wasn't on some sort of happy pill for their depression was a mystery. Unless, of course, they were. What did Miranda know—she wasn't a psychologist.

But she did know people, and behavior, and for a brief period of time, it had been her job to make sure people were happy. Now, she needed only to make sure that Benjamin was happy, or she'd be the one to suffer.

Miranda rubbed absently at her shoulder, a bruise forming there from an unfortunate incident with a doorjamb.

There was also the little matter of her plans being derailed if this party didn't go off without a hitch. This was for her. Though she didn't always seem to be a priority in Crystal Harbor, which she was finding hard to balance. Miranda had always come first in her previous life.

With the weather, the stupid mutt had gotten muddy footprints everywhere, and by some miracle, Ben had agreed to put her in a kennel for the weekend.

Just when she was about to have a full-blown panic attack, the sun had beat the clouds into submission, and the sky had turned blue and everything finally seemed right in the world. A sign that her plans were coming to fruition.

"Stop worrying," Benjamin murmured, brushing his lips against her temple. "The party's perfect. You're perfect."

Miranda smiled, but it felt like putting on a too-tight bra, suffocating. "Let's hope the town thinks so too."

He chuckled. "Since when do you care what Crystal Harbor thinks?"

Since it held my entire future in its judgmental little hands.

Being accepted, enamored, meant social capital, power. It meant her plans would come to fruition. Being shunned, a failure, left behind, meant years of her hard work down the drain and nothing to show for it. Miranda would have changed who she was for nothing.

The slightly damp, freshly cut grass stuck to the sides of her wedges, and she breathed in the faint scent of brine from Echo Lake, mingling with gardenias along the perimeter of their property.

Miranda stared into the watery depths of the lake, knowing what secrets it held. She shuddered.

Tables and chairs had been set up in their own garden, overlooking the lake, where a breeze ruffled the hem of her dress. The string trio was playing on a raised platform she'd had erected just for this very event, tuning their instruments. Her fingers tingled with nerves. The humidity dampened her skin, causing her dress to stick in places.

Every chair, every canapé, every godforsaken blossom in the centerpiece had been handpicked to ensure people liked her. Because if they didn't—Well, Miranda didn't want to consider what would happen if she didn't fit in here. Crystal Harbor didn't welcome outsiders. It tolerated them. And if this party didn't land just right, she'd never be anything more than the mayor's second wife. And what she needed to be was a close and trusted friend. There was no other way to lure them into what they had coming.

Benjamin had been skeptical about the price of the party—the lengths she was going to in order to make some friends—but as soon as he'd seen the buttery-yellow tablecloths, the floral centerpieces, the waiters carrying canapés, he'd pulled her into their butler's pantry and given her a kiss that made her want to drag him upstairs.

The only reason she hadn't was because they'd been interrupted by one of the tiny minions—aka her stepchildren—wondering if they could start bouncing in the bounce house. Miranda had been about to say yes, because why not, and it would get them out of her hair, but Benjamin had wanted them to wait until the rest of the children arrived.

Which seemed stupid, considering they didn't even know if there would be any other children in attendance.

And didn't he want to fuck?

But she kept her mouth shut. She was only their stepmom. And while she tried her best and followed the rules of what a mother should do in Crystal Harbor, she feared that was where her place ended. She was not a disciplinarian. More like a distant aunt. Not even a babysitter. Which was fine by her.

But now, everything was in place, and the guests were starting to arrive. The musicians began to play, the soft strings of their instruments floating over the garden.

Brad and his wife, Kennedy, had come first, and fortunately their kids, reeking of sunscreen, had been as eager to bounce as Benjamin's.

"This is great," Brad said, taking two mocktails from a passing waiter and handing one to Kennedy.

She glanced at Kennedy, and her severe, slicked-back ponytail, her expression so pinched it was a wonder she'd come to the party at all.

Every time Miranda had seen her, the woman appeared more like she wanted to run away. The disdain she showed Miranda had her wondering if she'd done a secret background check.

"We're so glad you could make it." Miranda pasted on her brightest, most practiced smile—the one she used to flash for social media back in New York, before anyone in Crystal Harbor had ever heard the name Miranda. She slipped her hand into Benjamin's. She was not partaking in the mocktails. In fact, she wouldn't eat anything either. Whenever she hosted, she made it a rule not to let anything pass her lips . . . Well, unless it was a you-know-what, but this wasn't that kind of party. She'd promised.

"A little fancy for a Saturday afternoon," Kennedy murmured coolly, lips pursed, eyes sweeping the party the exact way a lawyer might evaluate an opponent—assessing, appraising, calculating worth.

And yet, here she is. At my fancy party. Drinking my mocktails. Smiling at my husband.

Funny how often envy disguised itself as disdain. Miranda swallowed the retort she wanted to give, and fortunately didn't have to respond at all as the Olsen family made their entrance.

Ariel Olsen had been such a star. To see her now, a baby strapped to her abdomen, and four other children clutching at her legs and arms, seemed almost sad—except she had a radiant smile on her face. Not the tranquilized look she'd had at the store. Not the haunted, guilty expression she used to carry. Miranda cocked her head, studying her, wondering what had changed.

Ariel had five kids clinging to her and still managed to look luminous. Miranda had stepchildren clinging to her reputation as the perfect stepmother and she looked . . . What? Desperate for approval? She straightened her shoulders, going for the look she admired most—controlled, confident.

Ariel's husband, Shane, was what some people might call a snack. Rock solid, tall and handsome enough to draw the eyes of every person in the garden, including the men. If his younger brother had still been in town, they'd probably say the same thing about him, but Ryan had left Florida the moment he turned eighteen. People still talked about Shane's twin sister, Tara. How desperately sad it was she'd drowned. Poor Tara. Miranda wondered if anyone actually remembered her—or if they only remembered the story.

"Ariel." Miranda rushed toward her, tugging Benjamin along, just like they were old friends and hadn't seen each other in an age. For a split second, Ariel looked nervous, and Miranda guessed why. She didn't want her to mention the encounter in the store, and so she'd keep that to herself. A woman needed to have her secrets, and she needed to have a friend who could keep them. Miranda knew all about secrets. And Ariel was very good at keeping them.

"Thank you so much for having us," Ariel said. "This is my husband, Shane."

Miranda stared at her own reflection in Shane's aviator sunglasses, noting that a few of her strands had grown frizzy in the humidity. She waited a beat for recognition, always surprised when no one placed her beyond where she was. She smoothed down her flyaways. "Nice to have you both."

"I'm not sure we can stay long . . ." Ariel trailed off, her eyes scanning the garden.

"Can we, can we?" her children chanted, and Shane shooed them off toward the bounce house, straightening to shake Benjamin's hand.

Children were useful distractions. Everyone always cooed at the kids instead of looking too closely at the parents.

"They've been talking nonstop about your bounce house since we got the invitation."

"All Miranda's idea." Benjamin put his arm around her, smiling down at her with a pride that obtaining a stupid piece of manufactured plastic filled with air didn't seem to deserve—but she took it all the same.

Of course, the inflatable monstrosity was getting more compliments than her floral centerpieces. Which said everything about Crystal Harbor's priorities. Inflated distractions. Keep the kids busy. Keep the adults busy pretending.

"You look beautiful," Miranda said to Ariel. "I saw her on Broadway several times," she added to Shane and Benjamin for effect. "Absolutely a stunning actress."

Ariel stiffened, as if she expected her husband to be displeased at this compliment, but Shane smiled brightly, slinging his arm around Ariel's shoulder.

"My Ariel was the whole reason I even watched shows on Broadway. So proud of her accomplishments. Funny, our kids don't even realize how much of a star their mother was."

Is, Miranda wanted to correct him. But that likely wouldn't be appropriate. Ariel might not be onstage anymore, but people hadn't forgotten. Especially since her last play had been televised and could be streamed even now.

"A real celebrity in our midst," Benjamin said, nodding in that way he had that showed he was impressed but also distracted.

"Oh, but *Mayor*, you're the true celebrity," Ariel said, changing the subject. "I really like what you've been doing with the shoreline conservation."

Was that a hint of mockery in Ariel's tone? If it was, Benjamin didn't seem to notice.

"Well, you know, I've been a resident of Crystal Harbor since I was a kid. This town is really near and dear to my heart, just like it is yours. I don't want to see any part of it destroyed."

Ariel smiled and took a small puff pastry from one of the waiters, nibbling on it.

The scent of Gruyère and apricots twisted in Miranda's stomach. She wasn't hungry. Hunger was a weakness. Hunger was wanting, and wanting always came with consequences.

Miranda's stomach growled. Not only had she not tasted any of the carefully curated menu items, but she also had forgotten to eat earlier in the day. Maybe she could forgo her rule of not eating at a function?

But she could feel the other women's gazes on her. Feel their judgment. And she desperately wanted to feel the weight of their unspoken approval. And so, she went without. The storm had passed, but Miranda knew how quickly clouds could gather.

After all, the game was rigged, and rules were made to be broken. Just not by women like her—at least not where anyone could see.

Winning at Crystal Harbor wasn't about playing fair. It was about playing flawlessly.

And really, were they all so shallow they didn't see past her mask? Couldn't see who she really was?

Chapter Thirteen

Jennifer

The Fifteen Commandments of a Tradwife

> **Four:** Honor thy husband's ego, even when he cannot grill a burger without googling how. He is the king. You are the serene queen behind the scenes—smiling as he explains something you already know (again).

Music and voices filtered through Jennifer's open window off Echo Lake.

Echo Lake had a funny way of showing you the truth—reflections you didn't ask for, silence that bounced your thoughts right back at you. It never let her forget what she'd lost . . . or what she might still find if she stopped letting the people in her community define her.

Growing up along the water, the glistening soft surface used to feel like a promise—tubing in the summers between school years.

Parties on boats when she was in high school. Fishing. Kayaking. Late night skinny-dipping. The future wide open and spread out before her, so hopeful and happy.

Until that one horrible weekend in high school.

But now it felt like Echo Lake was taunting her—echoing back to her all the things she couldn't have, all the things she'd seen.

She whipped her damp hair away from her face—she'd been mopping her kitchen floor since the kids were out of the house and had the splinter to prove it embedded in her thumb.

The inhabitants of the massive house across the water were having a party.

Jennifer shivered. Parties made her nervous.

She poured herself a glass of iced tea and meandered onto the lanai with Shadow, the five-year-old yellow Lab she'd adopted. She kicked off her flip-flops and sat in a chair beneath her awning with her sweaty feet propped up, watching the party across the way. Shafts of sunlight stabbed through the awning where it had ripped in the last hurricane, and she'd not had the money to fix it. The salty breeze lifted strands of her damp hair, and the water lapped gently at the shore, a sound she used to find soothing. Now it sounded like applause she'd been excluded from.

Across the water, they clinked glasses, and she swore she caught the scent of a grill. Though that was probably someone down the street as she doubted a party like this one would serve burgers. More like shrimp on skewers and tiny crustless sandwiches. They dined on fine food, while she'd just scrubbed dried mac and cheese off the floor.

There was light music. Classical? Was that a string trio?

Shadow was curled up beside her, a solid body that kept her grounded. She absently stroked his head.

A massive red, blue and white bounce house was moving like mad, probably filled with a dozen or more kids shrieking with joy. The sight of it, the sounds of unadulterated childhood pleasure, made Jennifer smile before bitterness seeped into her belly.

Were her kids at the party, their feet bouncing weightlessly in the inflatable house, or were they with a babysitter? Would they grow up thinking she'd been the one who didn't belong? That it had been her fault?

Women's dresses, like bright flowers, dotted the green lawn between the flicker of white tent poles. They were all onstage, weren't they? Dresses as costumes. Laughs as cues. And if that party was a performance, she was just the woman watching from the wings—uninvited, unneeded, unseen.

She remembered standing in a garden like that once, smiling, wearing heels that pinched her toes—but at least she'd belonged. She could still feel the press of Jamie's hand at the small of her back as they'd attended similar parties, loving or threatening depending on the mood. A gentle kiss on her temple as Jamie told her she was the most beautiful woman in the world, and she believed him.

A ghost of a touch that lingered even now after all the bitterness and lies. Those subtle gestures, the fake compliments about her dress from friends, had given her a confidence to walk obliviously through that world.

The tea, despite its coolness, burned her throat. Or was that jealousy?

She should be at that party. Rubbing shoulders with the people of Crystal Harbor. Looked like practically the entire town was mingling in that coastal backyard.

Well, she was glad she wasn't there. She didn't want to be a part of that life anymore. And yet . . . she couldn't stop watching. Wondering.

A droplet of condensation from her glass left a damp circle on her shirt beside what was clearly a spot of bleach from her morning chores.

She bet Colleen was over there now, sipping cucumber water and telling a version of the parking lot story where Jennifer was the villain and she was the victim. Colleen was good at telling stories like that.

She'd say what she'd told Jennifer's manager—that Jennifer had accosted her with accusations that her husband was going to leave her. That Jennifer was hysterical. That no one should believe anything Jennifer had to say. Because Jennifer had a lot to say, and no one wanted a word of it to be spoken.

Colleen had portrayed Jennifer in a light that was the complete opposite of not only her actual character, but also the CCTV video her manager had watched—which was the only reason she still had a job. A job she was going to be late for if she didn't stop drinking tea and get into the shower, now that her chores had left her covered in sweat.

The bitterness, however, kept her where she was. Watching the party across the water. And it wasn't like she really wanted to be there. Not a single person who was eating fancy snacks and laughing over the music was a friend of hers. No one had stepped up to defend her during her divorce. And why had she expected it? None of them had stepped up before.

In fact, it felt like the entire town had shunned her. Well, not the entire town. Only the people who'd been in her personal circle.

Divorce was a sin.

Divorce was taboo.

Divorce was a disease.

But only for the woman.

They acted like she had leprosy or something. She hadn't just broken the rules. She'd shredded the whole damn tradwife handbook—and Crystal Harbor didn't like that kind of rebellion.

And Jamie? He hadn't suffered one bit. The man never did. Divorce hadn't cost him friends. Instead, he'd gained admirers. Women bending over backward to make him feel good, and men clapping him on the back as if they were happy for him to be rid of her. Single dads who remarried were heroes. Single moms? Just sad stories.

In fact, he was probably walking around the garden party like he was a king—his eye candy hanging off his arm with her dumb coquettish looks, her dress perfect.

Jennifer lifted the glass to her lips, paused. Why should she swallow it? She'd swallowed everything else for years. Suddenly the tea she'd sipped while ruminating on her past life was bitter. She didn't want that anymore. Without thinking, she threw her tea into the water. The glass sank, then bobbed once, floating with the tide like a piece of herself she couldn't quite hold on to.

Well, that was dumb. She'd liked that glass.

So, what—she wasn't invited to the party. She wasn't friends with fake people. Shouldn't that make her happy? Shouldn't she be glad that was no longer her life? That she could now live her life authentically for herself?

Except when she had been a part of the in crowd, she'd felt . . . special. Loved. Safe.

And now, what? Now she felt like an outsider.

But the question was: Had she ever really been an insider? Ever really been safe?

And who gave a fuck?

Well, *she* did.

And she didn't want other women to feel the same way. Maybe she'd form a club for single moms. Something fun like a wine and book club. A place to commiserate, but also to have fun and friendship. They could call themselves something clever, like The Next Chapter Wives Club. Did she dare hope to form a connection, even if it was just over dollar wine and cheap pizza?

There were so many more Jennifer Davises in the world, so many Colleens. Didn't they deserve to know the truth? The Colleens of the world had their stories. But she was ready to tell hers—not in whispers, not in shame, but loud enough to echo across the lake.

I know what happened to Tara. So does Colleen.

Chapter Fourteen

Tara

Summer 2013

I've never been part of the in crowd.

Never had the money for Hollister or American Eagle. My shoes are more Stevie than Steve Madden, and my dark hair has never seen highlights. Careful not to touch my mother's collection—her colors were too bright, the opposite of the dim light of her drug-induced haze—I wear only whatever makeup I can slip into my bag at the CVS.

But tonight, at the end-of-junior-year party, Brad Johnson—the hottest guy in school—invited me to Echo Lake. He's been dating Colleen forever, but they must have broken up. That's the only reason I can think of.

Brad isn't that smart. I've been tutoring him for his second round of algebra, and maybe that's why he's kissed me a few times, not realizing how dangerous it would be if Colleen found out. His note tonight promised something more serious. Seal the deal, *he wrote.*

Maybe I'm the not-smart one. But if Brad were my boyfriend, everything would change. I wouldn't just be the girl with a loser mom and an absent father. I'd belong. I'd have friends.

Not even my twin, Shane, knows I'm coming. He's working tonight, always working to keep up with the cost of maintaining his spot with the cool kid crowd. Being cool costs money. He shows up to the parties late, after he gets off work, like he's making an entrance. Somehow, he's pulled it off. I never have.

After making sure my younger brother, Ryan, is settled in front of the television, I pedal my bike—tires soft, no helmet because for the first time, I've straightened my hair, and I'm not letting the helmet undo my hard work. The bonfire's glow reaches me before the voices do, laughter and music spilling across the sand. The scent of roasted marshmallows and melted chocolate. Red Solo cups flash in the firelight as the popular kids dance.

I head toward the small boathouse, just beyond the dock—the meeting place Brad promised.

"What are you doing here?"

Colleen's voice cuts through the night, sharp as broken glass. She stands in a skirt the size of a napkin, chunky heels, bikini top glittering in the firelight. It's like she's been waiting.

"I was invited," I say, keeping my voice even, ignoring the goose bumps crawling up my arms.

She smirks, thrusting a red Solo cup into my hand. The liquid inside is deep red, staining the side.

"Well, then you need some punch."

"What's in it?"

She waves her hand like I'm an idiot. "Nothing bad. God, don't be such a pussy." Then she turns and melts into the crowd.

I stand there, staring into the cup. I lift it, the scent of fake cherries and sugar rushing up. The first sip is syrupy, clinging to my tongue, too sweet—like it's hiding something sharper underneath.

Part Two

Tittle-Tattles . . .

Chapter Fifteen

There's a pair of black leather sandals on the beach.

But not just anywhere on the beach.

The sandals lie discarded in the sand about twenty yards or so from a pier, yet to be lit by the sun. They were abandoned sometime in the middle of the night at high tide, far enough from the ebb and flow of the frothy waves that they weren't swept away.

Though they had come close more than once. They'd been discarded an hour before the peak of high tide, when the water laps its way up the beach to practically touch the place where humans reside. Just the barest hint of the tip of a wave nudged the sandals from their original place. A subtle push that had them float a few inches from their original place of rest.

There'd been a brief moment of hesitation before the sandals were separated from the wearer. Before the first body was laid out, positioned. Then the second. Before the click of a cell phone camera. The muted laughs. The nervous sounds.

Last night, the sandals had failed to keep the wearer on their feet. Failed to provide that barrier between ground and skin. The wearer had stumbled over the uneven sand until they'd kicked the sandals into a pile, dropping them as if they were disposable. And maybe they were. After all, nothing lasts forever.

Some might call the sandals flip-flops. But the owner of the sandals hated that term. Made it sound as if they were wishy-washy, unreliable. And these were not flip-floppers. They were *sandals.* They did not fall apart. They did not stain. They did not disappoint.

How long would it take before the earth reclaimed its bounty?

If sandals could be disappointed, these sandals would be. And they'd also be morose. For there was nothing they could do for the wearer. Nothing they could do for the person who'd once happily pulled them out of a shiny dark box, taking them from nothingness to a life that was well led.

The wearer was not coming back.

Once a body on the beach, then claimed by the water. Like the sandals. Discarded.

Unwanted.

Unnoticed.

Disposed of.

The sandals had been created with the purpose of being worn. A purpose they'd fulfilled. What purpose would they serve now other than to be buried in the sand, never to be seen again? Perhaps that was what death was. A vast nothingness. A loss of purpose. Of being forgotten. Of being buried.

If sandals could mourn, they would. If sandals could speak, they'd sing. They'd tell someone what they saw last night. What they heard.

But in the end, they were only sandals. Designed to be worn on feet. An awareness only in the imagination of the person who stared at them before walking away. Inanimate objects told no tales.

Not like people. Someone knows the sandals were on the beach.

Someone knows because they were there when the sandals were discarded.

The question is, will they tell, or will this be another secret buried? Will they come back for the sandals, discard the evidence of their existence and the presence of the body laid out and then swept away?

Perhaps the sandals were just something else to be discarded. Sandals littering the beach like an empty can of soda. A water bottle crunched in on itself. A cigarette butt flicked off careless fingers.

There were rules in this world. Rules on the beach.

But last night, there were many rules broken . . .

Chapter Sixteen

Ariel

The garden party felt surreal.

As if Ariel were not a part of real life.

The mingling scents of trimmed hedges and perfumed wrists made Ariel dizzy, as if she were onstage again, waiting for her cue under the heat of stage lights. And her feet hurt. She'd grown accustomed to her work boots, and now her feet barely fit in the same fancy heels she'd worn at after-parties in New York. Five kids later, she'd absolutely grown a shoe size.

The music was tranquil, and unbidden, her body swayed. The tune was specific—one she'd heard in the opening curtain call of a play so long ago she barely remembered the cast, the part or the title. And yet somewhere in the back of her mind, in the bones of her body, the familiarity of it seeded movement.

"They are lovely, aren't they?" Miranda asked, smiling over at the musicians. "We were lucky to get them so last minute. I wanted to surprise Benjamin. In New York, we often went to classical music shows, but we've yet to find a place down here."

“The Ringling hosts musical acts, and there’s a theater in Tampa too,” Ariel offered.

“Have you been?” Miranda’s eyebrows lifted with interest.

“Only once on a date night.” She smiled nostalgically, recalling how Shane had surprised her after the birth of Edith. Four kids later and they hadn’t been back. Not that he hadn’t offered, but because she was so tired. And because she had some sort of ingrained guilt about leaving her children to have fun.

It was one thing to go to the grocery store. That was a service to them. But to go listen to music? To listen to the rhythmic tunes of an instrument for no other purpose than enjoyment felt somehow . . . blasphemous.

“Well, maybe we can all go together,” Miranda suggested. “Ben would love it.”

Ariel glanced toward Shane, who was chatting it up with their town mayor. “Does, um, Mayor Peterson play golf?” she asked.

Miranda frowned for a split second before nodding. “You can call him Ben or Benjamin. We invited everyone here to make friends.”

Friends.

Ariel bit the inside of her cheek. That was something she’d also let fall to the wayside. In fact, she’d known Ben in high school. Had maybe once considered him a friend.

But five children made it hard to socialize.

She glanced down now, feeling that familiar prickle between her shoulder blades, and found baby Tara staring up at her—the same silent watchfulness she had from her crib, as if she knew the world was busy and she’d have to wait her turn.

She loved this age—their quiet, soft eyes like unblinking moons. But sometimes, in a certain light, those eyes looked too much like her aunt’s.

"I could use a friend, couldn't I, Tara?" Ariel said, but even as the words left her mouth, she wondered what she meant. A fellow mother to share the weight of invisible labor? A witness to the person she used to be? Or just someone who wouldn't flinch when she confessed how lonely it was to be surrounded by love and still feel adrift?

Miranda let out a little strangled sound, and Ariel glanced at her. "Sorry, just sipped the wrong way."

Except Miranda didn't have a drink.

"Want me to get you some . . . water?"

"No, no, I'm fine. Little Tara, is it? Tell your mommy she has a friend in me." Miranda stared at her a beat too long, and Ariel wondered what she was thinking. Was it Ariel's nails digging into the apple at the grocery store?

"She's adorable," Miranda said, reaching out to touch Tara's back, but her hand didn't quite reach it, as if she wasn't entirely comfortable in a role as nurturer.

Ariel watched the way Miranda studied her. She couldn't decipher if the woman was judging her or just interested. She'd grown quite jaded recently, believing even someone's kindness came with strings. Was Miranda's warmth genuine? Or was she like some of the other women in town, collecting allies the way she might collect recipes and Instagram followers?

"Thank you. Do you . . . have kids?"

Miranda nodded, smiled. "Stepchildren. Ben's kids are in the bounce house with yours."

Everyone knew the mayor was divorced. That his new wife was different from anyone else in their circles. Ariel wouldn't go so far as to call Miranda an outsider, but there were plenty of people who would.

She didn't like to gossip, though. Gossip was for the weak. And she was weak enough.

Brad approached with Samantha—both of whom Ariel had known in high school. They'd dated briefly, before Brad dated Colleen. Before Tara.

Ariel pressed her toes hard into the bottoms of her shoes, trying to ground herself. The world tilted anyway, like the air had thickened. Seeing all of them together again felt like too much—like the past had been quietly waiting in the corner for her to notice it, and now it was stepping forward.

She told herself it was nothing, just the crowded party, the lack of sleep. But the name still rang in her head, louder than the chatter around her. *Tara.*

"Ariel, always good to see you," he said. "My wife, Kennedy, works with Samantha's husband, Nathaniel." He pointed toward a duo in deep discussion. "Probably working." He rolled his eyes.

Nathaniel and Kennedy were both newcomers to Crystal Harbor.

"We missed you at the open gym for homeschoolers earlier this week," Samantha said to Ariel. "You look well today."

Well today. As if she'd shown up last time with mascara smeared and motherhood visibly unraveling. As if they all weren't coming apart at the seams beneath pastel dresses and perfect lipstick.

Ariel hoped her face didn't convey the fact that she was irritated beyond measure at Samantha's remark, her mind completely buzzing on the *you look well today.* "Good to see you."

Open gym was mayhem, with children running all over the place to exert the energy their mothers kept bottled up inside.

"I've been trying to convince Brad to bring his twins, but he's afraid they'll cause enough trouble to get the place shut down,"

Samantha said with a laugh. "But if we're all there, we can provide a united front."

Ariel cocked her head, keeping the smile in place as she imagined the three of them locking arms and bracing their legs against the onslaught of insane preschoolers. Funny that Samantha would mention it now when all of them had avoided each other since that summer before senior year. More often than not Ariel pretended she didn't know them at all. Wished she didn't.

"I'll look for you next time I'm there," Ariel lied.

"We should sit together at church," Miranda said.

"I'm usually in the Sunday school room," Samantha said. "Finger painting is good for the soul."

"Agree." Ariel stroked Tara's back until she closed her eyes again.

"Good baby," Brad said. "You're lucky."

"We are blessed."

A commotion toward the gate drew their attention as a horde of children rushed ahead of two scrambling parents, arms outstretched as if they might catch one of them.

The kids ran in a zigzag pattern away from their parents.

"The Christensens are here," someone called, as if they needed a formal announcement. Even though they were moving in a blur, Ariel would have recognized Colleen and Zachary and their brood of unruly children anywhere. Every time Ariel saw Colleen, the hair on the back of her neck stood on end.

If her kids ever behaved that way, Shane would lose it, and Ariel would die of mortification. There was no option for her children to act like hooligans.

Miranda laughed. Samantha groaned. Brad gaped.

Ariel kept her expression neutral, even though on the inside she was trying to tabulate the last time all of them had been standing within whisper distance of each other. And all she kept coming up with was a fire-lit night full of regrets and sadness. She glanced at Shane to see how he was doing, but he didn't seem bothered.

So, she pasted on a blank face, just like she had onstage when it was clear there was a commotion in the crowd. One should never break form. Never let the audience know that you know they are there.

Colleen lunged forward, fingers brushing the back of her son's collared shirt, but he tugged away at the last minute, the fabric slipping from her grasp. The momentum of the lunge, the tug, the running—all of it seemed to be too much for Colleen, who carried a permanent scent of alcohol about her, though she'd swear it was her kombucha.

She teetered on her impossibly high wedge sandals, spun as if looking for something to grab hold of, and then, quite embarrassingly, she fell.

Once, when a set piece had collapsed mid-show, Ariel had improvised so smoothly the audience thought it was part of the act. Life offstage wasn't so forgiving.

Ariel never broke character—not back then and not now. Not even as those around her rushed to Colleen's assistance, and Zachary caught up with one child, hauling him up like a suitcase.

Ariel stood, watching. She didn't laugh. She couldn't. The sight of Colleen's body crumpling at the base of the hydrangeas hit too close to home. If her breath hitched, no one noticed. If her heart sped up, she told herself it was just the heat.

She told herself she was grateful to be a spectator. That the spotlight had shifted from where she stood on this performative stage back to Colleen. But deep down, she wondered how long she could keep from becoming the spectacle herself.

Colleen was smiling. Smiling through the stumble took effort. Invisible labor, just like folding laundry or smoothing out tantrums. No applause. Just the expectation of grace.

Chapter Seventeen

Miranda

"Who the hell is that?" Miranda crossed her arms over her chest, annoyed that her tranquil party had been ruined by the newest guests. More annoyed that she had to pretend not to know just who Colleen was. Then she realized she'd just said *hell*, and crossed herself—though to be honest, she didn't feel all that remorseful. *Hell* was just a word. "I'm so sorry for my language."

Brad chuckled. "That is one fucked-up family."

"Totally fucked up," Samantha agreed with a perfunctory nod.

Miranda smiled, knowing she could be a little more relaxed. The whole purpose of this over-the-top barbecue was to draw them in. Make them trust her. People who might be enticed to enjoy a different sort of party.

"I guess I should be a good hostess," Miranda said with a clap as she wandered toward Colleen, who was being fawned over by at least a dozen other guests.

"Are you okay?" She kept her voice breezy, the perfect hostess, even as her shoulders ached from holding her posture just so. That was the thing about appearances: you couldn't drop them for even a second, or the whole illusion cracked. Even if you were annoyed.

Colleen's cheeks were flushed, and on first glance, one might think it was from embarrassment, but Miranda recognized a boozy flush when she saw one. Interesting . . .

"I'm so embarrassed. Please accept my apologies." Colleen touched her palms to her cheeks to cover the evidence she wasn't a good, sober Christian.

"Oh, don't be embarrassed. I'm sure everyone here has had a run-in with a little rebellion." Miranda gave one of her tinkling laughs that always drew attention. There was nothing real about it. Her laugh was as practiced as Ariel's face when the commotion happened. Actresses weren't all onstage. And she watched to see if what she said hit its mark.

Colleen seemed oblivious.

Miranda was so good at observing she should be some sort of spy.

"Let's go inside and get you cleaned up." Miranda reached out for Colleen, expecting the woman to take her hand.

Colleen looked down at her palm, which had a smudge of dirt from catching herself. She nodded and took the offered help.

Inside the house, the chaos of the yard was suddenly dulled. The added children had increased the screaming, making Miranda's ears ring. Why Benjamin wanted more of those, she couldn't understand. But she also wanted to be a good wife. Which meant making happy exclamations about making an effort to provide him with another little monster.

She led Colleen through the living room to the kitchen.

"Wow, it's so clean in here." Colleen's voice was full of awe as she took in the gleaming marble, spotless floors and shining kitchen fixtures.

"Cleanliness is next to godliness, Colleen, right up there with being honest," Miranda said with purpose.

Colleen flushed again. Miranda laughed. "The party is catered. I didn't have to prepare anything. No fuss, no mess." She'd also paid for a cleaning crew to come in, which Benjamin had agreed to for the party only. But not every party trick needed to be divulged. Let Colleen believe she'd spent her morning scrubbing.

Colleen laughed nervously, holding out her hands when Miranda wiggled the organic lemon hand soap toward her. She gave three squirts, filling the kitchen with the odor of the delicious citrus-scented soap, then turned the water to warm, watching Colleen scrub the dirt from her hands.

There was a beat of awkward silence, and then Miranda said, "When we walk outside, the day will start all over again. Fresh. New. Easy-peasy lemon-squeezy. Like nothing ever happened." Except so much had happened. And Colleen, well, she was one bad girl.

"Are you always so upbeat?" Colleen obviously tried to say it with a smile, but it was hard to hide the nervous little twitch at the corner of her lip.

Miranda shrugged and pointedly said, "Beats the opposite. Nobody likes a Debbie Drowner."

"What did you say?"

"I meant Debbie Downer," Miranda said with a laugh, then stuck her tongue between her teeth for effect.

Colleen's smile widened, but it looked more like lips peeling away from her face than an actual smile.

"Listen." Miranda licked her lips, folding her arms across her chest, and leaned in conspiratorially. "I have something that might take the edge off." If she hadn't guessed correctly about Colleen's little habit, this could bite her in the butt.

"What do you mean?" Colleen looked skeptical—but behind the skepticism was interest. A lot of interest.

"A little bottle stashed under the sink." Miranda winked. "My husband never looks there."

Colleen's eyes widened, then narrowed. She didn't move. Was Colleen a wild card . . . or the exact kind of woman Miranda needed in her corner? This was a test—for both of them. And Miranda wasn't sure who was passing.

Panic sliced briefly up Miranda's spine until a gleam lit in Colleen's eyes. A gleam she recognized.

Miranda tugged open the cabinet and pointed to where the clear bottle of vodka lurked. She was nothing if not a good hostess. A good friend. Always looking out for others. But mostly for herself.

"You . . . drink?" Colleen asked.

Miranda cocked her head to the side, neither denying nor confirming. "I bet more people outside in my garden do than are willing to admit it."

"This is a dry town."

"Whatever is dry must get wet." Miranda laughed, realizing what she'd just said could be taken more ways than one. "Kind of like what goes up must come down."

Colleen's laugh changed pitch halfway through—too high, too sharp. Unreal. Miranda made a mental note never to pour too much and never share too soon. She glanced toward the glass lanai doors expecting her husband to come barging in and demand to know what they were talking about.

"Won't someone notice?" Colleen glanced furtively toward the windows, biting her lip, her fingers ringing the hand towel into a cloth spiral.

Miranda dropped down to a crouch. The citrus bite of the soap lingered in the air, clashing with a hint of sweat and Chanel. The air was thick, intimate. Confessional. "Not if we hide."

Colleen crouched too. "I feel like I'm back in high school."

Miranda's blood chilled. "Stealing Mom's?"

She shook her head. "No, my mom was obsessed with following the rules. But my dad . . . He had a little nip every night, and I always finished off the last few drops when no one was looking."

"Naughty girl."

"It was necessary." Colleen rolled her eyes. "My mom was a number one fan of discipline. Any little indiscretion. In fact, she even taught new moms blanket training."

"Blanket training?"

"Yeah, it's when you start using a small switch on your baby. Around four months old. Any time they try to roll off the blanket, they get a little snap. It teaches them that their desires equal pain."

Miranda was horrified, not only at what Colleen had divulged but at how causally she'd shared it. "Holy shit. Your mom supported beating babies?" At least Miranda's mom was only absent. Off doing whateverthefuck or whoeverthefuck she wanted, leaving Miranda's raising mostly to herself and her grandmother.

"I'm not like my mom." Colleen glanced away and Miranda wanted to call her a liar. "But maybe if I was, my kids wouldn't be so insane."

Miranda shook her head. "No, no. I know plenty of kids who weren't blanket trained and have never been smacked in their life who behave. Like my stepkids." As wild as they were, they were pretty good kids if she were to rank them.

Colleen wrinkled her nose and reached for the bottle. Miranda couldn't tell if she believed her or not, but it made her want to ask Benjamin: Was his ex-wife . . . abusive? No, there was no way.

The kids were perfect, not a mark on them, and they loved their mother. They'd be afraid of her otherwise.

"To no blanket training," Miranda said, unscrewing the vodka, the cap clinking on the tile floor. A thrill zipped through her—but it was chased by something sharper. Not quite guilt. Not quite dread. Just a small twist in her gut that whispered, *Careful.*

If she were to grade whether or not this garden party was a success, this moment in the kitchen was an A-plus. Sharing a shot with Colleen wasn't just vodka. It was a shared secret. A pact sealed in citrus and sin. If only Colleen knew what Miranda had in store.

"And to new beginnings." Colleen took a long swig—so long Miranda worried she'd drown in it.

Of course Colleen liked new beginnings. But then again, so did Miranda.

She took a sip, too, establishing trust, and knowing at the same time she was also ruining her husband's trust. But what he didn't know wouldn't hurt him. The vodka burned a path down her throat, warming her insides as much as the sun had warmed her outsides.

"I like you," Colleen said, her mood improving as fast as it took the vodka to slip down her throat.

"I like you too." As Miranda tucked the vodka away, she caught a flicker of movement through the kitchen window—someone outside glancing toward the house. She smiled tightly, pretending she hadn't noticed. Hopefully, they hadn't either. "Now, we need something sweet to cover the smell." She pulled the breath spray from under the counter. "Say 'ah.'"

Dutifully, Colleen opened her mouth. That was a little too easy.

"Good girl." Miranda laughed as she sprayed.

A shadow passed too slowly across the patio. Was someone watching? Or was her paranoia getting the better of her?

"My turn." Colleen returned the favor, the cool mist of the breath spray stinging Miranda's tongue.

But their laughs were cut off by the sound of the lanai door opening and shutting. Miranda held her fingers to her lips, and Colleen nodded. The first time she'd had a big secret, she'd ended up almost dead. The last time she'd trusted a woman like Colleen, she'd found her secrets on a gossip blog the next day. But this wasn't New York. And Colleen . . . Well, would anyone believe an obviously unstable person?

"Miranda?" Ben's voice had the power to make her heart skip a beat—especially because she was doing something she shouldn't. Only in situations like this did she long for the life she'd created in New York City.

They waited a beat, and Benjamin's footsteps against the tile floor faded as he went in search of her in the opposite direction. If Benjamin had caught her . . . she didn't know what she'd say. Just that it wouldn't be the truth.

"Let's go," she whispered, grabbing Colleen's hand and tugging her out into the backyard as if they'd never been inside at all.

As they stepped back outside, Miranda's smile returned on cue. But inside, something prickled. She wasn't sure if she'd gained Colleen's trust—or opened the door to her biggest liability yet.

Chapter Eighteen

Jennifer

The Fifteen Commandments of a Tradwife

> **Five:** Thou shalt perform femininity as if thy life depends on it. Because it does. Lipstick is armor. Aprons are power. And nothing says "I'm fine" like fluttering lashes and a perfectly timed smile.

Ever since she was seventeen, after what happened to Tara, Jennifer had made a personal rule not to use social media. She'd not paid any attention at all since—well, until Jamie left her. Then, it felt like all she could do some nights was scroll until the tears dried up, or she'd spend hours laughing at various comedy sketches and cooing over kitten videos.

In the last year, she'd come a long way from those 2 a.m. scrolling sessions. But there had been the occasional motivating video that had helped her pull up her big girl panties the next day.

And maybe now it was her turn to pay it forward.

Or at least share her story.

The weight of her phone in her hand felt a whole lot heavier than its meager ounces. The weight of what she was about to do—even more so. Could she really put a message out into the world warning women against the stifling repercussions of being a tradwife? What could happen when a woman gave up her autonomy and bowed to her husband's will? Could she really share her story?

More important, she worried that sharing her story would dig up a whole lot of the past that needed to remain buried.

If Jamie—or anyone he knew, for that matter—saw what she said about him, about the life they'd led . . . he would be beyond pissed. And there was no telling what he'd do when he was pissed. Jamie had a temper. When he didn't get his way, or she'd done something he didn't like, well, he made it very clear. Sometimes with slammed cabinets and doors. Sometimes with three days of silence. Sometimes with threats that weren't said outright—but she still heard loud and clear. Other times, his anger took a more corporal method, as he'd put her over his knee and spank her like she was a bad child.

Now, with them sharing custody, he had leverage over her he'd never had before—the threat of taking away their kids. And she didn't like that.

So, if she was going to post on social media, she'd just have to create a new profile. Something untraceable. No real name. No connections. Something anonymous enough that no one—not Jamie, not one of the moms from church, not even her old book club—would ever figure out it was her.

Jennifer hovered her finger over the Create New Account button on the social media platform, hesitating for half a second before she clicked.

This needed to be done. If not for her own personal well-being—to get these things off her chest—then because she knew she couldn't be the only woman out there who'd depended on her husband and community, been coerced into a certain lifestyle and then dropped from the world she knew without a second thought. Left scrounging for purpose, her fingers slipping on the edge of a cliff made of crumbling rock.

Somehow, she'd managed to pick herself up. But every day brought a new challenge. And every day, she worried something else would be ripped out from under her.

Her own community had effectively canceled her. The realization hadn't come all at once. It trickled in—first when she wasn't invited to Bible study. Then when people she used to join for book club avoided eye contact in the grocery store. The final straw had been the church bulletin. A fall event she used to coordinate listed a new name under "Hospitality Chair." Her name wasn't even in the acknowledgments.

Trying to think of a handle, the only thing she could come up with was @CanceledTradWife. That name pretty much said everything she felt—and what her message would embody.

With the account made, and an avatar as her profile picture so no one would recognize her if her profile popped up, Jennifer again hovered over the record button for a reel. She turned the phone over in her hand again. It had become a lifeline after the divorce—a window into other people's joy, other people's pain. Could she really go from consumer to creator? What if no one cared? What if they did?

This time she hit record. The camera light lit up her face—which she did not like—so she turned off the light icon and moved to a shadowy part of her house. The silence was sharp, broken only by the hum of the fridge and the distant drip of a faucet she kept forgetting to fix.

If she was going to share a video, she wanted to start out anonymous, but she wasn't ruling out the possibility of revealing her identity later.

"I live in a small town in Florida," she started. "We're on the coast, and it's quite lovely, actually. The beach has white sand. The waters in the spring and summer are a gorgeous turquoise color. Everything about it is ideal, tranquil. What you might expect the most idyllic coastal town to look like. Except the tranquility of this town is surface level only. Not everything is what it seems."

Jennifer took a breath, pausing the recording. She pictured the linen apron she used to wear, embroidered with bright yellow lemons and verdant green leaves. The morning sun spilling through the window as she cracked eggs into a pan. The sizzle of bacon. Her children's syrup-sticky faces laughing over pancakes. Jamie's lips brushing her fully made-up cheek before he left for work. She'd believed in that version of life. Worshipped it.

She remembered the way Jamie used to leave his juice cup in the sink every morning. How she'd rinse it without resentment, humming as she wiped down the counters, already planning dinner. The feeling that her work meant something. That she mattered.

Now, those memories were suffocated by a feeling of foolishness. Of loss. Jennifer blew out a breath, blinking away the tears that came at being used, no matter how much time had passed.

When she was ready to continue, she mentally straightened her shoulders.

"I used to be a tradwife. Traditional wife. Think about your 1950s housewife. Beautiful dress. Full breakfast served to the family in the morning. Fresh-baked sourdough at night. I served my family. I served my husband. And I'll be honest with you—I loved every minute of it. Being a wife and a mother was my calling. I didn't care that people thought being a traditional wife was archaic. I ignored the feminists who said being a traditional wife was an insult to years of fighting for women's rights. I was happy. Until I got canceled."

She felt the weight of the word as she said it—like a gavel slamming down. Her hands trembled slightly, the phone wobbling in her grip. Her stomach twisted, a slow burn rising in her throat as if her body wanted to reject the truth she'd just named aloud.

Jennifer took a long sip of her Diet Coke, contemplating what to say next. She checked over her shoulder, instinctively scanning the quiet house. The blinds were closed in the front of the house, but open in the back facing the lake. Paranoia crept in. She lowered her voice, heart thudding in her chest.

"And I don't mean canceled by the internet. I got canceled by my husband. Canceled by a society I depended on. Canceled by my friends. By my church. I am a pariah in a town that is the only life I've ever known. Sneered at now for trying to make a living wage. Which, by the way, when you don't have any education or work experience, a living wage isn't really a living wage."

Had she said too much? Did she sound too bitter?

Jennifer shook her head, the shadowy reflection in the camera swimming on the screen.

"I'm supporting myself. I do get child support, but let's face it, ladies—it's not enough when your husband has the child half the time. Which I want. My kids love their father. But that's not what this video is supposed to be about. I'm not on here to complain about my divorce, or how many coupons I have to clip to put dinner on the table. I'm here to educate. I'm here to warn you. Those of you who serve your families and not yourself. Those of you whose identity is as a traditional wife—I was you once.

"There is no guarantee. There is no promise of a happily ever after. Those are just words.

"Tomorrow is not something you're owed. You, too, can be canceled."

Jennifer stared off toward the water in the back. The party was over, but she could still hear their laughter filtering on the wind. She could still feel the disappointment of not being a part of that world.

"We have to protect ourselves," she said softly. "From ourselves. From the world. From the fantasies and the lies." Jennifer looked back into the camera.

"Develop a skill that can be used in the workplace. Get your own bank account. Learn how to read a contract. Know how to file taxes. Save some money in your own account. I know those things sound boring or pointless—but freedom is taken for granted until you don't have it."

Just when had her freedom been taken? Was it that night on the beach in 2013 when Jamie had gripped her arm and said she'd better go along with the story, or was it the first time he'd grabbed her by the hair a week after they were married and asked what the hell she thought she was doing?

She was free now. That, she knew. Jennifer drew in a deep breath, the heaviness that had been pressing down on her lightening. Then she added one final thing. "You never know when your world is going to come crumbling down, and the traditional life you loved is no more. This is the beginning. I'm not here to shame anyone. I'm here to tell the truth—one video at a time."

Video complete, Jennifer hesitated over what to write as the caption. What if someone recognized her voice? Her living room? What if Jamie took her to court and tried to use this as proof of instability? Was telling the truth worth that risk?

She pictured other women stumbling across her video in the dead of night. Pictured them sitting a little taller, maybe cracking the window to smoke a forbidden cigarette, maybe googling community college classes, leaving the dishes in the sink a little longer.

Before she could delete the whole thing, she typed: Dear Tradwives: Please watch this before it's too late.

Her finger hovered for a full minute before she tapped post. When it uploaded, she tossed the phone face down on the couch and walked away. Her heart thundered. Her palms were sweaty. She opened the fridge, took out a string cheese and stood in the doorway chewing, as if her body didn't yet know her life had just changed.

Shadow nudged her leg, and she gave him the last bite of her cheese.

There was no going back. But maybe, just maybe, there was something ahead worth walking toward.

Chapter Nineteen

Ariel

For the briefest second, Ariel stared into the camera without blinking. Her mind was as blank as her gaze. But then her assistant, Harper, cleared her throat, gave a thumbs-up and mouthed, "Action."

Ariel's face made a metamorphosis into one of joyful anticipation. "It's Monday, friends, and you know what that means—we're making soup." She held up the packet of mixed herbs that she'd handpicked from her garden and a few others that were outsourced for the recipe. She could do this with her eyes closed—smile, speak, stir, sparkle. A well-oiled machine wearing a woman's skin. "Today's recipe is for a Cajun chicken noodle soup, and you can get the perfect mix of spices, grown by yours truly, right on our website. Nothing tastes better on a Monday than fresh, homemade soup."

Ariel set down the packet and shifted toward the pot of boiling water. "First, you'll put last night's chicken roast—picked clean, of course—into our boiling water. You'll want to let this simmer for about six hours for the most flavor. I put this one in this morning just before getting our kids ready for their lessons."

She picked up the lid of her simmering pot and showed the carcass submerged in boiling water. Not one of her precious six. Instead, she'd gotten this one from the grocery, unable to murder her feathered audience. She often felt like that chicken. Lowered into boiling water not by force, but by routine. One decision at a time until the heat surrounded her, and she'd stopped noticing how much it burned. She wiped the slight dampness from her palms onto her apron, which featured her six chickens—all still alive.

"While the stock is almost done cooking, let's chop our vegetables. For a traditional chicken soup, you'll have onions, celery and carrots." She waved at her wooden cutting board and all the vegetables on display there, wrapping her fingers around the solid hilt of her sharpened chef's knife. "But when we're making a Cajun soup, I like to add an extra ingredient of chopped bell pepper. I prefer red because red is pretty." Ariel smiled into the camera, then started to chop, her assistant bringing the camera in for a shot of her hands.

Her fingers moved faster, chopping at a speed some might consider dangerous. But what was a little thrill if not a dangerous one? Ariel used to be able to do the knife game—the one where you stabbed the space between your fingers at an ever-growing pace until you nearly came away with one less digit.

Of course, it hadn't happened to her, but late one night after a show, someone made a bet, and that someone now only had four fingers on their left hand.

Ariel had not always been good at cooking. In fact, when she'd been an actress onstage, she'd had to maintain her weight to fit into her costumes, which meant keeping a rather strict and boring diet. And on the occasion she'd binged on a late-night burger, there was always pulling the trigger afterward. One stab to the throat and boom, flushed.

Once she gave up acting, she decided she wanted to experience food in a different way—a healthier way. And if they were going to own a little homestead farm and try to grow their own food, then she was going to learn to cook. Shane, of course, had been completely on board. Growing up in his house, there'd only been cans of Dinty Moore stew and ramen. Meals were often eaten alone, especially after Tara was gone.

Hence, their current lifestyle jived pretty well for them both.

As she chopped, her mind kept wandering back to the garden party. There'd been such a feeling of disconnect with the other women present, most of whom she'd known since childhood. She'd wanted so badly to fit in, but there'd been an aura of *other* cloaked so tightly around her that Ariel thought she might drown in it. Or maybe it was caution. They'd vowed never to talk again after that summer in 2013.

The sense she got from their hostess, Miranda, was that she was somehow playing a role. And of course, weren't they all playing a role? Ariel had had to do just that herself more times than she could count—and not just onstage. Hosting a party was a lot of work. Even Colleen, with her dramatic fall—which felt almost manufactured; if not a cry for help at least staged. Performative. Was it desperation? Scripted? A power play? In Crystal Harbor, it was hard to tell the difference. Besides, Colleen used to always want to be the most important.

Ariel stabbed her knife into the cutting board, watching it wobble but stand upright. Her viewers seemed to like her little tricks, and she dearly loved to entertain.

She scooped the vegetables and put them into a pot of heated oil and garlic to simmer. "Time to sprinkle." She held up the spice packet, wiggling it back and forth before dumping the contents onto the sautéing vegetables.

She shifted on her feet, in her sandals she wore for filming, the straps scraping uncomfortably over the blisters she'd gotten from the garden party shoe choice—form over function, as always.

"While these get nice and sautéed, we're going to drain our stock so we can add it to the vegetables. Oh my goodness, this smells so good." Ariel closed her eyes, leaning over the pan and wafting the scents toward her face, the steam curling like invisible hands around her neck, tightening every time she took a breath.

Truthfully, it did smell delicious. On any other day she would have savored it, maybe even taken a picture for Instagram. But lately, nothing sparked joy. Not the garden. Not the fresh eggs from her chickens. Not even baby Tara's soft weight in her arms.

It felt like a storm cloud had taken up residence inside her skull, pressing against her eyes, settling heavy on her shoulders until she could hardly lift her head. She told herself it was just exhaustion, hormones, the sleepless nights—but deep down she knew better.

Ever since she'd given her daughter that name, *her* name, the past had started knocking again. And then the DMs and comments began. The kind that made her skin prickle and her chest tighten, the kind that felt like someone was just behind her, breathing down her neck. Watching.

And the worst part? She wasn't sure if she was more afraid that the messages and comments were real . . . or that they were deserved.

"Ariel?"

She popped open her eyes. Across the counter was her assistant, eyebrows raised in annoyance. "Did you fall asleep?"

Ariel laughed, sweeping her long hair over her shoulder. Her mascara itched at the corners of her eyes. She dared not smudge it, not on camera. Not now. Not ever. "Of course not. Have you ever just smelled soup? Let the steam rush over your skin? It's like an herbal facial."

Harper shook her head, staring at her as if she'd just asked if she'd ever committed murder. Ariel tried not to let the judgment of the younger woman get to her. Tried not to think about murder.

"Well, maybe you should try it. You might like it."

Harper, one earbud constantly in place, half rolled her eyes, as if catching herself in the act. "Let's get back to filming."

Ariel bit the inside of her cheek. She was perfectly within her rights to say she was the boss and could decide when they filmed—but doing so wouldn't earn her any points with her assistant, and already she was skating on what shouldn't be thin ice.

Ariel poured the stock through a strainer into the pot of spiced vegetables, then added the rotisserie chicken.

"Now for the special ingredient." She held up another spice packet, wiggling the Cajun seasonings toward the camera. "A little kick of Break-a-Leg Cajun Seasoning."

All her store's products had a touch of theater. Even her apron was for sale in her store. Her social media was constantly flooded with people tagging her while they cooked, wearing her chickens' faces.

Ariel had never been one to do things halfway. She always rose to the challenge. Liked to be the best. And with this little venture, there was no difference. She was almost to a million YouTube followers and had already broken that threshold on TikTok last month.

She finished preparing the soup, then ladled a healthy portion into a bowl.

"Let's test it out." She scooped soup into a spoon and poured it into her mouth. "Oh my chickens, that is delicious. Now the bread test!"

She always had a bread test. If it didn't pass the bread test, it was no good. She pulled out the sourdough she'd baked that morning and cut off a thick slice, accidentally nicking just the barest part of her thumb. Red droplets seeped into the bread. But she didn't want to stop filming. To show her assistant she'd cut herself. To waste even a moment on a Band-Aid. Onstage, there were no do-overs. So she ignored it.

Ariel took the blood-marred hunk of bread and dipped it into the broth before tasting. Savory, herbal, primal. At least the metallic taste of blood wasn't something the audience could sense.

"Even better." She smiled into the lens and held out the bowl of soup, keenly aware of her apron strings digging uncomfortably into the back of her neck. How long until they encircled her entire throat, suffocating her?

Her assistant called "Cut" and turned off the camera. "Nice. I'll have this edited and uploaded in an hour."

"Great, thanks." Ariel reached for a spoon left on the counter and held it out to her assistant, offering a taste. "Want to try it?"

"I'm good." The younger woman didn't even glance up from where she was tapping furiously on her phone with a perfectly polished manicure.

Ariel retracted the spoon, her smile tightening. "Suit yourself."

She placed it down quietly, like setting a piece of herself back on the shelf. "Same time tomorrow? I have some breakfast muffins I want to film."

"Sounds good," Harper said, twirling one of her braids like she always did when she was over it. Her assistant made busy work of cleaning up her supplies and not engaging with Ariel.

Outside, one of the sheep let out a sharp, defiant bleat. Ariel flinched. Funny how even the animals knew how to be heard.

Ariel watched her assistant, opening her mouth to try to make a connection that just wasn't there for the thousandth time. Why was it so hard to say the right thing? Maybe it was because she didn't understand herself. Just a woman in a pot, too numb to feel the boil.

How to get this young woman to understand her? She didn't want praise. She didn't even need help. She just wanted to be seen. Not as a brand. Not as a mother. Just . . . seen.

There was something empowering about being seen—truly seen—as a person, not just through the shallow rush of likes and views. In town, most everyone knew about her socials, her products. Some admired her hustle, others rolled their eyes at the attention she drew. But small towns remember everything, even the things no one says out loud.

Sometimes she scrolled her DMs late at night—women saying she'd saved their marriages when they didn't know how to cook, thanking her for her sourdough starter tips, begging for a collab. But would they recognize her without the apron? Without the filter?

Then again, if they really saw what was beneath the layers of skin, muscle and bone, Ariel worried she might never recover from their censure. To her audience, she was sunshine in an apron. A woman who had it all. If only they knew . . .

She ran her finger along the edge of the soup bowl, still warm. She'd been seasoning herself for years, hadn't she? Marinating in everyone else's expectations. God help her if the flame was still rising.

Chapter Twenty

Miranda

Miranda loved to come to downtown Crystal Harbor—except for the parking. Everything was parallel, and though she drove a tiny cherry-colored BMW convertible, her spatial awareness when trying to insert herself between two cars wasn't exceptional.

The town itself was a pure Italian Renaissance fantasy. Stucco exteriors in warm shades of cream and coral, arched doorways with wrought iron trim, a central fountain of mermaids and cobblestoned sidewalks lined with cafés and bright umbrellas gave the town its curated charm.

The last time she'd come into town, she'd bumped someone's Tesla a little, leaving the barest, tiniest scratch. When she'd gotten out to apologize, the blustery man had taken one look at her cleavage and said there was no need to exchange papers. Men were so predictable. It's why she'd pushed up her tits before even getting out of the car.

But today, she'd gotten lucky. Two open spaces, shaded by palms, outside the Harbor Café meant she could just pull right in.

Getting out would be another story, as the place would no doubt be packed in minutes.

The sun beamed down on her bare shoulders in her Lilly Pulitzer white sundress with a bougainvillea print. Purse slung over her shoulder, sunglasses perched on her nose, she sauntered toward the outdoor tables of the café, where she was meeting a few of her new friends.

Her party friends.

Not everyone was invited to this little brunch. Just the few chosen ones.

A girl had to have her favorites, didn't she?

Sometimes she thought she might have been insane, agreeing to play housewife with Benjamin. After all, she'd had a good gig in New York. Ben was great in bed, and his money was nice. The cars. The vacations and fancy dinners. But that's where the good parts ended.

A girl who'd had to take care of herself from the time she could remember deserved having a man take care of her for once. And not for a service. That was really the whole point of this marriage, wasn't it? Free sex. Free labor. What traditional wife in her right mind didn't realize she was providing services? A servant.

Well, at least Benjamin was willing to make some allowances, given he'd met her in New York, and she'd seen a side of him he didn't present to the world.

The night he'd walked into the club, and she'd decided he was hers, she'd come up behind him, the music pumping, the lights strobing, and tapped him on the shoulder. He'd turned around, a very alcoholic Manhattan at his lips, and looked her up and down as though he was a man dying of thirst and she had the key to the fountain. Miranda had dragged him onto the dance floor, and he'd promised her the world.

There were some perks to being a kept woman.

Loving Benjamin meant loving a version of herself she still wasn't sure fit right in her skin. In New York, she'd been loud, wild, untethered—exactly how she liked it. Free from her past. Here, she'd traded stilettos for espadrilles, dinner reservations for car pools and covered dishes. Sometimes she caught herself smiling too wide, like a woman in an ad for a life she hadn't meant to order. Here, she wasn't free.

The clocks were ticking, and she was running among them checking off lists—some to keep her life in order, others to set it spinning.

A yellow sundress of commotion by the sidewalk caught Miranda's attention. Colleen. The woman was a mess. Had she driven here in that state? She could barely walk. Miranda stood and rushed over to where Colleen was trying to straighten her wedge leather sandal, which had fallen off—probably because it wasn't buckled. Karma was a bitch.

Miranda knelt before Colleen, buckling her shoe. "Are you all right, hon?"

"Yes, yes," Colleen said, waving her hand away. She didn't smell like booze, but her pupils looked a little too big for this kind of sunshine. And when she laughed, there was something hollow about it. So, what was it? Pills? "Just rushed out of the house before the kids could wrap their claws around me and drag me back."

Miranda reached for Colleen's hand to steady her, and for just a second, she wanted to ask if she was *really* okay, if she suffered from nightmares, guilt. And wanted the real answer—not the brunch, prepared-response version. But she didn't ask. Instead, Miranda laughed. "Sounds like a horror movie."

"Sometimes it is."

How true the words. The shoe secured, they walked back toward a table where a waiter was putting down glasses of water. Before they'd taken their seats, Brad, Samantha and Ariel arrived.

Ariel looked completely different from when Miranda had first seen her in the grocery store. She looked refreshed somehow.

"Good morning," Miranda said, hugging everyone before taking her seat.

"I think I'm going to get a Diet Coke," Ariel announced with a grin. "I never drink soda."

"Me too," Samantha chimed in.

How sweet. "I wonder if they can make me a mock mimosa?" Miranda offered, testing the waters to see if anyone said they wanted a real one.

Colleen's eyebrows shot up. "Yes."

"I'm going with a dirty Diet Coke," Brad said.

"Dirty, do tell?" Miranda sat forward, waiting to see just how far Brad would go—whiskey, rum?—then realizing how fucking stupid that was. In New York City, they'd be trashed already.

"Add some creamer to it. My gosh, it's like heaven." Brad looked ready to cream his pants over a fucking soda. He wasn't even being suggestive. That was the wildest part.

"Oh," Ariel crooned. "Creamer? That is dirty."

Miranda hid her disappointment. "I've never had that."

"Don't waste your time," Colleen said, eyeing Miranda over her sunglasses from bloodshot eyes.

Miranda grinned. "Too dirty?"

"Not dirty enough." Colleen waved over the waiter. "Two dirty

Diet Cokes for my friends here, and two mock mimosas, light on the mock if you know what I mean." She winked.

Miranda's eyes bulged, and Ariel, Samantha and Brad swiveled their heads toward Colleen.

"I'm kidding," Colleen said with a laugh that sounded as fake as Miranda's love for cleaning toilets. "Of course we want real mock mimosas."

The waiter glanced around the table like he hadn't understood a damned word, then nodded and walked away. Ariel's smile tightened at Colleen's joke, and she adjusted her napkin without looking up, putting her silverware back into perfect order. So, the princess had boundaries. Noted. Then again, Miranda hadn't found a boundary she couldn't break. Challenge?

"You had me going there for a second," Brad said, shaking his head and blowing out an exaggerated breath.

"Zachary would kill me." Colleen laughed.

"Would he?" Samantha teased. "Or just give you a good spanking?"

"I've never had champagne," Ariel said, coming off ethereal and making Miranda a little nauseated in the process.

"Not even when you were on Broadway? No celebratory cheers?"

She shook her head. "I've never had a drop of alcohol in my life." She shrugged. "It's a sin."

"Hmm," Miranda said. "If drinking alcohol is a sin, have you ever wondered why Jesus changed the water into wine?"

"Good point," Colleen offered, reapplying her lipstick unnecessarily.

"The wine back then wasn't strong at all," Brad said. "Practically water."

"Because you're a time traveler and would know?" Miranda teased.

"They just didn't let it ferment as long." He shrugged.

"That's true, I heard it on a podcast," Samantha mused.

"Interesting," Ariel said, her voice detached.

"Do you ever get bored here?" Miranda asked, glancing at the perfectly cleaned and styled street. As if the town had been built like a movie set and all the people within it, the actors.

"Bored?" Brad asked.

"Like you're sitting around and feel like you have nothing to do?"

Brad chuckled. "You need a baby. Babies keep you busy."

Suddenly, the lovely warmth of the day felt sticky and oppressive.

Ariel studied her silently. There was a lot more happening behind her eyes than what was coming out of her mouth. "I think I know what you mean. You need a hobby. What were your hobbies before coming here?"

Partying. Sex. Drinking. Revenge.

"I liked to organize events," Miranda said.

"Your garden party was so lovely." Ariel nodded. "I still dance and sing. But like Brad said, my kids keep me busy."

"Have you never wanted to work?" Miranda asked Brad. It was really strange that he was a stay-at-home dad. Like, she knew men did it, but she'd never actually met one.

"Being a full-time father is work." The way Brad said it, a little on edge, made it seem as though this was a discussion he'd had before—and a platform he often had to defend. "Just because I'm a man doesn't make it any less important."

Miranda nodded along, but something about the way Brad gripped his glass—tight, knuckles white—made her pause. She wondered if he practiced that speech in the mirror.

"Oh, of course not," Miranda soothed. "I just was curious. Did you always want to be a dad?"

"Yeah." Brad sipped his water. "I used to be a criminal lawyer. It's how Kennedy and I met, but she loved working more than me, and when we had the twins . . ." He shrugged. "It was the logical decision."

Ariel, Samantha and Colleen watched Brad, their expressions shuttered. Oh, if only Miranda could pry open those brains and pick around inside.

"And thank you for inviting me to brunch," Brad said. "Not many women around here have accepted me as part of the pack."

Miranda turned to him slowly, letting her sunglasses slip just enough to meet his eyes. She held the stare a beat too long—just long enough to make him wonder what she was thinking. Flirtation? Appraisal? Dismissal? He looked away first.

"The pack?" Miranda laughed. "You make us sound like wolves."

"Some women are," Colleen said.

Miranda laughed again, but her smile didn't reach her eyes. Did Colleen count herself as one?

"Well, you're welcome anytime," Miranda said to Brad.

"Careful, Miranda," Colleen said with a smirk. "Keep acting like queen bee, someone might swat you."

Miranda licked her lower lip, ready to tell Colleen exactly what she thought, when the other woman threw up her hands, eyes wide. "Kidding! I kid. Of course Brad is welcome."

"Don't be so sure about that," Brad said. "Men tend to get jealous."

"Of you?"

"Of other men."

"I'm sensing a little history here." Miranda tilted her head to the side. "Did you two used to . . ."

"Ages ago." Colleen waved her hand in the air.

Miranda grinned as she watched the four people at her table squirm.

Miranda wasn't so sure Benjamin was the jealous type. When they'd been in New York, before they'd been married, they'd played a game where she would pretend to seduce another man until Benjamin swooped in. One time it had even gotten so far as her pushed up against a wall with another man's fingers inside her.

Miranda suddenly felt like a stranger at her own table with these people whom she knew. The laughter, the clinking glasses, even the warmth of the sun—all of it felt a little too bright, a little too far away.

Would Benjamin want to watch her with Brad? Did she want Brad?

The waiter returned with their drinks, and when she sipped her mocktail, she was decidedly disappointed all over again.

She set the drink down. Too sweet. Too safe.

Like everything else in this town that claimed to be real.

Chapter Twenty-One

Jennifer

The Fifteen Commandments of a Tradwife

> **Six:** Thou shalt not covet thy neighbor's divorce lawyer. Even when your husband forgets your birthday and "accidentally" gropes his secretary. Forgiveness is free, divorce is not.

At one point in her life, Jennifer was fairly certain that her entire personality was constructed like a round of sourdough bread—soft on the inside, hot enough to melt butter, with an exterior shell that was crisp and came to a perfectly curated peak.

What sort of woman compared herself to bread?

Even now, she mixed the four ingredients—flour, salt, yeast and water—from memory. Her hands measuring, stirring, kneading in a meditation of creation. She was the bread, and the bread was her. One with the bread. Sticky dough covered her fingers, and she reached into the powdery tub of flour to sprinkle more onto the dough.

She glanced toward the darkened kitchen window as she breathed in the familiar yeasty scent. The hour was before dawn, and it would be a few more before the kids would wake to fresh-baked bread that she'd slather in homemade strawberry jam. There were some traditional habits that were hobbies, and she wasn't interested in breaking those. There would be the comforting warmth of the oven, the mouth-watering smell of baking bread mingling with the sugary, berry scent of the jam she'd made the night before.

With the dough set to rise, she picked up her cell phone, surprised to see dozens—no, hundreds?—of notifications. Startled, she stared for a moment, flicking through the unending line of notifications, trying to decipher exactly what was happening.

Her first instinct had been to worry about her children, even though she knew they were nestled asleep upstairs with Shadow resting in the small hallway. The number of notifications and dings going off indicated some sort of disaster.

The notifications were all from TikTok—thank goodness, not an emergency. But also . . . What the heck?

Jennifer sat on the cold tile floor, her back pressed against a cabinet, the scent of rising dough clinging to the air like a comforting blanket. She clicked on the app notifications and her shadowed face, hair tossed up in a messy bun, popped up on the screen followed by the sound of her voice. *We have to protect ourselves. From ourselves. From the world. From the fantasies and the lies.*

If she wasn't listening to herself speak on screen, she wouldn't recognize her own voice, which sounded oddly . . . confident.

All of the notifications were from the post that she'd put up last night—it had garnered so much attention. Hundreds of likes and comments. More than she'd ever get through in a single day, let alone the hours she had to wait for her bread to rise.

Was this what it meant to go viral? She swallowed hard, the implications whirling around in her head. Panic. Fear. Exhilaration.

"Oh my God," she whispered, then crossed herself for taking the Lord's name in vain. She might have left her community, her church, but that didn't mean she didn't still believe in God. As cliché as it sounded, the Lord did work in mysterious ways.

Like right now, with her phone and the video. As she stared at it, the numbers continued to tick up. She really was going viral right before her very eyes. This was insane. And terrifying. What if Jamie saw? What if someone recognized the outline of her face and told him? She could picture his own face turning red. Imagined him swerving down the road, running a red light, hopping a curb and storming up to her door. A single fist slamming against the barrier until she answered.

Jennifer shook herself out of the nightmare. Jamie wouldn't do that. He couldn't do that. They were no longer married, and he no longer had any say in what she did . . . but he could punish her all the same. Take her children from her, which he'd threatened more than once. He wouldn't scream. He'd do what he always did—smile in court, and twist every word until it was her fault.

She could still hear the way his voice dropped when he said, *Careful, Jen. You don't want to make me look bad.*

Her thumb hovered, heart clenching every time a new comment popped up. Her breath caught on the mean ones, released in shaky exhales at the ones that were kind. Fear of what people might be saying seemed to never ease. Would they disagree with her? Tell her she was stupid? Rage at her and say that it was all her own fault?

Well . . . there were a few of those. A flicker of guilt wormed its way through her chest. She shouldn't have opened up herself, and potentially her kids, to this kind of scrutiny.

Maybe you shouldn't have gotten married so young.

You made your bed, now sleep in it, idiot.

Why should we care? Get over yourself.

No wonder your husband left you. 🙄

But there were others that warmed her heart. Provided the validation she hadn't known she needed.

You're so brave. I'm happy you got out of that situation!

Thank you for sharing this. It gives me hope there's a chance for me too.

Ugh, I have to work two jobs to pay the bills and keep my kids fed. The ex is a total scam artist.

You're my hero!

Your kids will thank you one day. Keep on keeping on, mama.

The mix of reactions was surprising, and at the same time, it wasn't. More than one of them rattled her to her core. And just as many lifted her up. How surreal that a personal post, where she'd poured out her heart, her worries, had become popular content in less than twenty-four hours.

Jennifer had worried that by posting, she would get a lot of flak from haters. That was the way social media worked—especially if you shared something personal. There was something about the anonymity of a keyboard that gave strangers the guts to lambast others. To judge. To be rude. To hate.

And there were certainly plenty of haters here. Her past self would have been one of them.

But there were just as many people sharing love. Just as many people who were inspired.

And those were the ones she'd wanted to reach in the first place—to inspire women to take care of themselves. None of them were guaranteed a happily ever after. And as much as she loved to read about sweep-you-off-your-feet heroes in the romance novels she'd snuck when Jamie wasn't looking, she also knew those were fantasies. At least, they had been in her reality.

She'd take the kids to the library for the children's reading hour, and while they were having a grand old time with the librarians and other kids, she'd sneak off to the stacks and pull out a book. Her heart had pounded with each turned page, from a strange cocktail of shame and exhilaration. She'd stayed until she could hear her kids' voices as they ran through the stacks trying to find her, devouring every stolen sentence. Then she'd mark down the page number and come back to pick up where she'd left off next time. The only books she'd ever checked out from the library were cookbooks, gardening books, religious texts and, of course, approved children's books.

There was always a list of approved reading material from Pastor Joseph that all the women in the community abided by. Because what one read and took into their brains was important. And according to her old community, only the approved books with the right messages were the suitable thing to read.

All it had taken was an afternoon spent accidentally reading a non-approved book for Jennifer to realize that edict was a bunch of garbage. People who read thrillers weren't out there murdering and maiming people. Women who read romance weren't suddenly leaving their husbands to find their medieval knight in shining armor, or to join a motorcycle gang, and reading a novel about two people of the same sex falling in love hadn't turned her sexual preference. Love was love.

She glanced toward the coffee table with its basket of knitting, which held seven romance novels and thrillers she'd checked out from the library this week. One book a day to devour. She had an entire adult reading life to catch up on. And no one to tell her she couldn't. But she still kept the books hidden. Afraid that one of her kids would see them and tell their dad about it. Not on purpose or out of spite. Just randomly, casually—the way children sometimes did. Letting loose hints and clues and confessions without realizing it.

That was how she'd found out about her husband's new wife before she was his wife. The kids had found a tube of fuchsia lipstick in a bathroom drawer. Jennifer had never worn lipstick when she was married to Jamie. And when she'd learned about the lipstick, the first thing she'd done was go and buy the exact color and try it on. She'd expected to feel ridiculous, a fraud. But instead, the mirror showed someone sharper. Someone just beginning to see herself again. She used to think that lipstick belonged to someone else. Now she wore it like war paint.

Sometimes she wore it now when she read her novels.

Her phone buzzed with incoming comments and likes—or hates.

After two hours of scrolling, when it was time to punch down the dough, her blood was buzzing with anticipation for another video. Why lose momentum now?

And then it came to her: *a then-and-now picture.*

Her, out of the shadows.

Jennifer put on the fuchsia lipstick. She tapped some flour onto her nose. Pulled on her apron—the one she'd used for decades. And she took a selfie with her perfect dough.

On TikTok, she uploaded a side-by-side of her baking bread before the divorce—pale, drab, a smile that looked haunted—and the second picture now, where she looked playful, peaceful, and . . . dare she say, feisty? There was something straighter in the set of her shoulders. Again . . . that confidence she'd noted in her voice had somehow found its way into her posture too.

Her finger hovered over the post button on TikTok. Again. She took a breath, steadied herself—and tapped.

Another idea came to her then, and she bit her lip, wondering if she had the guts to do it. If she was going to send a message out into the world, it was probably important for her to post this one. She searched for the name of a woman she knew in town, watched her video and then did a stitch. A warning to other women. Not a mockery but a message about the dangers of embracing the tradwife lifestyle. She wrote as her caption: *This life might look peaceful, blessed, but what happens when the camera stops rolling? When the curtain is lifted? Not everything is the way it seems.* Again, she hesitated before posting. But before she could change her mind, she pressed the button to post.

Maybe that was why her community didn't want women to read romance novels—because they were empowering. She was as feisty as a Highland lass. As fierce as a magazine editor marching down a boulevard. As brave as a woman who'd inherited an inn and had to fix it up.

She didn't think of herself as a writer. And though she'd only posted a couple of times, each caption, each video, each stitched story, was starting to feel like the beginning chapters of her own story. Already, she had dozens more planned in her mind. A way to keep track. A way to be heard.

Jennifer was taking back her life. She was going to be the hero of her own story.

A loud *thwack* at her front door had Jennifer bolting forward. Shadow gave a low growl, slinking toward the door. Maybe it was just the newspaper delivery boy. Except she didn't subscribe to the newspaper.

Jennifer crept toward the door, peeking out of the tiny peephole and seeing nothing but the very first rays of dawn. She opened the door to see if the newspaper boy had accidentally delivered the paper to her house, but it wasn't a newspaper wrapped in plastic on her porch.

It was a loaf of bread. The bright white, red, blue and yellow packaging of Wonder Bread, smashed from where it had hit against her door. The price tag sticker very clearly stated the grocery store where she worked.

What the actual fuck? She glanced up and down the street, seeing no one in sight. Not a single movement, and yet she could feel eyes watching.

Jennifer picked up the loaf, only to find it had been cut underneath, and all the slices spilled out. *Asshole.* Fine, food for the birds.

She picked up the plastic to throw it away, and kicked the slices into her meager garden, only to reveal a note: *Wolves dress up too.*

A creak upstairs brought her back to reality. She needed to finish making breakfast. After throwing away the garbage, Jennifer punched down the risen dough, marveling at how something could collapse—and still rise again, stronger than before.

Fuck the person who'd thrown the bread. Fuck whatever message it was they were trying to send.

This dough would rise again. And so would she.

Chapter Twenty-Two

Ariel

The woman staring back at Ariel in the mirror was as familiar as she was unrecognizable. She used to see a woman on the edge of Broadway brilliance, with glowing skin, sparkling eyes and a smile that promised the world.

Now, the angles of her face were sharp and highlighted the lines she'd traced since the first time she played with makeup. And there were hollows there now—dips in the frame of her face put there by moments of strain that felt like an eternity in the making.

A sharp knock on the door startled Ariel. She gasped, pulling away from the bathroom vanity to stare at the door. Glad for no longer having to gaze into the hollowness reflected there, no longer wanting to scratch her own eyes out. She swallowed, her throat dry, as the white wood shook from the knuckles on the other side.

"Ariel, what are you doing in there?" Shane groused. He always liked to make sure his hair was more perfect even than hers. "We've got a video to make—hurry up."

Ariel swallowed the sudden panic in her chest, gripping the edge of the marble vanity so tightly that her fingernail broke. She gasped at the pain and stuck the finger in her mouth, the jagged edge of the nail rough on her tongue, and the barest hint of metallic blood.

"I'll be out in a second. I just broke a nail."

The excuse slid off her tongue as easily as Shane would later slide into her. As easily as all the lies that seemed to come out of her mouth every day, and as easily as the truths she kept silent. She stared down at the broken fringe of her now ragged nail. A little line of blood seeped across the top and mixed with her saliva.

There had once been a time when the act of taking out the nail clippers, the nail file and her polish would have been a simple task. But now her fingers felt heavy as she gripped the drawer handle—one that felt like a thousand pounds—and fumbled through the contents until her fingers found the cool metal of the clippers.

"I've got a tee time in thirty minutes. Clients don't like to wait. We need to get this done." Shane's voice sounded irritated from the other side of the door. He never enjoyed making the videos they needed for their social media to keep the farm products selling.

She supposed she could've made the videos on her own, but the whole point was to show their audience that these wholesome products were made by a loving, beautiful family. People would look at them and think, *If I use this product, I can have a family like that too.* Sometimes, when she rewatched the videos, she thought the same thing. Like an out-of-body experience—realizing, once the video ended, that it wasn't really her family she'd just seen on-screen.

But that's what commercials were, right? Lies disguised as beauty. Manipulations that played on your desires. She'd worn this role so long, she wasn't sure where the costume ended and her skin began.

With her nail fixed, Ariel forced herself back into the place she'd been for what felt like eons. She adjusted her face like a mask, sculpted not with clay but with obligation. When she opened the bathroom door, Shane was standing in the hallway, leaning against the wall, arms crossed over his chest, one ankle hooked over the other.

His brow was furrowed, lips pursed in irritation. When had he gone from being excited about making these videos with her—sharing their life with the world—to it being a burden? It had been a recent development. She was sure of that.

Maybe as recent as the changes with her.

Ariel flashed him a smile. The kind of smile they both knew well. *I'm sorry for taking so long—and you look handsome, if that helps.*

The irritated lines of Shane's face melted, and he grinned back at her, going from the husband who had changed recently to the man she'd fallen in love with.

She supposed she wasn't the only one good at acting. Humans were good at deceiving each other, whether for entertainment or some other agenda. The only thing was—Ariel knew what she was hiding. She had no idea what Shane was keeping hidden from her.

Downstairs in the kitchen, their assistant, Harper, hunched over the island counter. Her fingers frantically scrolled her phone. Hearing them approach, she glanced up, panic on her face that made Ariel's heart skip a beat. Something was wrong. Really wrong. Ariel hadn't seen that kind of panic since opening night at the Gershwin Theatre, when the understudy forgot her lines and half the cast spiraled.

"What's the matter?" Shane sounded as worried as Ariel felt, which only made her heart jump more.

Harper didn't say anything—her mouth opened and closed like she was choking on megabytes, the cell phone dangling from her fingertips like a weapon used in a crime.

"Harper?" Ariel shuffled forward, her feet gliding across the slick wooden floor they'd spent hours agonizing over at the design shop.

Before the assistant could hold the phone back, Ariel snatched it away, scrolling through what Harper had been looking at. Her brow wrinkled in confusion.

Just comments on a social media post—people saying horrible things about whoever had posted a video.

At first, Ariel didn't understand what she was reading. This couldn't be about her. Why was Harper freaking out? But then it became very clear. Reality slammed into her chest, knocking her back a step. It was the chicken soup reel they'd filmed. The one where she'd zoned out mid-shoot, her smile had slipped—not long, just enough to show the ghost behind it.

She looks haunted.

Free Ariel.

They probably don't even make their own products. It's all a sham.

No one is that beautiful. Something's off.

I heard they don't even raise those chickens. Free range my ass.

Didn't his sister die?

"Is this about . . . *us*?" Shane's voice was full of rage.

Ariel glanced at her husband, his cheeks flaming. Tears formed in her eyes after reading the horrible things people said about her—about their video—questioning the integrity of their products, their lives.

She questioned herself enough. But seeing the doubts typed out by strangers made them feel *real*. They weren't . . . wrong. But to question her integrity? Not just her appearance, her performance, but her life. She was used to mean comments, but they didn't usually call her a sham.

To bring up Tara . . .

A text popped up, and then another, messages from friends asking if she was all right. Clearly, they'd seen the video and comments.

Shane grabbed the phone, scrolling. His face turned a shade of red rarely displayed. He handed the phone back to Harper, his teeth gritted.

"Take this down. Get these reported. These people are harassing us. It's going to ruin our product."

"But there are thousands of them."

"Well, then, you have some work to do, don't you?" Shane glanced at Ariel, his face unreadable—and firm at the same time. His phone buzzed in his pocket, and his eyes flicked down before he silenced it without checking. Ariel's stomach twisted. He never ignored his phone. "We're not doing a video today."

He turned around without letting her argue and walked toward the garage.

She rushed after him, grabbed his arm—and he turned back around, glaring down at her with startling anger. He stared at her hand where it gripped his bicep, and she let go. He'd never looked at her like that before, with disdain and . . . indifference.

"Don't go." Her voice came out sounding whiny. Scared. As if the little girl inside her—the one who'd been afraid for the last nine months—had finally surfaced.

The muscle in the side of Shane's jaw flexed, and he hesitated, eyeing her. "I need to get some fresh air. And it's my job, Ariel."

Numbly, Ariel watched him walk through the door. She almost begged him. Almost apologized, she didn't know what for. But she swallowed it down. Willed her tongue to still.

The wall around the door shuddered as he shut it firmly behind him, as if it were a finality. As if she wouldn't be walking through that door after him. And she didn't.

She stood there. Her stomach knotted. As if she were in a scene she didn't recall auditioning for. Resentment and bile rose in her throat.

Then she rushed toward the bathroom to throw up, lifting the toilet seat to find a blue foamy letter *M* in the toilet, courtesy of one of her children. Of course it was the letter *M. Mother. Mirror. Monster.* She wasn't sure which fit her best anymore. Bile burned the back of her throat, and she tried to swallow it down, fishing for the bathtub letter, holding back her vomit. Even in her worst moments, motherhood was waiting, bright and artificial and impossible to escape.

Once the toy detritus was retrieved, however, her body let loose.

She was as jagged as that broken nail—splintered at the edge, held together by will.

It wasn't as if she hadn't had bad reviews before or seen the things people said about her online. No one in show business could escape that kind of scrutiny.

The thing that was bothering Ariel the most was that the lies she'd been telling herself—the lies she'd been trying to convince herself were true—had seemingly been brought to the surface, their layers peeled back, her insides exposed for all the world to see.

All it would take was one more slip and the whole truth would come out.

She flushed, wiped her mouth and stared at the mirror again—half expecting not to see a woman at all, just the costume she'd sewn herself into. The worst part wasn't the comments, or even Shane. It was that somewhere, deep down, she was starting to agree with them.

Chapter Twenty-Three

Miranda

Sitting in the quiet of her closet, with Benjamin off to his office, Miranda hit play on the old cell phone she kept in the secret lockbox.

On the screen, someone asked, "What day is it?" The background of the club was purple and pink, the music thumping.

A younger version of Miranda's face flashed on the screen. "My twenty-first birthday!"

It wasn't her twenty-first birthday, but when she'd left her old life behind and started a new one in New York City, given the line of work she was in, a new identity was important, which included a new birthday. She'd just switched the numbers. Instead of June 8, her new birthday was August 6. Easy to remember, not that she would ever forget.

Miranda's memory was a fireproof vault.

On-screen, several women from Miranda's scene cheered into the camera, raising shot glasses into the air. Miranda could practically taste the sweet and tang of the lemon drop shots. She closed her eyes, swayed to the music and the cheers on-screen. That had been the first birthday she'd celebrated in her new life in the city, ignoring the previous ones. And it had been the start of what she would come to think of as her enterprise. Big parties, rich men, deep friendships—the kind that only happen when you text a friend to come get you out from under a mark who's passed out mid-fuck.

The cheers on-screen cut off abruptly and Miranda opened her eyes. The battery had died on the old cell phone, but the memories still played in her ear. Though she'd shunned her past, blamed those people from her youth for her later misfortunes, without them, she wouldn't have become the woman she was. She wouldn't be here, fulfilling a decade-long dream.

Since leaving New York City, Miranda rarely scrolled on social media. It was hard enough to look at the life she'd left behind—to see the people she missed at a rooftop party, a curated picture on the subway of her wearing red-bottom heels, the life she hadn't exactly wanted to forgo. She missed the rhythm of the city—the buzz of espresso machines, the chaos of a hopping club, the way the bodega guy by her apartment knew her name. Here, her biggest thrill was a charity luncheon where someone brought lemon bars instead of brownies.

The only time she scrolled now was to look up recipes that might entice her husband or things she could make for the neighborhood barbecues and bake sales that would impress her community and endear her to them.

These days, her posts were strictly homemaker-core. @MayorBsWife posted natural makeup tutorials. The perfectly folded napkin. Posts that would make people believe she was something other than what she really was. Anything else only made that itch beneath her skin grow frenzied, like a million ants dancing along her skin.

And those uncontrollable yearnings, the need to do things that this town wouldn't approve of, would only get her into trouble. They'd be horrified if they'd seen her social media content from her old life—shots at a Technicolor club, scantily clad models at a fashion show, sleepy, makeup-smeared eyes at 4 a.m. #LifeOfTheParty. But a girl had to do what a girl had to do, didn't she? And let's face it, she'd had a lot of fun doing it.

For some reason, this morning—after documenting her day at the spa, getting her nails and hair done, mingling with the crowd—she started scrolling on TikTok. The subtle pink of her acrylic nail swiped absent-mindedly. She told herself she was looking for a dinner recipe. A savory meal that would make Ben's tongue dance. However, the first thing that popped up was what was trending.

Tradwives in small towns, rejecting feminist ideals and "taking women back in time."

That was odd. Miranda bit her lip, her manicured nail frozen over the screen. She should X out of the app. She should put her phone in her purse and head straight to the grocery store. She should do a lot of things. But curiosity was getting the better of her.

It sounded a lot like what she'd noticed when she first came to town with Benjamin. What he had wanted from her—living like it was 1950. She remembered stories of her mother's childhood, of a mother who stayed at home, always had dinner on the table by five, a demanding husband, chores, depression. No life. Just living *for* the family.

When Miranda had heard those stories, she thought they sounded completely miserable. Her own mother had, in fact, shunned such things—so much so that she was rarely even around. Miranda had spent most of her childhood taking care of herself and counting on her grandmother for rides. Rare was it that her mother picked her up from school or made a home-cooked meal.

The parallels between her life now and those stories hadn't really struck Miranda . . . until just now.

She started to scroll through the various tradwife posts. Pictures of smiling wives with dead eyes in puffy skirts, hair done in 1950s styles, food prepped and on the table, martinis in hand—it was all very reminiscent of a time long gone. Except these women were standing in modern kitchens with modern appliances, recording their lives on cell phones, hashtagging the crap out of their content like they'd just discovered social media. #Tradwife #Homemaker #TraditionalWife #FeminineNotFeminist #SAHM #TraditionalValues.

Miranda glanced down at her own dress—a vintage-inspired Chanel that a woman in the 1950s would never have dared to wear. She'd never have pictured herself here, but it was exactly where she needed to be. Pot roast on the table; polite lunches with Ariel, Samantha and Brad; playing along as if she were in on the joke.

The irony wasn't lost on her: She'd once laughed at influencer culture, rolled her eyes at women who filmed their morning routines like it was cinema. Now she was one of them—posing her napkins and smiling just so while timing her sourdough reveal with golden-hour light. Every detail curated, every scene staged. The whole performance carefully designed not just to help her blend in, but to hide the real work she was doing—the work no one here would see coming until it was far too late.

Then she came across a video that made her heart skip a beat.

It was a side-by-side sketch by some random person online—some nobody with little influence until now—who had decided to take up a mantle against a lifestyle they clearly knew nothing about. And right next to them was the beautiful face of Ariel. Ariel dancing on her farm, gathering eggs from her chickens, her smiling face bright and beautiful. She looked luminous, even in a grainy frame. Miranda hated how easily beauty still clung to her.

There was no other reason for the post but to make fun of the life Ariel had formed for herself.

The comments were even worse.

Stepford Wives cosplay much?

You're selling submission as empowerment.
Good luck when the divorce hits!

Privileged influencer playing house. Gross.

Pick-me.

Anti-feminist puppet.

Cruelty masked behind a screen. These weren't just trolls—these were bored, bitter people who hid behind their keyboards, spitting poison they'd never dare to in person. She knew that kind of vitriol. She'd felt it burn once, years ago, until it had nearly pulled her under. One wrong word, one ill-timed reaction, and a person's whole world could be swallowed by the tide.

Had Ariel seen this? She was already brittle enough, if anyone had been paying attention. Miranda made a mental note to call her later. Check in. See how she was holding up. Sometimes kindness softened people enough so you could see what was underneath.

Ariel took pride in the life she'd built, though Miranda could tell she missed the life she used to lead. That was something they had in common, though for very different reasons. Miranda liked to think her own past had made her harder, sharper—but even steel could bend.

Sometimes she caught Ariel staring, lost, like someone trapped behind a pane of glass. Like at the grocery store, her nail sinking into the skin of an apple, eyes fixed on something no one else could see. Miranda had seen that look before—on her own mother, after her youngest brother was born.

Postpartum, maybe? Guilt over something she'd done?

Was Ariel getting any kind of care?

Miranda's irritation flared. *Don't react. Don't get dragged in. Don't give them anything.*

One comment mentioned Ariel's "crazy eyes." Another said she was probably medicated into submission. Miranda's hand shook. She didn't know who posted the video, but she knew what they were trying to do. Cancel Ariel. Ruin her. And she wasn't going to stand by and let it happen. Ariel still had a part to play, whether she knew it or not.

The only person doing any canceling today was going to be Miranda. She tapped into the comments: If looking hot AF while making soup is your version of oppression, maybe go cry into your microwave dinner.

Her finger hovered over the post button, sunlight catching on her diamond ring. She stared at the glint like it might explode. One wrong move and everything would detonate. Her pulse ticked in the side of her neck. She could almost feel Benjamin's career collapsing under her nail—and the aftermath of his anger would not be confined to his office. There was the issue of self-preservation.

There was also the issue that if she spoke up publicly, if she commented, reposted, defended—there would be a spotlight on her. And that meant people from her past life would see where she was. What she was doing. They might say something, post a picture of her online partying at an exclusive, taboo club. All it would take was one blurry photo—her in fishnets and eyeliner, a glass of champagne mid-toast—and the whole illusion would collapse. And then the people of Crystal Harbor would see who Benjamin had really married. That was definitely not information she wanted getting out. Benjamin certainly didn't.

It would ruin his career. And it would ruin her plans.

So, the only thing she could really do to ensure Ariel didn't falter was to be there for Ariel, quietly. Privately.

With an irritated groan, Miranda deleted her reply in the comments and then flashed off a text to Ariel, asking if she wanted to meet at the farmers market to get some fresh fruit and make pies together. Something they could do to get out of the house and talk. A gentle way to check in.

As she scrolled through more posts—checking to see if there were others about Ariel—she came across another one that made her blood run cold. The bitch might put herself in shadow, but Miranda had a good eye.

There was *no way* Benjamin had seen this yet. And she was going to make sure he *didn't*. The witch could call it reinvention, but some things were too permanent to be remade.

Everything they'd built, everything she wanted, was on the line now—and it wasn't even her fault.

Social media was a toxic place. Keyboard warriors with no lives deciding to pick up causes and screw with people.

Well, she wasn't going to let them screw with her. It wasn't just her reputation on the line—it was the illusion of their perfect life, and she'd spent too long curating that illusion to let it fracture now.

Miranda grabbed her keys off the hook and headed into the garage. She slid into the creamy leather interior of her red BMW, which purred to life. She backed out of the driveway, barely missing a woman pushing a stroller. Miranda waved in apology, ignoring the words her neighbor yelled after her. She'd have to take her something later to say she was sorry and that there'd been an emergency with the dog. No one would know the dog was in the house and not in the car.

Hopefully, that would be enough to make up for almost killing her family.

Extreme times called for extreme measures.

And Miranda was not shy about the extreme. She knew how to play dirty. She'd just been trying not to. She knew people in PR. People who could make a scandal disappear overnight or amplify one just as fast. It wouldn't take much—just a single call to an old contact, someone still grateful for what she once did for their launch party. She hadn't used those favors yet. But she still had them. She wasn't powerless. She was just . . . hiding.

Chapter Twenty-Four

Jennifer

The Fifteen Commandments of a Tradwife

Seven: Thou shalt be fertile and multiply—but never complain about it. Breastfeed like a goddess, bounce back like a Barbie. If you're tired or overwhelmed, meditate. Tradwives don't whine.

"What's a bitch?"

The word hit her like a slap—not just because of what her son said, but because Jennifer had heard it before. In a whispered fight behind closed doors. Jamie's lips curling as he threw it out like a punctuation. Jamie's wife threatening her this morning. Wearing a sheath dress that probably cost more than Jennifer made in a day, her blond hair curled around her shoulders; there'd been hate in those oddly blue eyes.

The vitriol had escalated when Jennifer refused her demands.

Surprisingly, Jennifer hadn't even flinched as the psycho had threatened her on her front porch until a neighbor opened their door to peer out. Then the fury had magically disappeared, and she'd walked off with a fake "Bless your heart, take care."

But now, hearing it through her son Craig's voice? It nearly gutted her.

Jennifer swallowed the memory with a dry throat and whirled around to stare at her son sitting innocently in the back seat of their minivan. Craig's tiny face was tilted to the side, a curious expression dimpling his brow. The other three children stared at their brother. Athena, two years older, likely knew *exactly* what a bitch was, judging by her expression.

She couldn't believe seven-year-old Craig had just said *bitch*. Suddenly hot, Jennifer hitched up the air-conditioning a few notches, letting the cool air soothe her overheated face.

"Bitch," Bailey, all of five, popped the word off her tongue as easily as the word please. "Bitch."

Beside Athena, Dominic's eyes were wide enough to reflect the afternoon sun as he elbowed Bailey to make her stop repeating the word. And Shadow barked in time with the repeated curse word.

"Where did you hear such language?" Jennifer worked hard to keep her tone neutral, not wanting her son to see how his question affected her. Not wanting the other children to notice either.

"Scotty said, 'Your mommy's a bitch.'" Craig shrugged, as if he hadn't just used a cuss word. A word spoken so innocently from his sweet mouth—not used in the same malicious context the original utterance had likely taken—struck her painfully in the center of her chest.

Jennifer faced the windshield, unable to look into Athena's knowing eyes or at Dominic's twitching mouth, which meant he was sure to tell Craig and Bailey any second exactly what that word meant.

Craig had no idea Scotty had actually said something so nasty about her. *Bitch.* Or that he'd repeated the word most likely from his own mother. Jennifer was not a bitch, even if Scotty's mom, Colleen, thought she was.

Sucking in a deep breath through her nose, Jennifer blew it quietly out of her mouth before she turned in the seat, the cracked and aged leather creaking loudly in the silent minivan. She offered her son a smile she didn't quite feel. "*Bitch* is not a nice word, sweetheart. And it wasn't very nice for Scotty to say that."

Craig winced. "Is he gonna get in trouble?"

The innocence and kindness of her son in that moment sent warmth cascading through her chest, and for a brief second, she thought she might cry. Jennifer turned back to face the pickup line that was slowly moving forward, unable to look at Craig's sweet face. She sat back against the seat, too warm because she used her air-conditioning only sparingly. Her sweaty palms scraped against the wheel. The soft polyurethane was a jarring contrast to the roughness of her hands—earned from scrubbing floors, chopping vegetables, holding it all together. A reminder of the softness of her son's voice against the harsh word.

Why did she feel as though she was having an out-of-body experience?

Why the heck was Scotty calling her a bitch? What exactly had his mother said? Maybe something about the parking lot.

Maybe the answer was even worse than that. Maybe Colleen

had seen Jennifer's anonymous TikTok account. It had been a mistake to come out of the shadows and post her face online. And Scotty's mom wouldn't have kept the discovery to herself. The conversation could've easily been overheard by a seven-year-old lounging nearby.

Jennifer thought about posting again. Something snappy. Something that would put Scotty's mom and all her sanctimonious cronies in their place. Something that would put Jamie's replacement wife in her place. But the thought of her kids seeing it one day stopped her cold. Instead, she would post something on the power of words, and the power of silence. Her stomach twisted.

"I don't think he would get in trouble unless you said something to the teacher about it. I'm definitely not going to call his mother because it's none of my business. But I will tell you this, son. It wasn't a very nice word, and he's wrong. Sometimes people say things like that because they don't understand the meaning. I'm guessing that's the same thing with Scotty. He probably thought it meant something else."

"Like pretty or nice?" Craig asked.

Jennifer smiled as she stared at the red light, waiting for it to change so she could be done with this conversation—forever, although she knew she wasn't going to stop thinking about it. "Yes. Exactly, sweetheart."

Oh, how the innocence of youth was so often destroyed by the vindictiveness of adults. If there was one thing she'd always strived for, it was to grow good humans. And if there was one thing it appeared this town was trying to do, it was the opposite. Jennifer knew that from experience growing up here.

Could a few social media posts really turn the community against her more than they already had?

They drove slowly through town, and something felt off.

People she used to wave to as she passed openly turned away. The shop owner she often saw sweeping outside—who always had a friendly smile—glared at her as she drove by.

Was it just her imagination? Or was hearing the words of Colleen seep through her own son's mouth an anonymous warning of what was to come?

Had Jamie's wife started a rumor? Ruined her as she'd threatened to do?

Jennifer rounded the corner into her neighborhood, driving slowly down the street, pretending she didn't notice the neighbors glaring at her. One even raised a fist at her car as she passed.

Her nerves were nearly shot by the time she pulled into the driveway of their tiny bungalow by the lake. Everything looked normal as she opened the door and her four children climbed out. They marched in perfect unison, their pretty little heads bobbing in a row until they reached the front door. Athena turned around, shock in her eyes, and then turned back toward the door.

Jennifer's gaze followed her daughter's and her heart skittered. Athena wasn't the type to overreact.

The door had been covered in slime. Not just any slime. Eggs.

Someone had come by and egged her door. Maybe Jamie's wife. Maybe Colleen.

A crumpled note, reeking of sulfur and yolk, sat on the mat—the mat that said *All Are Welcome Here* in some sort of ironic message. She should throw it out. Burn it, maybe. But she just stared at it, wondering who exactly was being welcomed anymore. Maybe she should order a new mat. One that said *Welcome Unless You Have Opinions.*

"Oh my goodness," Jennifer said. "Looks like we got Halloween early!" She laughed, as if she wasn't disturbed by the sight in front of her.

Her kids laughed nervously, not wanting to disappoint.

She scooped up the note, staring at the egg yolk congealing in rivulets down the glass that outlined her door and had to nudge Shadow from licking up the remnants. When she opened the screen door, one of the shells cracked under her heel with a soft pop. She ushered the kids inside and then filled a bucket with soapy water to clean up the egg wash before it destroyed the paint.

Only when she was outside by herself did she open the note and read what it said: *Thought you might need some eggs for that shit cake you're about to eat.*

Jennifer glanced up sharply, feeling eyes on her from afar. Earlier, someone had left an anonymous note in that loaf of bread: *Wolves dress up too*. She'd decided it was a kid, probably thought it was funny. But now it definitely felt more like a threat. Someone watching, waiting to pounce.

Jennifer thought back through her life, the reasons why someone would want to threaten her. Besides her tradwife warnings, there was only one other thing she could think of, one night and one person, and that person was dead.

One of her neighbors passed by with her dog. This time the woman *stopped* and smiled.

"Oh, goodness. What's happened here?" she asked, staring at the mess Jennifer had started to clean up.

Was the woman truly just walking her dog? Or had she stopped to admire her handiwork? In this town, even the kindest smiles might be laced with venom. Jennifer shook her head. Her neighbors had always been nice to her. This was ridiculous. Just a prank. Just like the note had been a prank.

"Are you okay?" the woman asked. Was that real concern in her voice or the kind of faux empathy that bought time to gossip later?

Jennifer nodded, blinking back tears, her throat swelling with the need to release the sobs she'd been holding in since she got in the car and heard her son say that someone at school had called her a bitch.

She managed to force a laugh and waved at her door. "Just doing a little cleaning. You know how it is—all the salt from the water."

Her neighbor nodded and walked off as if nothing had happened. As if this encounter—and the egg mess—wasn't real.

Jennifer turned back to the door, picking up the soapy sponge and scrubbing. She wanted to get it done, to get these eggshells off her porch, to move on with her life.

But all she could hear was her son's voice in the back seat, asking if she was a bitch.

And then coming home to Athena's shocked face.

No matter what she said. No matter how she spun the story.

Someone was out to get her.

Someone must have seen her TikToks. Recognized her flour before-and-after pics. That was the only thing she could think of. She was sure of it. Because Tara was dead, and Tara was the only one who might have wanted to hurt her.

There was no hiding from what she'd posted. Even if she deleted it, the likelihood that someone hadn't taken a screenshot was not high. The only question was, how many others had seen it too? The new video she posted about not being able to afford both groceries and gas had felt good in the moment—cathartic. Real. But now she wondered if that realness had been a mistake.

If Jamie's wife had come by with threats and demands, was Jamie next?

Athena opened the door just a crack as Jennifer swept up the last of the egg. Her daughter whispered, "Are you really okay, Mom?"

I'm not, but I have to be. Jennifer nodded, smiled, but it didn't reach her eyes. Coming inside, she made sure her face had that plastered-on smile, a grin from ear to ear for the other children, sitting at the kitchen table working on their homework.

"Who thinks we should make chocolate chip cookies?"

Four hands shot up in the air, their grins matching hers. Except theirs weren't practiced.

"Do we get cookies every time someone eggs us?" Dominic asked, the picture of innocence.

Jennifer laughed. Too brightly. Almost convincingly.

Chapter Twenty-Five

Ariel

Ariel rubbed her arms in the darkness of the barn, a chill sweeping over her skin. A piece of hay was stuck between her toes, and she bent to pluck it out. The smell of earth and sweet feed clung to the rafters. She was wearing only a thin, gauzy nightgown—appropriate for the Florida heat and the AC not turned down to the proper temperature—but now that she was outside, where the temperature had dipped without the sun, goose bumps covered her skin.

Her mouth still tasted like a hint of the cinnamon in the apple pies she'd baked with Miranda that afternoon. The text from Miranda had been unexpected. The baking had been pleasant; they'd even taken a selfie. But there was something about Miranda that threw her off. A strangeness to her eyes, a distance in her smile.

An old mirror leaned in the corner, long forgotten, its glass clouded—but Ariel didn't dare look into it tonight. She couldn't seem to face herself. Not after all the comments she'd read online. Despite the comfort of Miranda, Shane, it was hard to move past the meanness.

The glass of the mirror was streaked with time, warped at the corners like it could barely remember her. She used to love mirrors—used to pose in front of them in costume, rehearsing lines. Now her reflection felt more like an interrogation.

Just like any other night when her house was asleep, she'd snuck outside to watch old videos of herself performing onstage—the lightness of her body as she glided across the planked stage, dancing, singing, pretending to be someone else. The sticky haze of stage makeup, the spotlight heat on her skin, the adrenaline rush of that final bow. She could still feel the sting of spirit gum under her wig cap, the director whispering, *You were magic*, as she convinced the audience she was someone else.

It reminded her of the life she was currently living, or pretending. But who was she pretending to be?

She wasn't even sure she knew who she was to begin with. So much of her life had been spent acting, playing roles, picking apart someone else's traits and adopting them—morals, values, likes and dislikes, even weaknesses and strengths. Was that what life was supposed to be? A constant stacking of other people's identities?

Sometimes she'd forget how to answer when someone asked what she liked—because half the time, she wasn't sure if it was her preference or something she'd borrowed from a character, a role or a script. And sometimes she remembered the roles she hadn't played—the words she hadn't spoken when they might have made a difference. The difference she could have made in someone's life—maybe she could have saved it. Staying silent had been a sacrifice she was willing to make in order to secure her future.

A creak behind her had her spinning in fear. The strange stalker texts were coming with more regularity now. Thankfully, it was

Shane who took up the space behind her—a shadow in the night. But she knew it was him by the outline of his frame, the flop of his hair, his scent.

"What are you doing out here?" Shane's voice was filled with sleep, and the sound was familiar, comforting.

She rubbed her arms again, smiling at his form, unsure if he could even see her in the barn's darkness—the only light was behind her, cast from the television screen where she'd watched her old video. But she imagined the glow framed her face like a halo, making her look like an angel.

"Just watching this video of myself from high school. Look at me—I'm Anastasia." She gestured at the screen. The applause had been loud enough to shake the floorboards. Now, even her own breath felt too loud in this space.

The real Anastasia had probably died when her whole family was massacred by revolutionaries. Although, for years, people believed she'd survived. Some had even tried to pretend they were her to collect an inheritance.

At least Ariel hadn't gone that far, pretending to be someone else to collect money. Or had she?

To be fair, the videos she posted online to sell their farm products *were* a kind of pretending—an encouragement for people to live the life she had: in a traditional, peaceful, God-loving family. But those things weren't lies. They were real. She loved her husband. She loved all of her children. She loved the life she was leading. She believed in the products they made. She believed in raising good humans, who'd also contribute to the world.

Someone had once told her that the purpose of life was to create life. If that was true, she was fulfilling her role.

"Is that . . . Tara?" Shane stared into the screen, and there in the background onstage was his late sister, playing the role of a Russian court member.

"Yeah." Ariel bit her lip, watching Shane stare at the grainy footage of his dead sister, knowing how much he missed her.

"It's cold out here." Shane stepped forward, pressing his warm hands to her cold shoulders, and in an instant, warmth flooded her body. She leaned up, and he pressed his lips to hers—kissing her the way he always had, with love, with passion. She used to take that for granted. Until she realized that some women weren't satisfied with their husbands. Until she realized she might not be satisfied in the end either. But the lead-up was always great.

Ariel cataloged the kiss—pressure, duration, the way his hand slid down her arm and didn't quite close around hers. She wondered if he was kissing her or the version of her she used to be. The one he still needed her to be.

"Come back to bed, sweetheart," he said, grabbing her other hand and pulling her to her feet. His hand lingered on her wrist a second too long. Not possessive, but close. She wondered if the warmth in his voice was genuine—or just habit. "You've got to get up in a few hours, and you're going to be exhausted if you don't get some sleep. You've been doing too much lately. And if you're staying up all night out here watching old videos, you're not going to be any good to anyone tomorrow—especially yourself."

Ariel nodded, knowing he was right. There'd be no time for a nap. She still hadn't dealt with the fallout of the social media comments she'd seen on their assistant's phone, and that was something she'd have to address in the morning in a video.

Part of her knew that doing the video was good—for the brand, for the family, for her reputation. But the other part resisted. Why should she owe anyone anything? It wasn't her fault people had posted judgmental comments. Let them judge. People who judged weren't good people. And by addressing them, wouldn't she just validate their points? Invite more scrutiny?

A life she hadn't even really wanted to put online was now being dissected.

People were so quick to judge—especially when they had no idea what they were talking about. Jealousy bred contempt. More often than not, she suspected it was jealousy. Jealousy of her children, her husband, her life.

One comment had called her "a Stepford Wife with a ring light." Another said she looked like she was blinking in Morse code for help. She hadn't slept since.

What if the brands she'd partnered with pulled their funding, their support? If the moms at the farmers market co-op where she sold her products froze her out entirely, she might never be invited back.

What if their neighbors—already skeptical of outsiders—stopped waving altogether? One bad clip and everything could tumble like a stack of mismatched blocks.

And the stalker messages . . . Those felt more sinister, more personal. As if someone had a vendetta against her that ran deeper than jealousy.

Her mouth opened in a silent moan when she thought of her children seeing the comments, doubting her, questioning their life. But she clamped her mouth shut just as quickly, knowing that was impossible. She and Shane didn't let their kids have social media. They were homeschooled. And no adults in their circle would be so cruel as to show them . . .

But lately, her oldest had started asking questions. About followers, about YouTube. About why Mommy got dressed up just to talk to her phone. Kids always noticed more than adults gave them credit for.

And so did meddling bullies. What the online army didn't realize was that she wasn't just lucky. She was a hard worker. She'd busted her butt to get where she was. She hadn't been lucky—she'd been relentless. Hadn't she earned the right to be proud? She practiced her lines until they were perfect. There'd been sacrifices for as long as she could remember. Dancing until her feet bled. Singing until her throat ached. Sleeping in the wings backstage between acts. Investing every dime she made into her future even if it simply meant forgoing dinner in order to buy a new pair of dancing shoes.

Ariel had grit.

She made sure that in every aspect of her life she worked herself to the bone to get where she was. She wasn't going to let a few idiots online take that from her.

Shane pulled her through the barn door, closing it behind them. The video still played silently on the TV, the ghost of her past its only audience now.

The yard looked like a painting—serene, still. But she felt misplaced in it, like someone had cut and pasted her from another scene entirely. Even the grass felt unfamiliar under her bare feet. She walked beneath the night sky, the stars reflecting in the pond and the dew glistening in the yard. And she wondered what she could possibly say to make people understand. To make them go away.

Whoever had started this was going to have to answer for it. One way or another. She had sacrificed too much to let someone else tear it down. If they wanted a reckoning, she'd give them one. Maybe she'd find the words. Maybe not. But she wasn't going to vanish without a fight.

The barn's murky window reflected a version of herself she barely recognized. She wondered if her reflection in the dusty barn mirror would recognize this version of her—tired, exposed, angry. Or would it just turn its back?

A flicker of motion near the fence caught her eye—but it was just the wind rustling the hedges. She could feel a gaze like a thread pulling at her spine. Maybe it was a neighbor. Maybe it was a super fan stalking in the dark. Maybe it was nothing. But the world was full of watchers now—waiting to catch her slipping, to record, to stitch, to post, to judge.

Was that a faint glint blinking in the darkness beyond the fence? Was it a flash of a lens? A pale eye in the dark? Or just the wind catching on something sharp?

Her skin prickled. She wasn't sure who was watching. But someone was.

She reached for Shane, wanting to point, but the light was gone, the darkness mocking, and her husband was too far ahead.

Chapter Twenty-Six

Miranda

Miranda slammed the pregnancy test down on the bathroom sink so hard it cracked against the edge. No two lines. Once again, she'd failed. There'd been a bit of nausea the last few days she couldn't attribute to anything. And her period was two days late.

Fuck. She needed to be pregnant to secure her position. Needed it so people would believe she was here with Benjamin for the "right" reasons.

Benjamin's minuscule mutt stared at her in accusation, and she slammed the bathroom door to keep it from looking at her.

If she couldn't fulfill her duty to Benjamin, what was to say he'd keep her around? The whole point of their marriage on his part had been to start a family. His entire campaign centered on being a wholesome family man. And sure, he had kids with his ex—but none with Miranda. And without a hand on her pregnant belly, she just looked like a side piece.

And if he kicked her to the curb, she'd never be able to finish the real reason she'd come to this godforsaken town.

Before leaving for work that morning, Benjamin had told her the donor gala was moving forward in a few months. Pictures of their happy, growing family—her precious bump—would be part of the printed program. Except there was no baby. There was nothing growing inside her at all.

Every teenager freaked out about getting pregnant just from sucking face. At thirty, she was closer to being a geriatric pregnant woman than not. She could practically hear her eggs mocking her.

If she wanted to keep her place as his wife, she needed to fulfill her part of the bargain, didn't she? What good was a woman if she couldn't get pregnant?

They'd spent hours picking names. Designed a nursery Pinterest board filled with cream linens and mahogany cribs. Tasteful neutral colors for paint and curtains. The empty bedroom was right upstairs, waiting for her womb to fill it.

Her fingers hovered over her phone, ready to google false negatives, but she stopped. That hope was more dangerous than the truth.

She let out a guttural groan, smashed the test down again and threw it in the trash—then immediately realized he might see it. That would be a disaster. If she had to hear him say *It'll happen next time* one more time, his face growing ever more skeptical . . .

She emptied the trash, stomped down to the garage and buried it deep in the bin, closing the lid with a finality that made her want to scream all over again.

Shaking with rage at her own body, she marched back inside, yanked open the bottom cabinet drawer and pulled out the flask she'd once offered to Colleen during the party. She stared at the clear liquid as if it mocked her. Drinking herself into oblivion sounded appealing, but it wouldn't solve anything.

There had to be another way.

Maybe she should call her doctor. Maybe this was a fertility issue. But she knew the problem couldn't lie with Benjamin—he already had plenty of kids. What if it was her? If it was, Benjamin would drop her like a bad habit. Then again, her life before Benjamin had only ever been a means to an end—a carefully curated stage set, all glimmer and masks, designed to get her exactly where she was now. She hadn't come to Crystal Harbor by accident. She had chosen this marriage, this town, these people. Every step had been deliberate, right down to the smile she wore when she arrived. And she wasn't leaving until she got what she came for. A fat bank account was just one item on that list.

Miranda unlocked her phone and clicked on the internet app to google the wording from her prenup, "Clause 6D: No issue, no settlement," a phrase she'd asked Benji about, not understanding that *issue* referred to children within the marriage. What popped up on the internet, she didn't like. Without a baby, there was a chance the settlement she'd earned could evaporate.

She should've read the prenup more closely. Back then, she was too busy tasting champagne, picturing big diamond rings and imagining the day she'd collect what she was really owed. Now all she could focus on was Clause 6D, where her worth was summarized in two sterile words: *no issue.*

Her search spiraled, and she ended up on a Reddit forum called "Issue of the Marriage," reading about how one woman faked a pregnancy and miscarriage once the ink was dried on the page.

Maybe she could fake a pregnancy. Get someone else to pee their pregnant positive urine on a stick. Ariel was always pregnant. There was a good chance . . . It wouldn't be the first time a woman used someone else's baby to save her own skin.

Miranda frowned. She wasn't above lying, but faking a pregnancy felt lame, old, dried-up and pathetic. She was not pathetic. But then again, she didn't really want to be pregnant. She'd be a terrible mother. She wanted revenge.

Annoyed and beyond frustrated, Miranda stomped upstairs to her bedroom, yanked off the designer dress she'd worn to shop in town and pulled on top-tier athletic shorts and a matching light pink tank top. Even when she was working out, Miranda made sure she didn't look sloppy or desperate. The only thing that might get her through the rest of this day without committing murder was a long run.

As she exited the house and started on the trail that circled the lake behind their home, a small sense of mourning crept in. She kind of actually liked where she lived. The access to money. The quiet solitude of the lake and the beach. Knowing that all of these people had what was coming to them.

She needed to be patient. It had only been a few months. Ben wasn't going to drop her just yet, and if she ramped things up, maybe she'd get what she came for before two lines showed on the pregnancy test. Catastrophe averted.

But patience had never been one of Miranda's virtues.

A woman like Miranda didn't get ahead by waiting. She found the friends she wanted, the outlets she craved and the life she deserved by taking them. She'd stepped over plenty of bodies to get where she was—and maybe she needed to start treating this new block in the road the same way. If she couldn't get pregnant the right way, maybe she'd just have to find a different way.

Sweat dripped down her spine as she rounded mile four. The houses along this path were all familiar. She knew who lived in each one. The couple on the corner who always argued at seven o'clock every evening like clockwork, the husband who snuck home for lunch and drank a bourbon on the porch. The mother who sat rocking on the porch while her infant screamed inside.

At night, when the lights were on, you could see right inside. Watching people eat dinner. Watching them watching television. Watching them strip out of their clothes and into pajamas. Watching them fuck.

It was one of the things she liked most about Crystal Harbor. Everyone watching. Everyone seen.

In the city, she'd kept cameras off and curtains drawn—most of the time. Privacy meant power. Here, it was the opposite. Let them see just enough to feel superior. Just enough to underestimate her.

As she rounded the last bend, she slowed. Mrs. Henley was trimming her roses, pretending not to notice Miranda, but the subtle shift in her body told a different story. The woman was a gossip. Last week, she'd caught the old cunt whispering to her equally cunty acquaintance outside of church about how Miranda had yet to get pregnant despite her low-cut dress. She'd nodded and smiled, and swore inside her head that if they didn't shut up, she'd fuck their husbands—make them beg, then leak the footage to the church Facebook page.

Miranda straightened her shoulders, smoothed her hair and added a hint of sway to her hips. She smiled with all her teeth. Only when she turned the corner did she notice the sting from her clenched palm where her nails had broken the skin.

Even now, she could feel Mrs. Henley's eyes on her. The rest of the neighbors peeking from behind curtains. She didn't mind the stares. In fact, she counted on them. People were easier to control when they thought they were in on the show. So, let them ogle. There was a moment in time when she'd hated the idea of eyes on her. But now, she loved being watched. Being desired. Being coveted. And yes, she knew from church that was a sin. But she didn't tell anyone. Once a sinner, always a sinner, right?

For a moment, she remembered the way Benjamin looked at her the night he proposed. Like she was redemption. Like she'd already forgiven herself. She almost believed it too.

She was trying—*really* trying—to take things slow. To make sure everything was perfect. But the dark part of her, the part she'd caged when she said yes to herself, to her true desire, was restless. Clawing. Wanting to be seen. Wanting to take.

Maybe it was time this town met the real Miranda. The one who once lit cigars for billionaires while they whispered secrets they shouldn't. The one who knew how to make a scandal disappear—or ignite. The one who never lost a game, because she wrote the rules. The one who could make a girl disappear.

A grin spread across her face as she ran—one scenario after another dancing in her mind, each more depraved than the last. By the time she reached home, though, she'd halfway convinced herself to keep that Miranda locked up.

For now.

But it all depended on whether she got what she wanted.

She was tired of playing by the rules.

Tired of pretending.

Once inside, Miranda opened her calendar app and added an event for tomorrow: *Message Beth for a coffee.*

She hadn't spoken to Beth in years. Last time she did, someone lost custody of a million-dollar painting and a two-million-dollar inheritance, which had set Miranda up nicely in the city. But Beth never asked questions. Only asked for fees.

Beth wasn't her friend. Beth was the problem-solver. The woman who once forged a will when it looked like one of Miranda's lovers was about to kick the bucket. She'd also forged Miranda's birth certificate and social security number so she could get a driver's license and get married.

Miranda didn't need that kind of help . . . not today.

But she liked knowing all of her options if her plans went sideways. Coffee to go. One sugar. No forgiveness.

Chapter Twenty-Seven

Jennifer

The Fifteen Commandments of a Tradwife

> **Eight:** Thou shalt weaponize thy domestic bliss. Have the best sourdough. The cleanest baseboards. The most obedient children. Be so perfect that other women cry in the produce aisle.

Jennifer had finished posting her latest video, sharing some of the invisible rules of being a tradwife and how it damaged future generations' perspectives, when her cell rang.

Jennifer stared at the caller ID. Jamie's name flashed, and she counted the seconds. She considered not picking up. Letting it ring forever.

Her stomach twisted. He must've seen the egg-stained porch on the Ring camera he insisted on having access to, or maybe Athena told him. That's all it would take—a mess, a rumor, a neighbor whispering—and he'd use it as ammo.

But then, he must have seen his wife's visit too. Heard what she said.

So, she didn't want to answer the phone. But the last time she ignored his call, he'd phoned the school and said there was an emergency, and he couldn't get in touch with her. He'd known exactly how to make her look like the irresponsible one, because of course she'd answered the school's call on the first ring. The entire exchange had been humiliating.

The kids had talked to him before bed, and she was positive there had been some sort of relay about the eggs that had been smashed on her front porch.

Jennifer wasn't really in the mood to hear about Jamie's opinion on the matter. He had chosen not to be in her life, so why should she give him any sort of consideration? Then again, as the father to her children, did she owe it to him to answer the phone and at least see what he had to say—even if it wasn't going to be something she wanted to hear? She hated that his voice still had the power to yank her out of her own mind and body.

No matter the fact that they were divorced, and he'd already remarried, Jamie seemed to think that he still held a place of authority in her life. The caller ID flashed again, and the voicemail symbol popped up. She'd waited too long. Her thumb no longer hovered over the green answer key. Instead, she set the phone down. But no sooner had she done so than it started to ring again.

This time, she picked up right away, her nerves still firing inside her chest from having been married to him for so long and knowing that he hated to wait for her to answer.

"Hello?" She said it like a question, as if she didn't know exactly who was calling or why. And it made her wonder—why did people say hello with such a question in their voices whenever they saw who was calling from the caller ID? As if their brain didn't want to process who it was. Or maybe that was just her.

"Jennifer, what the hell with the eggs? And bread before that? Is someone planning to make a sandwich on your front fucking porch?"

The lamp in the corner of her tidy living room flickered. The dishwasher clicked faintly in the kitchen—normal sounds that suddenly felt too loud in the silence that followed Jamie's voice.

She imagined the kids had told him about the eggs, but the bread was definitely from him snooping on the Ring camera. So why hadn't he mentioned his wife's visit?

Was it possible his wife *also* had access to her Ring camera and had erased her little stopover?

Jennifer sighed, hoping that the sound of her heavy breathing didn't pass through the microphone on her cell. Jamie didn't like it when she sighed. He thought it was a sign of disrespect. Didn't understand that sometimes people needed a soothing mechanism when their hearts were racing and they were holding their breath, waiting in anticipation—or in fear—of what was to come next.

"Probably just some teenage kids in the neighborhood." Jennifer's fingers dug into her palm, her other hand gripping the phone so tight that it was sure to leave marks. Although, she'd been starting to think it wasn't teenagers.

"You have no idea who threw food?" His tone was accusatory, as if he too hadn't likely tried to decipher it from the camera that had glitched and all she'd seen was a blur both times.

"Of course not." Jennifer tried to keep her voice calm, to keep the emotion she felt welling in her chest from seeping through the phone, knowing that if Jamie had any idea how irritated she was at this phone call, she was in for it.

Sensing her unease, Shadow sidled close, nudging her, and she was glad for his company.

"Well, it makes me think that there's something dangerous going on in that neighborhood you live in with our kids. Maybe it's time they spent more time at my house. Over here we're not getting assaulted."

Jennifer sat forward on the couch, gripping the edge of the cushion. He wouldn't actually take them. Would he? She pictured their backpacks no longer by the front door. Their shoes in the basket—vanished. The house hollowed out by the absence of small voices calling for Mommy.

Then she thought about Jamie's new wife, who wore pearls to school pickup—and how much easier it would be to slide Jennifer out of the picture if she seemed unstable. If she became a story he could spin.

Before, when he had left her, he hadn't been married, and he needed her to take care of the kids. They were collateral to him. But now he had a new wife, new life, and he could push Jennifer out completely if he wanted to. And he would. She knew he would.

"It was just a prank," Jennifer said. "You know how kids are. You remember being that age—they pick random houses and throw eggs. They do other things . . ." Her mind stalled, tunneling back to the summer of 2013, the firepit. The prank. Jennifer swallowed. "It's safe over here. I promise. The kids love it here too. They've got friends in the neighborhood. They've had enough disruptions in their lives lately. Let's not give them another one."

The words were out of her mouth before she could pull them back, and she knew instantly that Jamie was going to retaliate for her taking a stand. He didn't like it when she told him what to do or even had a whisper of authority in her voice.

"How dare you?" Just as she suspected, Jamie was seething on the other end.

She got a faint glimmer of satisfaction from hearing the irritation and anger in his voice and knowing that she was too far away so that he couldn't instantly do something to make her regret it. But what about his wife? Would she suffer his rage?

"Listen, Jamie, I'm not trying to make you mad," she said. "It's just a fact. Let's try not to disrupt them. They've had enough."

And so have I.

But she kept that last part to herself. First, he wouldn't care—that's why he left her to begin with. And second, it would only make him mad and want to retaliate even more.

"Well, you better have cleaned it up."

Like muscle memory, she was hit with a flashback. The sting of his palm, the sound of the plate crashing, the spaghetti splattered across the tile like blood. The silence afterward had been its own heavy kind of punishment.

His berating continued on the other end. "That's just an embarrassment waiting to happen, for someone to see that mess on the front porch. And if I hear one more thing about this, then we're going to revisit this discussion—changes in their lives be damned."

Jennifer had been banking on his laziness, on his not wanting to actually take full responsibility for the children they'd brought into this world. She was certain he rather liked the arrangement of seeing his kids only part time. Kind of like a friend who held babies until they fussed then swiftly gave them back. But she took his threat seriously. She needed to make sure that nothing like this ever happened again.

She could already see the court waiting room with its polished floor and wooden walls. The clipboard with her name misspelled. The lawyer Jamie could afford and the one she'd have to beg for pro bono.

"I agree." By offering him an agreement like that, she made it sound as though it was his idea—which was what he liked. To be in charge. For all of the ideas to be his.

"Also, what are you doing working at the grocery store?"

Her stomach tightened. A reflex she feared she'd never lose when he accused her of something. The back of his hand, just in a different form.

This was not something she felt was any of his business, and he knew exactly what she was doing working there—given that after her portion to the private school, he didn't provide her enough money to survive off of, or at least for her to give the kids a life they were deserving of.

"Working." She didn't feel like she owed him any more of an answer than that, and it was obvious anyway. He was only asking to be rude. She hated how defensive she felt. As if working was something to be ashamed of, instead of what kept her and the kids afloat.

"What happened to the diner?"

"I make more money at the grocery store." Not that it was any of his business.

"I heard something about you causing trouble in the parking lot. I hope I don't hear anything like that again."

Jennifer tensed all over again, the back of her neck sending a shooting pain through the base of her skull. Divorce didn't mean that she'd got rid of this guy. Even now, he could twist her insides with a single sentence.

"Thanks for your concern, Jamie. Really, I appreciate it. But it's getting late, and I've got to get the kids up early in the morning for school. I'll talk to you later."

And then she did something she never had the guts to do when they were married—she hung up the phone without saying goodbye.

Feeling exhilarated at having won something in that conversation, even if it was just by ending it, Jennifer stood up from the couch, tossed her phone into the corner of it and marched over to the little table by the front door where she kept the mail.

She opened a drawer, taking out a key, and then unlocked a second drawer, opening it to reveal a flash drive sitting in the center. None of her kids, fortunately, had figured out that this was here yet, and she decided that now was probably a good time to move it—just in case.

She plucked up the flash drive, holding it between her thumb and forefinger, staring at the little piece of plastic that held all the information she could ever need if she wanted to get retribution against Jamie.

Photos of the abuse. A threatening voice memo he never meant for anyone else to hear. A confession of a cover-up from years ago. If a judge saw and heard even half of it, he wouldn't just lose the kids—he'd lose everything.

She held the drive like it might burn her—because it could. And part of her wanted it to.

All it would take was one word from her and handing this flash drive over to the appropriate party—and then she wouldn't have to worry about his threatening phone calls ever again.

This slim drive was a weapon in plastic casing. Jamie wouldn't be able to control her—not if she ever found the courage to detonate.

But she'd never do that to her kids. Take away their hero. He'd never laid a hand on them. And in their eyes, he was the best dad ever. Jamie might have been a shitty, abusive partner, but she did feel confident that when he was on daddy duty, he was a good playmate.

Later that night, she filmed a video. She didn't post it—just saved it in drafts. Her face was blotchy, her voice too shaky. But she said what she needed to say: that being a wife didn't mean being silent. That safety wasn't always what it looked like from the outside.

The fact that she didn't post it, though, was proof Jamie still held a heavy hand over her.

Chapter Twenty-Eight

Tara

Summer 2013

The boathouse is dark, the only sounds the creak of the wood as I step through the door, the lapping of the lake against the pilings.

"Hello? Brad?" I ask, sipping the icky punch. I don't usually drink, and already the fuzziness is creeping in.

Hands wrap around my waist from behind, tugging me against a hard chest.

"You made it. Didn't know if you would."

I smile and turn in his arms, holding up the cup. "Sip?"

"What is it?"

I shrug and giggle. "Red magic?"

Brad takes a long gulp, then leads me to an uncovered canoe. I settle on his lap, and he kisses me—tasting like cherries and sin.

We kiss for what feels like forever, in that dizzy, floating way that makes time stop. But then . . . something tilts. My body feels heavy. My thoughts slide away before I can grab them. I feel really drunk.

Our kisses and touches have become more like sliding and sloshing parts.

In the back of my head, I hear a voice. A girl, but I can't see who it is, my vision is blurry.

"I don't feel so good," I mumble. Brad mutters something similar but I can't make out the words.

Hands—not his—pull me up. I stumble, feet sinking into wet sand, the breeze off the lake raising goose bumps on my arms. I'm trying to see straight, but everything feels like I'm seeing it through surrealist lenses. Like I'm Picasso or Salvador Dalí.

"You made a mess," a girl says, and then my shirt is gone. My pants.

"Hope you're not attached to those," another girl says with a laugh as she throws the clothes into the lake.

Cold air hits me, and I hunch over, trying to hide my naked body. Brad is beside me, bare skin pale in the firelight, still out cold.

"God, you're so desperate?" a boy says.

"As white as Wonder Bread," says his date.

I blink, trying to understand, trying to make out the faces of the girls, the boys. I try to shake Brad's shoulder but end up falling beside him. Camera flashes burst in my vision—white-hot, blinding. Someone is taking pictures.

I squeeze my eyes shut, pretending I am anywhere else, wishing I had the energy to run.

Chapter Twenty-Nine

Ariel

Ariel stood behind her table underneath the tent in the shade at the community bake sale, hyped up on adrenaline and Diet Coke. The chirp of birds intent on pecking at forgotten crumbs mixed with the clatter of folding chairs and the shrill giggle of sugar-high toddlers.

Samantha stood in front of her table, arms over her chest, commiserating with Brad. "It just doesn't make any sense. Why would someone take the clothes off my line, soak them in vinegar and throw them all over my lawn?"

"And you don't have a camera?" Brad was saying.

"It wasn't working that night, we checked."

Ariel watched the exchange, hearing what Samantha was saying but not comprehending. That was really freaking odd. "A prank?" she suggested.

"A rude prank. They could have damaged my dresses."

Ariel swiped a bead of sweat from her upper lip. It wouldn't do to sweat all over her goods. Also, these two having a complaint session in front of her station wasn't going to sell her goods either. She picked up a napkin to dab behind her neck, the paper smelling of sugar. The sticky sheen on her fingers from passing out scone samples tugged at the napkin fibers as she wiped them again.

Normally, this type of event was exciting for her. She got to show off the baked goods that she made with her herbs and spices—like the yummy rosemary and cheddar bread, the savory chive and sausage muffins, not to mention her berry scones. The warm, sharp scent of cheddar and herbs battled the vanilla-sugar haze wafting from the neighboring table.

"Oh, I need to get back to my table," Samantha said as she rushed toward the line forming for her lemon bars.

"Baxter, no!" shouted Brad as he took off after one of his toddlers, who was climbing a table.

Ariel breathed a sigh of relief when the last of her bread was sold, and she could count down the minutes to the bake sale coming to an end. Every dollar exchanged. Every glance from the crowd. Each one made her wonder just who had left those comments on her page. There'd been plenty of anonymous, nasty remarks made about her and her family.

Every time the line waned, she found herself scanning the crowd, searching for some clue as to who had been at her house, hiding in the bushes. And she knew they'd been there. Not just from a feeling, but because an anonymous message had shown up in her Instagram app with a picture of her walking into her own house.

Pressing her hand to her stomach to settle her nerves, she practiced her breathing, then yanked her hand away when someone shot her that speculative look that people saved for pregnancy. Well, she wasn't pregnant with a child. She was carrying something else entirely: anxiety, swelling fast into full-blown panic.

The way these people devoured her baked goods reminded her of the story of the "Little Red Hen," only this was a little bit more heinous. They wanted all the goods, but they didn't want to do the work—or rather, they didn't want to be nice to her for them. Maybe this time, the hen should keep the bread to herself. The hen might've baked the bread with love—but that didn't mean she couldn't serve it with a knife.

Her fingertips tingled, not from heat but from the creeping feeling that someone was about to confront her.

"Ariel, darling." Miranda came forward, looking as gorgeous as always—put together, the picture-perfect model citizen, the mayor's wife. Miranda had never done anything to make her question their friendship or whether she might be someone else, hiding behind the rumors about her, but there was just something different about Miranda. Something hidden. The way her smile looked too practiced, her eye contact landing precisely on the *ing* in *darling*—as if scripted. Ariel had tried not to let it bother her before because she, too, kept secrets, but now that she was eyeing everyone as a potential enemy, there was something off about Miranda.

"Miranda, you look lovely," Ariel said. "Are you not selling anything today?"

Typically, the mayor's wife always had her own table filled not only with baked goods—setting an example for the rest of the community—but also with the mayor's propaganda. Little stickers and pins that people could put on their shirts and kids could smear with grimy fingers after eating a chocolate chip cookie or brownie.

Miranda waved a hand in the air, rolling her eyes, a big smile on her face. "I've already sold out. Everyone just loved the cereal that I made, and the little granola bars and protein muffins."

An unexpected flash of jealousy forced its way through Ariel's limbs. But it wasn't as if she could show that to Miranda. They were friends, at least she thought they were. Friends weren't supposed to be jealous of each other. But Ariel had always been the most popular bake sale person at these things—and now she was having to compete with Miranda?

They were quintessentially different in their outward appearances: Ariel with her subtle homemaker style and Miranda wearing Louboutin wedges exuding city-life chic wherever she went. Even when Miranda insulted someone, she said it like a compliment. Her charm was a blade wrapped in expensive French satin.

Ariel's booth was handmade, rustic, authentic. Miranda's now-empty table was sleek, branded, possibly catered by someone else. What was more important in Crystal Harbor—what was real, or what looked good on Instagram?

"Oh no, I'm so sad. I had really wanted to try your granola bars."

"A little secret," Miranda said, "I have more at home that I saved just for you guys. I'll bring them to the barbecue tomorrow."

Ariel nodded. She'd invited everyone over for a barbecue in the guise of celebrating her daughter's birthday. But really, it was surveillance. She wanted to see who was studying her house—her things—a little too closely. She'd watch who lingered near closed doors. Who'd slip inside to peek in drawers when they thought she wasn't looking. Let them eat cake—but she'd be the one watching who pocketed the silver.

What did they say? Keep your enemies close and your friends closer? Or was it the other way around? In this town, it seemed like they were one and the same.

Two women walked by at that moment, their hands held close to their mouths as they whispered. The women's voices dropped, but their eyes didn't. One gave a tight-lipped smile. The other tilted her head, like Ariel was a zoo exhibit. One of the whispering wenches pulled out her phone. Maybe she was taking a picture. But then Ariel caught a glimpse of her own social media feed. Coincidence—or had she just caught the source in the act?

Ariel wanted to shout: *You know I can see you whispering and staring, right? You're not even hiding it—you're doing it to my face, only I can't hear what you're saying. So, do you want to share?*

Miranda turned around to stare at the women, having followed Ariel's line of vision.

"Bitches," she murmured, and gave Ariel a wink.

Ariel's face flamed red when it was obvious the women had heard exactly what Miranda had said. Said bitches looked at them both with disdain, shaking their heads as if they were the ones in the wrong. And actually . . . maybe they were. Ariel didn't typically go around calling people bitches, but if the shoe fit?

Suddenly, Miranda reached forward and gripped her hand. "Listen, you don't deserve to be talked about like that." She rolled her eyes. "Anyways, if you ever want to jump someone in the parking lot, just let me know."

Ariel only half smiled. She wasn't the violent type—most of the time—but the idea of jumping someone in the parking lot and punching their daylights out sounded pretty nice about now. She laughed and said, "Thank you."

"Anytime." Miranda winked again and then walked off. The crowd parted for her like she was royalty. No, not royalty—something more dangerous. Someone worshipped. Untouchable.

Ariel smiled as Miranda walked away, but inside, she was still replaying the exact timing of that wink and what it really meant.

She wondered if the granola bars really were for her, or if Miranda had said that to test her reaction.

Miranda had gripped her hand at just the right moment. Everything she did was perfectly timed, like she'd rehearsed every interaction. Even the warmth in her voice felt algorithmic. And maybe that was the most dangerous thing. What parts of Miranda were real?

A child ran by, swiping a scone. His mother chased after him, dropping a five-dollar bill on the table as she went. Ariel collected the money with a shake of her head.

Shane sidled up to her. "That looked intense. Everything okay?"

"Kids are all hyped up on brownies and cookies, I guess."

"No, I meant you and Miranda. That didn't look like just bake sale banter."

She nodded, wondering who else besides Shane had been watching their exchange. "Just two girls being silly." Ariel side-eyed Miranda cautiously.

"I don't know if I trust her," Shane said.

His words reinforced her own thoughts.

"Oh, she's just being nice," Ariel said, dismissing him, not wanting to think on it another second.

"Just be careful . . ." Shane said, and then, as if he didn't want to finish his sentence, shook his head.

And it was okay. Ariel wasn't really sure she wanted to hear what he had to say. Or maybe, deep down, she already knew. She wasn't the only one handing out goods today. Smiles. Lies. Wrapped in wax paper and charm. Just like granola bars.

A scream ripped through the bake sale, slicing straight through the hum of conversation.

"Ohmygod, Riley!" A mother dropped to her knees, hands scrambling to pry her child's fingers from their mouth. Blood seeped between chocolate-smeared knuckles, dripping onto the grass. A brownie lay discarded at their feet.

"What happened?"

"Did she fall?"

"Did she get hit?"

The mother's voice cracked into a wail as she pulled a jagged shard of glass from the child's tongue. Gasps erupted around them.

"Glass! There's glass in the brownie!"

Her wild gaze swung toward Colleen, who stood frozen, her apron's brownie-shaped letters spelling *Warning: May Contain Fudge* standing loud against the backdrop of accusation.

"I . . . I don't know. There was no glass when I baked them. I . . ." She faltered, her words tripping over the stunned murmurs of the crowd.

That's when Ariel saw her. Miranda, leaning against a tree at the back of the crowd, arms folded. Not shocked. Not horrified. Watching. When their eyes met, Miranda's mouth curled—not quite a smile, not quite a smirk—before smoothing into a slow shake of her head, as if to say, *What a shame.*

Ariel's stomach flipped. Miranda wouldn't.

Would she?

Chapter Thirty

Miranda

Miranda wasn't really into sports, but she knew that one thing most couples loved to do was get together with other couples to cheer on a team over good snacks and usually enticing drinks. Most of these people thought an amusing night out was comparing grocery store memberships—but Miranda gave them slushies. Bright, fizzy. Pity they weren't boozy enough to fog up their spotless little consciences.

She invited Colleen, Ariel, Samantha and their husbands—plus a few others who didn't matter nearly as much but made for excellent background noise.

Oh, and Brad and his wife, of course. Kennedy was a snore—the kind of woman who rearranged her kitchen drawers for fun and bragged about her court case wins like anyone cared. She was even obsessing over Benjamin's stupid little dog, like the thing was cute or something.

All of them had been talking about *Ted Lasso* over smoothies the previous week, so Miranda thought it would be entertaining if they watched a British soccer game together. The theme of the party was fun—or what passed for it in a town where spontaneity died at a bake sale. Especially after Colleen's brownies were found tainted. What a pity.

Miranda had been the first one to jump to Colleen's defense. How could anyone suspect her of putting glass in brownies? Unless of course she was too inebriated to notice—but it wasn't Miranda who said that. How ironic that it was Colleen who was saved from drowning in suspicion. In the end, the mother was blamed for not checking what her kid was eating.

Everyone dressed in the colors of the team they were going to cheer for, and they were taking a poll on who would win. She made fancy snacks like shrimp cocktail and crudités, although she just preferred to call them vegetables. There had been crostini with toppings, cheese with fig jam and a cheeseball that she made herself from a recipe she found on some woman's TikTok.

By the end of the soccer game, they were all hyped up on sugary slushies, their bellies full of tasty snacks, their hearts warm with laughter. And Miranda felt a smug satisfaction at how easy it had been to undo their uptight defenses.

They all cuddled up on the massive sectional couch together, their bodies pressed into the cushioned space. Time for the next box to be checked on her to-do.

For those on her special list, Miranda stroked arms, squeezed a leg here or there, let her laugh linger a second too long. Each touch was a test. A probe. Just enough to register, not enough to alarm. Who might lean in, who might pull away, who might be open to trading a little more than conversation.

Benjamin, as always, was oblivious. Good. The last thing she needed was him sniffing around her motives like a curious cat with nothing better to do.

He'd warned her not to test the waters here with some of the games they'd played in New York. That he wanted to lead an upstanding life, be the pinnacle of the community. That Crystal Harbor wasn't into wife swapping. But Miranda knew better. She was already charting the currents, had preselected the couples she'd pull under. Of course she'd agreed with him, because why wouldn't she? Benjamin would never know the truth, even if it stared him in the face. Even if it fucked him every night before bed.

But Brad had felt that squeeze. She was almost sure of it—the shift in his posture, the flick of his gaze. If he flinched, she'd retreat. If he leaned in, well . . . that opened doors. And Miranda loved a door that wasn't quite shut.

Although she wondered if Shane had an idea, because he kept side-eyeing her with a curious look, as if he was trying to figure out just what she was up to. Shane struck her as the kind of man who liked to be near the fire, not in it—perfect for her purposes. A spectator, not a snitch.

This was the kind of game she was good at. The only one she ever really won. And she never played for fun. She played to see who would bend first.

When she cleared a few of the plates from the coffee table, Brad followed her around the couch to the kitchen side of the open-concept area that faced the family room.

"I love your party," he said.

There was a noticeable shift in the air. Miranda also felt a sudden well of nausea. The sickening-sweet cherry syrup from her drink threatening to make an appearance. She swallowed it down.

If there was going to be a power dynamic that wasn't there before—she was going to be the one on top.

"Oh, thanks. I used to throw a lot of . . . get-togethers in New

York. I really miss it." Miranda tilted her head just enough to let her hair fall over one eye, her lips parting in a half smile. She flicked her gaze toward the couch to see if Ben was watching. He wasn't. "Maybe I'll host something a little . . . flashier next time."

"Oh, yeah?" Brad eyed her. "I went to a party or two when I was in New York. Kennedy and I used to love going to clubs. Man, those people really knew how to get into it."

Kennedy at a club. That seemed like an oxymoron.

"Oh, I bet that was really a lot of fun. I can't imagine all those people with all their dance moves and, you know, excitement, the exhilaration." Miranda sighed longingly, wishing that this was one of those clubs right now. She stared at Brad—the way his hair drooped over his forehead, the way he filled out his shirt. Back at her club, he would've been the prime choice. Women would've lined up to get a piece of him. And she would've been one of them.

If she couldn't go back to her old life, then her old life was more than welcome to come here, at least by her.

"Maybe we can convince Shane and Ariel to host a theater-style after-party," she said coyly with a little shrug of her shoulder. "We could all watch one of Ariel's old shows, just like we watched this soccer game, with snacks and fun slushy drinks—and then maybe she could teach us a few dance moves."

Miranda laughed as if what she'd said was funny, but the laugh had another intention. The way she laughed was a way to entice—to get people to do what she wanted. She was an expert manipulator, and she knew it. Her laugh drew people in, made them forget their own moral compass in order to follow hers.

"I don't know about that." Brad chuckled, too, as if they were sharing a joke. "I get the strong feeling Ariel's not really into that sort of thing anymore."

"What about you? Would you and Kennedy host a party?"

"Maybe." Brad eyed her as if he wanted her to give an invitation. Miranda knew she was stepping into dangerous territory right now. And she liked it. Reveled in the thrill. The pause before a fall. The second before a yes. She wanted him to tip.

He broke eye contact, gesturing at nothing in particular. "You're a great host."

"Oh, I don't know if anyone would want *me* to host again," she said, letting the mock humility roll off her tongue like honey. She watched Brad's reaction closely, waiting for him to take the bait.

His eyes returned to hers. "I think they would."

Hook, line, sinker.

"Well, maybe that's what I'll do." She giggled, not out of amusement, but calculation. Her voice pitched just sweet enough to sound innocent, just suggestive enough to land. "A Broadway-themed party—with all the songs from Ariel's old shows. And you can relive your clubbing days."

She let the words hang.

There. Let's see how that sits. With Brad. With everyone in the room. She watched them all, watched *him* especially. If he smiled too quickly, she'd know.

"Well, if you're hosting it, I'm sure everyone would want to join." But the way Brad said it wasn't as if he was talking about his wife, their friends—it was as if he was talking about himself.

He took the dishes out of her hands, his fingers brushing hers as he headed toward the sink. His skin was hot, searing her own, and there was a hitch in her breath, a flush of the forbidden. A spark she hadn't felt in a long time—a spark of exhilaration at being bad.

Miranda followed him to the sink, not sure what she was going to do when she got there, but feeling as if she needed to somehow return his gesture. To let him know that maybe she had a spark of interest too.

"Hey, you two." Ariel's soft voice floated across the kitchen, and Miranda practically jumped, a pile of crackers on a plate spilling to the floor.

"Oh my gosh, you startled me." Miranda dropped to the floor to pick up the scattered snacks, and Ariel rushed over to help. How much had she seen?

"I'm so sorry. I didn't mean to startle you." Ariel laughed.

"I was just thinking about how much fun I've had tonight and how I'd love to throw another party like this with everyone—such a good group—and I'm so glad that I finally have some friends I can hang out with."

"Yeah," Brad said. "Miranda was even talking about hosting a Broadway party in your honor."

Miranda caught it—the too-wide smile, the way Ariel's fingers faltered as she set the crackers down. Cracked in half, just like the moment. A slight tremble came into her hand. Miranda studied that tremble, studied her new friend's face, saw the fear, the anxiety—and saw how quickly it went away as Ariel replaced that look with a smile. Ariel wasn't going to be as easy to win over as some of the others. Interesting. *Maybe she's not as sweet as she acts.* Miranda was going to have to up her game.

"That would be fun." Ariel's grin was brittle as she stared at Miranda then into the family room, where Shane was chatting with Colleen's husband, Zachary. It was clear from her expression that she was uncomfortable, sensed, perhaps, the underlying vibe

Miranda had been trying to keep hidden. "Shane, I think it's getting late, and we'd better get going."

Shane looked disappointed, and Miranda couldn't blame him. It was only nine o'clock. Benjamin walked into the kitchen then, a lock of hair falling over his forehead, the grin on his face one that reminded Miranda of exactly why she'd gone after him. He was fucking hot.

"So, this is where the fun is all happening, huh?" Benjamin said. "Kitchen party."

Colleen wandered in next, not as wobbly as she was the last time she'd seen her, though perhaps that was due to Zachary's hands, which always seemed to be settled on her hips. No wonder they had so many babies. Or maybe Colleen was sobering up—less sway, clearer eyes. Disappointing. Colleen was pliable when she was pickled, and pliable was what Miranda preferred. "Kitchen party?"

Miranda almost laughed when Colleen's eyes went straight to the sink, and she licked her lips as if she could taste Miranda's hidden stash of booze under there. Naughty.

"Maybe you can help me convince Shane and Ariel to stay a little longer."

"Oh? Are you guys headed home?" Colleen put on a good pout.

Before Ariel or Shane could answer, Kennedy followed everyone else into the kitchen and tucked her arm through Brad's—the party now truly taking place around the marble island. Miranda's guests swarmed the kitchen like bees to honey—her honey—too naive to notice she was all sting.

"Oh, I need to leave too." Kennedy glanced from her expensive, sparkling watch to Brad as if to say *agree with me.*

What a party pooper. *Take the dog with you.*

"Well, anyone who wishes to stay—I thought that we could go outside and roast a few marshmallows, make some s'mores over our firepit." Miranda held up the plate she'd prepared before everyone arrived. They wouldn't see the irony in it like she did. It looked like a charcuterie board, except it was filled with marshmallows, chocolates, graham crackers and other yummy little things. "This is my signature sweet charcuterie. I call it Temptation."

"Just one?" The way Brad was looking at Kennedy was as if he were a child begging for a treat. *Please, Mommy, let us stay.*

Shane did the same thing to Ariel, even putting his hands together in prayer and getting down on his knees in front of her. "Just one, babe. Just one, please?"

Miranda's lip curled in disgust, and she forced herself to turn it upside down. Jesus. Begging for marshmallows like they were front-row seats at a Disney movie. As if they'd never had a puffy, sticky, burnt marshmallow in their lives. God, sometimes she hated this town.

Everyone started to laugh, and someone said, "Please, sir, I want s'more?" in a British accent, just like a child from *Oliver*, only twisting *some more* into *s'more*. Funny. Miranda snorted.

"Promise I won't keep you too late." Miranda smiled sweetly, her hands holding out the charcuterie board. "We all work too hard not to enjoy the sweets that life has to offer."

Miranda glanced at Benjamin, giving him a wicked wink, a promise for later, and for the briefest second she saw a look of hunger in his eyes. The old Benji wanting what he knew she could provide. Maybe he was finally remembering who he thought he married. The New York party girl. Only he didn't really know the full extent of what she was capable of.

Now the real party was about to start. She'd see who grabbed the decadent dark chocolate first. Who hesitated to roast. Who succumbed to temptation and devoured every morsel.

Dark chocolate, sticky hands, graham cracker crumbs in glossy smiles. Let them think this was the end of the night. She knew better. Temptation never ended with dessert. It just started there.

Miranda was ready for the next phase of her plot. Crystal Harbor was about to relive a story it thought it had buried.

Chapter Thirty-One

Jennifer

The Fifteen Commandments of a Tradwife

> **Nine:** Thou shalt not speak ill of the patriarchy (unless it's cloaked in concern). "Oh, I just feel like men are wired differently . . ." is tradwife code for "He's a disaster but at least he takes out the trash."

The air clung to her skin like a soaked towel after a swim on the beach. The back of her shirt was damp before they'd even reached the monkey bars. Of course, it was hot—this was Florida—but Jennifer still held out hope for a breeze that never came.

She shifted on the park bench, the metal slats sticky beneath her legs, and took a sip of her rapidly melting iced chai. The coolness hit her tongue like a promise she didn't quite believe. Shadow panted, partaking of the water she'd poured into his travel drinking bowl.

This was supposed to be a breather. A rare spring afternoon with all four kids home, no appointments, no school drop-offs, no overtime shift at the store. Just bikes, doughnuts and a trip to the park like they used to do—back when outings didn't feel so hard-earned.

Playing at the park where she'd played tag as a child, and where as a teenager, she'd . . . Jennifer swallowed, swiveling her head toward the oak that was older than Crystal Harbor, remembering a night over a decade ago where she'd met under the trees and made a vow she didn't want to pledge. To keep a secret forever.

She flicked her gaze away. Not wanting to remember what that promise had cost her, and everyone else. Most of all Tara.

Ever since Jamie's call, she'd been waiting for something to tip. For the sky to crack open, for the ground to give way. It always happened like that—peace, then pandemonium.

Athena was reading in the shade of a different tree, the palm fronds waving back and forth in the gentle breeze, fluttering the pages of her book.

Dominic was running back and forth with a few boys from school he'd recognized as soon as they arrived; already a grass stain marred the front of his shirt from tackling a ball. Off running on the path where he'd learned to ride a bike without training wheels just last summer. And Craig and Bailey were on the swings.

Jennifer watched her children, keeping an eye on all four—which wasn't always easy considering how active they all were. The only thing that was making it slightly less hard today was Athena's lack of energy and her concentration on her new book.

The difference today was that none of the mothers were coming up to chat with her. There was no small talk. No plans being made. No chatter about what Mrs. Baker in art had made the kids create this week, or that the gym teacher had forced someone's child to do something they didn't want to—like climbing the ropes and touching the bar at the top.

Jennifer had always hated climbing the ropes, too, but she found it built character. Didn't it? Or maybe it was just traumatizing, depending on the child. Right now, she felt like the fractured kid who'd been pushed out of the hopscotch line.

Jennifer sipped her iced chai. It was a treat she'd picked up for herself on the way to the park. They'd walked from their house, the kids actually riding their bikes and scooters while she tried to keep up. They stopped at the corner bakery, and she got a tea. Each of them had gotten a fancy doughnut before they'd headed over to the playground. Reclaiming joy wherever she could.

This was something they used to do when she was married to Jamie, when money was no object. And it was something that she had stopped doing after the divorce as she tried to make ends meet. But since she'd started working at the grocery store, she'd had more income, and it had made buying special treats for her kids a little easier. And truly, she thought she deserved a treat too. She worked her ass off.

The sweetness of the chai lingered on her tongue, grounding her—for a moment—in the present.

They used to sit on this same bench—Jamie checking his emails, she passing out juice boxes and segments of the clementines she'd peeled that morning. Back then, she thought exhaustion was the worst thing that could happen to a mother, maybe more so than Jamie's occasional heavy hand. Now she knew better. It wasn't the fatigue but the judgment. The silence. The way people disappeared without ever saying goodbye.

But the peaceful moment didn't last. The hair on the back of her neck started to prickle, and she didn't want to look up—she was pretty sure there was somebody watching her—but not wanting to look and not really having a choice were two different things. Instinct warred with curiosity, and curiosity won out.

She glanced up to see several mothers standing in a circle, pointing in her direction, whispering as if she wouldn't see their nasty behavior. The chai curdled in her stomach.

Jennifer thought of the Wonder Bread. The eggs. Who would be so petty?

The chaos that whirled inside her from that one vision undermined the calm of the park. The innocence of children laughing, shouting, birds chirping, all of it soured by the squadron of finger-pointers.

The divorce had been over a year ago. Why were they still talking about her?

But the question was rhetorical, because deep down, she knew the reason. Someone had seen her TikTok videos. Had seen how she spoke the truth about her marriage and the toxic culture of this town. How she'd tried to encourage other women to stand up for themselves. Pointing out those things went against the tradwife commandments. Not that they were written down anywhere. More like they were just known. Invisible rules that she'd broken.

The incident with Craig's friend at school repeating his mother's vulgar language made it pretty obvious she'd gained a few more enemies in Crystal Harbor.

It was partially why she hadn't posted anything recently. Although she hadn't taken down the account, she'd removed commenting, needing the space. Space from the comments. Space from the fear of Jamie's retribution.

Just to mess with them, she lifted her phone and took a picture.

She could hear their gasps of outrage from here, as they swiveled around, giving her their backs.

Jennifer finished her tea, walked over to the trash can and popped it into the recycling bin. A glance at all four of her children showed each of them in the same position. Bailey was trying to get off the swing that Craig was pushing her on.

Jennifer hurried over, helped her daughter off the swing and then watched the two of them run up the stairs to the slide. As she sat at the bottom to catch Bailey, she watched as the other mothers resumed whispering and talking about her out of the corner of her eye. And then one of them started to approach, tucking her tight brown bob behind one ear, her lips pursed.

Fuck.

"Jennifer, right?"

Jennifer slowly looked at the woman, recognizing her from PTA meetings she hadn't been to in forever, and high school before that. Mallory something.

"Yes?" Jennifer glanced back at Bailey, who was rushing up the stairs for another slide run.

"I just thought I'd let you know that the things you were saying online were really inappropriate." Mallory—or whatever her name was—had a patronizing tone, her head bobbing like a buoy in Echo Lake.

Jennifer drew in a heady breath. A bead of sweat traced her spine, slow and deliberate, like even her own body wanted to flee, one drop at a time. She wished she hadn't thrown out her empty cup of chai; she could have tossed the ice cubes into Mallory's smug face.

A part of her had been waiting for this moment—although she was surprised it hadn't happened at the grocery store, and a little bit relieved that it hadn't ruined her job. After the parking lot incident with Colleen Christensen—hypocrite extraordinaire—she knew she was one mistake away from being fired, even though CCTV clearly showed she wasn't at fault.

"I'm not sure what you're talking about," she managed to say in a controlled way, as she made a mental note of where each of her kids was once more. What she truly wanted to say was *fuck off, Mallory.* But knowing the group of Karens she was surrounded with, there was a high probability this conversation was being recorded, especially after she'd taken their picture. She could see them now—phones angled just right, ready to capture her "meltdown" for likes and smug PTA group chats.

"Have a blessed day, Mallory." She knew that line would sting more than anything else. Women like Mallory hated being dismissed with sugar.

Jennifer didn't bother waiting for her to give another excuse for approaching, or to continue the conversation further. Instead, she started to walk away, gently tugging on Shadow's leash and calling for her kids. She'd claw through an alligator-infested pond before letting Mallory ruin the day.

Besides, it was hot as hell, and she was certain her kids would appreciate an Italian ice, which, considering they'd already had doughnuts, was an extra special treat. Bribery worked well.

But the woman followed her as she tried to track down Dominic.

"I think you *do* know what I'm talking about. I think you know *exactly* what I'm saying."

Jennifer didn't respond. She didn't need to.

Let them whisper. Let them watch. She was done apologizing for surviving, for opening her eyes. Maybe it was time she came clean about the night over a decade ago too.

Jennifer turned without a word.

She reached for Bailey's hand. The day wasn't over yet, and she was determined to end it with sticky palms, wind-kissed cheeks and laughter—sugary and defiant—echoing off the lake. And no one—not Jamie, not Mallory, not the whole damn town—was going to take that from them.

Chapter Thirty-Two

Ariel

Ariel basted butter over the bread that she had formed into a circle, cutting an X in the top. She'd shaped the dough like she shaped herself—round edges, no sharp corners. Making bread usually soothed her. But today, even the soft dough and warm butter couldn't settle her nerves. They'd stayed too late at the party, and people had been acting overly friendly. Bordering on crossing a line. What line, she didn't know. It just felt . . . off. Too flirtatious, maybe? The kind of flirtation that wasn't overt, just charged enough to make her wonder if she was imagining it—or being warned.

She might've been married for years now, but she hadn't forgotten what flirting looked like—and that party had it in spades.

She thought back to the backyard—how they held their marshmallows over the fire, how Miranda had leaned forward and snatched the blackened marshmallow off Shane's stick before he had a chance to put it between his graham cracker and chocolate. The feelings that had stirred in her chest in that moment had been a mix of anger and jealousy. But an act like that had to have been innocent, right? It wasn't like Miranda was after Shane or something. She'd done the same thing to Brad. She had a handsome husband, Benjamin. They seemed very happy together.

But having everyone together again after years of avoiding each other felt . . . strange. And this morning she'd woken to another anonymous message: A fire pit by the water's edge. Feels familiar. Nothing like a night with old friends. Echo Lake keeps its secrets well.

Whoever was stalking her had watched them all last night. And the reference to old friends and Echo Lake's secrets . . . Ariel couldn't shake that whoever was sending her these messages might know what happened all those years ago. She couldn't tell Shane. He had no idea. Telling him could destroy everything.

As she swirled the melted butter around the risen dough with a basting brush, Shane marched into the kitchen, an angry look on his face, and for a split second she thought he knew. But he slammed down an orange pill bottle on the island counter. The thud echoed in her chest. Cold marble against her fingertips grounded her—barely. Even as the smell of butter, warm and nutty, normally comforting, suddenly made her stomach churn, she was simultaneously relieved that this was what he was angry about and not the other secret she held.

The baster stilled in her hand, her palm hovering over the bread. And her heart—she was fairly certain—stopped working behind her ribs.

Mommy's little helpers. Multiple responses ran through her head all at once. How to handle his reaction, the inevitable explosion that was about to come. What would be safest?

If she deflected, he might leave it alone. If she lied, he might get louder. If she told the truth . . . Well, that had never gone in her favor before.

"What's this?" Shane's raised brows and the challenging twist of his mouth told her that he knew exactly what it was. His palm pressed into the bottle cap like he might crush it into the marble. And if he didn't know what it was when he found it, then he certainly must have when he looked at the label, which gave her name and the prescription. And what had made him dig through her drawer to find the secret compartment where her pills were held anyway?

Or had she forgotten to put them away? She'd been so tired this morning when she'd taken them out, so tired when she'd popped the lid. Ariel could picture the bottle on the counter. Could picture herself pouring the pills into her palm, throwing them back and drinking them with water running from the sink. But she couldn't remember putting them away . . .

Ariel realized she'd been staring at the bottle. The silent beats passing between them making the air grow thicker. How long had it been since he asked the question? Half a second? Half a minute?

Finally, she swallowed down the panic rising like dough in her throat. "I won't demean us both by pretending you don't already know the answer to that." Ariel set the baster in the sink with calm precision, opened the oven and put the bread inside to bake. Her grip on the handle stilled the tremble in her fingers but did nothing for her knees. The kids had not yet risen, and she was going to make them toast this morning with the jam she'd made yesterday—strawberry, their favorite.

"You're right, I do know what this is." He tapped the lid forcefully, his knuckles white, the bottom part of his finger bent. "I want to know what it's doing in our house."

Ariel turned around to face her husband, her hands folded in front of her, trying to look as demure as she possibly could. She knew the choreography by heart—chin down, hands still, voice soft. Anything less might be a spark to kindling. She'd rehearsed it for years. Defer. Agree. Defuse. Never ignite. "I wasn't feeling well," she said. "My doctor gave them to me."

"What doctor?" There was a red coloring to Shane's cheeks, and the line of a vein in his neck pulsed.

"*My* doctor." She didn't feel the need to elaborate on that. His anger was precisely the reason why she hadn't told him about this before. She knew exactly how he felt about these things. He'd made it clear years ago, and with each subsequent pregnancy, her depression afterward had gotten worse and worse. And then Tara had been born, and the storm of memories returned. Every time she looked at her baby she saw a ghost. But Shane thought that those were things you could just overcome with willpower. Why didn't he seem to understand when someone's suffering was beyond their own control? As if she wanted to feel so empty inside. As if she wanted to have to force herself to feel emotion.

Deep down, she knew why he had an aversion to pills. His mother had abused them, left him and his sister, their younger brother, to their own devices, and then Tara had . . . died.

"I thought we talked about this."

Ariel bit the tip of her tongue to keep from scoffing at his remark. The only talking they'd ever done was him telling her there was nothing wrong with her and she didn't have postpartum depression, as if he'd gone to medical school and knew anything about it. Besides, he was categorically incorrect. Shane was so smart about so many things, but not this. His mind too skewed from his past to see sense.

"No, I don't recall that we have." Ariel marched toward the fridge on lightened feet, knowing she was tempting her husband to get angry by dismissing his words, but at the same time not really caring. In fact, she felt a little bit of exhilaration at the idea of irritating her husband. She was always so calm, so malleable, so giving, so nice. What would happen if she wasn't nice anymore?

The old Ariel would've apologized. The old Ariel would've cried. But she couldn't find her anymore.

"Ariel." Shane drew in a deep breath. "If you're not feeling good—*not good enough* that you need to go and get medicine for it—then that's something we should've talked about." His voice was soft, but his hand was still curled into a fist beside the bottle of pills.

Ariel stilled her hand on the handle of the fridge, the coolness of the metal against her palm somehow calming, the hum of the fridge's compressor a soothing pat on her back. The way he was talking right now, the sound of his voice was soothing—and confusing.

She turned around slowly to face her husband once more, examining his face and trying to get a gauge on his emotions and thoughts. But what she saw before her was something she'd never seen before: deep concern.

"The truth is, Shane, I didn't think you would understand or approve." She swallowed, pulse hammering, wishing that she wasn't having this conversation right now. Wishing that she'd been awake enough to put her pills away, because she was pretty sure now that after she popped that lid, she'd left the bottle on the counter and strolled out of the bathroom. "I didn't want to worry you. And I thought it best to just handle it on my own." She shrugged, hoping that would be a good enough answer for him.

Shane frowned, tapping the bottle again. "How long do you think you have to be on these things?"

Ariel tried to offer him a comforting smile, although she found that to be a little irritating, considering it was *her* who needed the comfort more than him. She could feel the smile stretch too wide, too stiff—like the leather of a brand-new dance shoe. "Not much longer, dear."

Shane nodded once, succinctly. "Good. I . . . It's not good for you to be on pills."

Ariel hid the seething inside her and nodded. He would never understand. "Of course, Shane."

And maybe it wasn't good for *her* to have a husband who refused to understand. Who looked at everything through a lens of his past.

She used to love him. She wasn't sure what she felt now.

He was so different before . . . Empathetic, romantic, charismatic . . .

She remembered the man who wrote her poems on the back of receipts. Who once braved the Lincoln Tunnel at the worst rush hour, missing his flight, just to bring her a bouquet of roses before a show. In high school they'd not really talked much, though they ran in the same circles. It wasn't until she'd come home during the holidays her last year in college that they'd gotten more acquainted, both of them waiting for a cab at the airport, recognizing each other enough to see if they wanted to ride together.

They'd hit it off from there, and he'd come to visit her in New York. She remembered the way he used to trace hearts in the sugar from packets at cafés. Now he traced circles on the pill bottle, like she was no longer Ariel, his wife, but a problem to be solved.

Guilt swirled inside her. The pressure was building, an ache she couldn't swallow anymore. And maybe, she thought, it was time to tell the truth—the whole truth—even if it meant dragging the past into the light. No. She'd never do that to Shane. He didn't know what really happened that night, and he never would. She'd carry it alone, because she loved her kids too much to let the truth rip their family apart.

Chapter Thirty-Three

Miranda

Miranda stood in her bedroom, admiring her reflection—the silhouette of her body in the black lace lingerie she'd picked out just for tonight. Her blond hair had been freshly processed, lashes extended, body waxed, and a fresh pack of her blue contacts had been delivered just this morning.

She was always one to dress to impress, but tonight was different.

Tonight was *special.* A chance for her to wrestle back some control in her life, to be *herself.* To play in a world that was forbidden.

She pulled a red dress over her head, feeling scandalous, then swiped on a fresh layer of matching lipstick. It clung to her like confidence—fabric over fear. It had been a long time since she felt like she belonged in her own skin.

Benjamin stepped out of the bathroom, water still glistening on his skin from the shower. He eyed her up and down, a hungry grin spreading across his face—familiar from the days they'd spent in New York, when their love had been forbidden because he was still married at the time—and a moment like this would have exhilarated her beyond belief.

"That dress," he said. "It's incredible."

Miranda walked slowly toward her husband, ever the actress. She trailed her fingers up his chest to his collarbone, then his neck, and gave a slight hug to his ear. "I can always take this off right now if you want me to." She leaned forward, her teeth scraping enticingly against his earlobe, leaving behind a smudge of red. She'd need to reapply—but the art of seducing one's husband was more important, wasn't it?

Benjamin groaned, his still-damp hands gripping her waist and tugging her close. She leaned up into him, pressing her lips to his, kissing him like there was no tomorrow. Because maybe there wouldn't be after tonight. When she was done, her lipstick was smeared on his face, and she smiled.

"How does it feel to be tagged?" She giggled.

He glanced behind him in the mirror and groaned again. "Oh geez, now I've got to get in the shower all over again."

She lifted her dress, revealing the lacy panties underneath. "Want me to give you something else to wash off?"

Benjamin fell to his knees in front of her, another exaggerated groan on his lips. "You're killing me, Miranda."

She laughed. "Well, I hope not—I need you around for a while longer."

The doorbell rang, pulling them apart. Miranda tweaked his chin, gave him one last red kiss, then straightened her hair, fixed her lipstick and sauntered down the stairs.

A sultry sound mix she'd created and added to over the years played on the house speakers, filtering in lightly in the background. She passed by a mirror on the landing, noting how incredibly good she looked. Unrecognizable as the girl she once was. If they wanted to judge her, they'd better do so after the party. Let them whisper tomorrow—tonight, they'd all be hers.

Tonight was a night no one would forget. This was going to be the party of the century for Crystal Harbor—a party people talked about for years to come. And if it went well, it wouldn't just be a party. It would be the beginning of something else. Something thrilling. Something hers. Something that no one could take. Not her reputation. Not her power. Not her sense of being wanted—for who she actually was, not the version everyone expected her to play.

The invitations had gone out to only a select few. Miranda preferred subtlety when it came to creating chaos. She planned to seduce them all. They liked to play innocent, but Miranda knew better. There was a darker side to them all, and if she could draw it out, well, she'd use that to her advantage.

Miranda passed the living room, the silk pillows strategically tossed on the couch, soft candlelight that flickered, and the air was thick with the scent of citrus and something darker—like heady wine left too long in the sun. One of the candles by the piano dripped wax in slow red rivulets, creating pools of hardened crimson on the wood. It reminded her of an event in New York City—when wax wasn't just decor, but foreplay.

The tile was cool under her bare feet, grounding her for a moment in the ritual of greeting and seduction. She'd left her shoes off on purpose, a contrast to the sexy dress. Down-to-earth in a way the lace underthings weren't.

Blowing out a breath, she steadied her damp palms. Tonight was either going to make all her careful planning worth it, or it was going to blow up in her face.

She answered the door with a basket in hand and held it out

to her first guests: Brad and Kennedy. Brad wore a pair of white snug slacks and a brightly colored blue Hawaiian shirt that showed off his tan, while Kennedy looked more . . . boring in a skirt and blouse that belonged in a courtroom rather than a get-together. Kennedy had courtroom energy. Brad had couch-cushion stains on his soul. She knew which one was already halfway undressed. She'd seen the way he looked at other men's wives, at her. Tongue tucked in his cheek like he was holding back a secret. Or maybe a confession.

"Cell phones and keys right in here." She tapped the basket coyly with a long French-manicured nail.

"Cell phones?" A flash of panic spread over Kennedy's face. "What if the babysitter calls?" Kennedy's hand fluttered to her collarbone, like she was trying to keep her dignity buttoned up.

"You're welcome to check your phone anytime you want—but party rules. We don't carry them through the house."

Miranda smiled kindly, generously, hoping that would be the end of the objections. It wasn't as if she could outright tell Kennedy that having a phone at this type of party was probably the last thing someone would want. A lawyer should know better than to leave evidence, but if she warned her, there was a risk Kennedy would depart—and she didn't want to do that to Brad. Seemed like he hadn't gotten any in a long time. Tonight might just be his lucky chance. Besides, the only cameras in the house were hers, and nobody needed to know about those.

"Where's your dog?" Kennedy asked.

Miranda rolled her eyes. *God, obsessed much?* "She's at her babysitter's house."

Not wanting to hear another word about the stupid dog, Miranda led her new friends into the kitchen, where mocktails were lined up on the counter along with all sorts of delicious appetizers. Brad had already clocked the faux bar. Kennedy was still scanning for exits. Miranda handed Kennedy a drink and watched as she lifted it to her mouth—then paused. Instead of sipping, Kennedy only stared at the cherry red, bubbly liquid.

Kennedy sniffed it. "What's it called?"

"Miranda Special," Miranda said. Her signature mix of equal parts cherry, pomegranate, lime and a little powder that made people say yes. "I promise you'll love it."

No one ever asked what was in a Miranda Special. That was the point. Trust, or the illusion of it, was tonight's first game. Miranda made it a point never to give away her special recipes—especially not at a party like this. She needed inhibitions lowered, and sober people had way too much sense.

She handed Brad a drink and took one for herself. "Cheers to you both." Energy clung to the bare skin of her arms as she raised her glass and sipped, the mocktail leaving a tang of the forbidden on her tongue. A tang of remembrance.

Brad sipped fast. Kennedy didn't sip at all.

Miranda noted the grip Kennedy had on her glass—white-knuckled. One well-placed comment, one flicker of doubt, and she'd bolt. She'd seen that look before. It always came just before someone reserved their husband an Uber and went home early—alone.

The doorbell rang, and Miranda skipped around the counter toward the foyer just as Benjamin was coming down the stairs, a waft of his spicy cologne with him. Delicious. She smiled at him, sliding her hands over his shoulders and kissing him lightly on the cheek, leaving behind a red imprint of her mouth. His shirt was still damp at the collar, sticking like doubt. Was he nervous?

He smiled at her, but his hands didn't quite relax. His fingers stayed curled at his sides—like he wasn't sure whether to reach for her or stop her.

Together, they greeted Shane and Ariel. Shane looked like he was dressed for a golf outing in snug chinos and a Polo, while Ariel looked ethereal as usual in a flowy bohemian-style dress.

Shane's hungry eyes devoured Miranda's body, making her feel a little queasy. She smiled dismissively. Shane wasn't her target, but his interest was a good sign that this party was headed in the right direction.

Ariel didn't notice—and for that, Miranda was glad. But when she glanced up at Benjamin, it was clear he'd seen Shane's gaze. He possessively wrapped his arm around her shoulders. That only made Miranda smile wider. Jealousy was the name of the game. Made things fun. Let him mark his territory. It made her all the more curious who'd be sniffing around it by midnight.

Benjamin smiled, but his eyes flicked toward the guest list on the table. She knew that look. He wasn't worried about the guests. He was watching her—like she was the fuse, and he wasn't sure how long the wick had left. And that made her want to climb him or claw him. She'd decide depending on how he reacted tonight. One thing was for certain, Benjamin had better not get in her way. She'd played demure up until tonight, but she wasn't going to be subjected to his rule anymore.

The doorbell rang again. Miranda hurried through the hall, pausing once more to check her appearance in the mirror. She caught a glimpse of her own expression—perfect. Too perfect. She paused, pressing cool fingers to her collarbone, feeling the pulse there. She looked like the version of herself she used to miss—the one from Manhattan who wore perfume like armor and once danced on a table at 3 a.m. enjoying every minute of being a party girl. But now the confidence looked like costume jewelry. Real from far away. Fragile up close.

There was a tinge of edge to her excitement. A reminder that this wasn't just any party. This wasn't just for a little fun. With all her careful planning, the one thing she hadn't planned on was . . . guilt?

Miranda shook it off. Guilt was an emotion she refused to acknowledge, like french fries on a menu.

As she led Colleen and Zachary, Samantha and Nathaniel into the kitchen, Miranda thought she saw a flicker of light across the water out the back window—like someone watching. Or recording. Her smile didn't falter, but her skin prickled.

She'd spent so long curating every detail. But control was a slippery thing. It wasn't just her guests she had to seduce. It was fate itself—coax it into cooperation, charm it into silence so the truth could unfold in all its perfect glory.

One wrong glance, one misstep, and it would all burn down.

A chill spread down her arms. She blinked—and the light was gone. But there had been someone. In New York, being watched had been foreplay. In Crystal Harbor, it was forewarning.

Chapter Thirty-Four

Jennifer

The Fifteen Commandments of a Tradwife

> **Ten:** Thou shalt keep secrets close. The truth is a fragile thing—best tucked away beneath the linens where no one dares look.

Most people on Friday nights had plans with their friends. Maybe a movie they were going to go watch. Trying out a new restaurant. Or maybe they were going to take a class, learn something new. Or take an intimate moment with their partner to discuss the week—activities, events or just a recap.

Jennifer still tapped on the TikTok app out of habit or maybe some masochistic impulse. After figuring out how to block Jamie and his wife, she'd turned the comments back on. Even her original videos were still getting comments now, stitches, mostly from strangers with usernames like Sassymom88 or TrueTradwife. The judgment was brutal, but sometimes . . . sometimes the DMs weren't. Sometimes, a woman would thank her. Whisper that they were scared too. It gave Jennifer the courage to consider making a new post even though she hadn't in weeks.

But not tonight. She clocked off the addictive app, indulging in something else entirely.

Her kids were all tucked up in bed, in her bed, watching a movie while she sat on the back porch with Shadow and a hot mug of tea that was bitter from steeping too long. The porch cushion stuck to the backs of her thighs, dew-damp and unwelcoming. She was in the dark, no lights on. She didn't want anyone to know that she was out here. She liked to be the one spying, not the one spied on.

The air smelled of damp grass, charcoal ash from someone's earlier barbecue and the sharp citrus of her lemon balm tea. Across Echo Lake, the party people were at it again, lights blazing. She could see straight into the kitchen, where they were dancing, grinding on each other.

A hollow ache throbbed behind her eyes. And a question she couldn't quite answer: Why couldn't she look away? She wasn't jealous, exactly, not so much as she was reminded of just how alone she was on a Friday night.

Of how another Friday night, years ago, had turned out differently.

How could the neighbors stand it? Couldn't they hear the music? A pounding, sultry beat alerting everyone who lived along Echo Lake of an after-hours event.

Though she couldn't make out the lyrics, the bass beat floating across the lake felt like it was thudding in her chest, a second heartbeat she didn't want. The pulse of the music sent a rush over her limbs.

Glass clinked. Laughter—too loud—spilled through the windows and into the dark like a secret escaping.

How desperately she wanted to hop into her neighbor's canoe and paddle across the lake, climb out, sneak up to the windows and peer inside. To see who these dancing shadows were. Without binoculars she was just too far to recognize any of them. But she wouldn't be surprised if she knew each and every one of the attendees by name. If they weren't the very same ones who'd partied here all those years ago.

She wanted to hear every word. Every conversation. Every little juicy morsel. They weren't innocent—she knew that. Because she was watching one man grind on one woman and then move to another to grind on her. A bare leg flashed in the window, skirt hitched up, silhouette framed in kitchen light like a scene from a movie she wasn't supposed to watch.

Why were the curtains open? As if they wanted everyone to see . . .

Though for most of her marriage, Jennifer had felt like she'd been kept inside a locked box and her childhood innocence dashed the summer before her senior year, things had opened up to her in the last year since her divorce. The box wasn't gone. It was just bigger now. A box with a porch and a view and no locks, but still, somehow, she felt constricted. She might have been let out of the locked box of her marriage, but she was still trapped here. Subjected to scrutiny, like finding out that her kid's friend's parent thought she was a bitch. Or that the ladies at the playground thought she was somehow personally attacking them by expressing her views.

But there were some things that remained hidden to her. Like the history of her husband's new wife. She'd gone on what she thought was a deep internet dive but came up empty-handed. A reverse-image internet search had brought up only a few promotional images at clubs in New York City. So the woman liked to party. Hardly shocking. Though to some in this community it might be.

There was of course the possibility that the woman was so clean there was nothing to be found. But Jennifer didn't believe that. The woman was hiding something, she was sure.

This type of party was what she imagined a swingers party would look like. The way they were dancing around like they were drunk on lust was unnerving. Not because she was ashamed of lust. Hell, she wouldn't mind a nice man showing her a little romance. But . . . there was just something so off about the party. A knot twisted in her belly, and she had the strange compulsion to stop something bad that was about to happen. Not the sex. Sex, as she'd learned from reading her romance novels, was beautiful and not about power.

She used to think she'd missed out on passion. But if this was it—this writhing chaos in someone's kitchen—maybe she was better off without it.

She squinted her eyes as if that would help her discern through the distance just who was inside. There were four couples—eight people—and she couldn't quite make out who was who. Just the shorter bodies of the women, the taller bodies of the men. And the way they danced across the kitchen in lustful, undulating waves. Bare arms, skirts raised to expose legs.

If someone asked why she kept watching, she wouldn't have an answer. Or maybe she had too many: loneliness, curiosity, spite. None of them made her feel any better. She told herself it was concern. But concern didn't make your hands sweat or your breath catch when a man dipped his hand below someone's waistline.

She watched one woman grab a man by the hand and pull him deeper into the house, disappearing a few moments later. And another woman looked around frantically, and then her hand was grabbed by someone else, and she was led in the opposite direction. Jennifer wondered if that woman's husband had just been taken away from her, if she even knew what was happening at this party. Was she just as innocent as Jennifer had been in her own marriage?

Had Jennifer ever been to a party like this? one might ask. Well, the past was best left in the past, now, wasn't it? A flash of Jamie's wicked grin, but not at her, at someone else . . . A subtle encouragement to rub another man's shoulders. The discomfort at the touch of another man, while her husband encouraged her, saying, *There are times when rules are meant to be broken.*

Did Jamie's new wife like to break the rules? Is that why he fell for her?

Jennifer shook her head, as if that would force the weird flashes of her past to go away. She took a long, slow sip of tea, letting it scald the back of her throat. Only it didn't quell the acid building in her stomach. If only she could somehow lift a bullhorn, turn on an announcement and tell everyone inside that house they were about to fuck up a whole bunch of stuff. But her warnings always fell on deaf ears—that was plain and simple. And most people thought she ought to mind her own business.

Would she warn them if she could? Stop them from making a mess of things? Or did part of her want to watch it burn?

Well, there was no way Jennifer was going to go back inside her house instead of watching the chaos about to unfold. She was trapped by her own need to watch their lives be smashed. This was too juicy. This was too much. This was everything she couldn't stop watching.

Jennifer pulled out her phone, prepared to video what was happening. She'd delete the video. Probably. But just knowing she had it made her feel like she had power again.

Then a figure stopped in front of a window.

Staring out.

Directly at her.

The figure stilled. One hand lifted to their brow, as if shielding their face from the light. Jennifer's pulse slammed in her ears. Her breath caught. The mug trembled in her hand. She didn't blink.

A breeze cut across her arms, raising goose bumps. It wasn't cold. Just the kind of night that reminded her she wasn't alone. Her first thought wasn't fear. It was guilt. As if she'd been caught with her hand in someone else's diary. And not for the first time . . .

She fumbled the phone into the cushion, but it was too late. The glow had already given her away. She leaned forward and shoved her phone deeper beneath the cushion. The glow vanished, but not fast enough.

Did they see her? Or were they just looking into the dark? Her whole body stiffened, waiting for a sign—Laughter? A wave? Nothing came. She strained for recognition. But she would have sooner been able to name the components of a star than the face at the window.

A mosquito landed on her leg, and she smacked it away, the sound too loud. Perhaps this little bloodsucker had been sent as a reminder. She was still letting her past suck the life from her. The mosquito had taken what it needed and left her itching. Just like Jamie.

The truth was, while she'd been ejected from one life, she couldn't stop obsessing over it. And the scariest thought was, if she'd been given the choice, she would have remained.

Echo Lake held all their secrets. But maybe watching theirs come undone right now helped her pretend, just for a moment, that her secret still mattered.

Chapter Thirty-Five

Ariel

Something was wrong.

Ariel felt funny. Lightheaded, almost. She felt light all over, untethered. Not *good* light. *Wrong* light. Like her bones had turned to mist but her heart weighed a thousand pounds. As if every care that she'd had for the last year had simply disappeared. The music sounded like it was playing underwater, or maybe from inside her own ears.

Was this what letting go felt like? Or was this something being taken from her?

Everyone else around her seemed equally happy, giddy, free from families, pain and worries. She felt like this only when she took her pills, but she hadn't taken any in the last two days since Shane had flushed them down the toilet and told her to do more yoga. She looked down at the cup in her hand, half full. The glass felt too smooth, like it might slip away from her fingers and shatter just to spite her.

She sniffed her drink for what might have been the thirtieth time, but smelled only the fruity mocktail of whatever mixture Miranda had made. The Miranda Special. Was there something in this? Some sort of drug inhibitor? A molly? Ariel had never been into drugs. She didn't know what it was supposed to feel like when she took them. And though she'd seen plenty of people in the city under the influence, there was one person who came to mind. *Tara . . .*

Ariel blinked away the ghostly images.

Maybe it was just the fact that she was at a party. Her kids were safely at home, tucked into bed by the sitter. She and Shane were finally having a night out with adults. It felt freeing. Except somewhere in the back of her mind, she knew that that wasn't the case—there was something else going on here. She swayed a little bit on her feet, trying to see if any of the other women noticed.

Samantha was dancing with her husband, a little bit inappropriately too—in fact, grinding on him like they were at some sort of club. The walls looked like they were pulsing with the music, though she knew they weren't. Right?

Colleen seemed like she'd arrived having taken something before even sipping the mocktail, and from what Ariel could see, she was on at least her fourth. Why was Colleen's husband watching her when she swayed? Not in concern. Like Zachary was . . . waiting.

Kennedy was sitting on the couch, lounging in a way that was supposed to be sexy. She assumed. She'd never even seen Kennedy look anything other than uptight—it was rather odd. Sitting beside her was Samantha's husband, Nathaniel, whispering too intently. He was leaning close, his elbow on the back cushion, not quite around her, but still close enough that it was only another slight inch and he'd be touching her shoulder.

In the kitchen, Miranda was laughing at something Shane said, and she kept slapping Brad in the chest. Both men looked enamored. Ariel remembered when Shane used to look at her like that. Now he and Brad looked at Miranda like she was a secret they were dying to taste. What the heck? Benjamin was eyeing his wife hungrily and giving Shane and Brad dirty looks. This was so strange. There was absolutely something wrong about tonight.

Colleen's husband came up behind his wife, his fingers dancing up her thighs. And all the while Ariel stood watching like she was on the outside of whatever this party was—a ghost peering in through the window. A reporter from the village paper taking notes. Like history was repeating itself.

Did no one else seem to notice that they were losing all their inhibitions in this one moment as Miranda's sultry mix played over the intercom?

Ariel wanted to go home. She moved closer to Shane, slipping her fingers into his, twining them. He glanced down at her with a faraway smile. The floor felt like it was breathing beneath her heels—just a little. Just enough to make her doubt it. She leaned against his shoulder, partly to establish her place as his wife, but also because she was having trouble balancing. Miranda eyed her with an unreadable expression and took a step back.

"Hello?" Shane nodded at Ariel then glanced toward Miranda, as if she'd done him a favor and they shared some sort of nonverbal communication that she wasn't privy to. What the hell was going on?

"Shane," she asked, "do you mind if we get going soon? I'm starting to feel a headache coming on."

Shane glanced down at her, disappointment wrinkling his brow. He didn't want to leave. Why would he, when temptation was knocking at his door?

She shook that thought from her mind. These were her friends. They were all just being friendly. Not flirting. Not making promises they shouldn't. And Shane wasn't going to go off and sleep with someone else. She almost laughed out loud at that thought.

"Want me to drive you home?" Shane asked.

Ariel nodded, glad that there hadn't been an argument and he was willing to leave. They didn't live far and could have probably walked, but they'd driven instead.

"Okay, no problem. I'll drive you home and then I'll just come back. Benjamin promised me a round of poker."

The words hit her stomach like spoiled eggs. He said it casually, like it was normal. But it stunk. And poker? Ariel hadn't known her husband to ever play a game of poker in his life. He liked to hold on to his money, not lose it. She didn't know what *poker* was code for, but it sure as heck wasn't cards.

"Yeah, it sounds like fun. Benjamin's going to teach us a few tricks," Brad added.

Miranda squealed. Her laugh was too loud, too rehearsed. Like she was performing a version of "friend" Ariel didn't recognize. "I love watching Benji play," Miranda said. "He's so good." She touched Ariel's arm, this time giving her elbow a gentle squeeze. "Oh, won't you stay? I have Advil if you're having a headache. Maybe you just need some water." Miranda turned and rushed out of the room and then came back and beckoned Ariel to follow her.

Shane gave her puppy eyes, and so she relented. It wasn't very often that they got out these days, and maybe one of the things that she should be working on was more of a social life. And besides, she lied—she didn't really have a headache. She just felt weird. Loopy. She wanted to go home because the wrongness kept sharpening and she wasn't sure if it was the company or this weird mocktail.

And every time her gaze unfocused, she swore she saw Tara in the room with them.

Was this it—the moment she finally went crazy?

"Here you go." Miranda extended her arm, a cool glass of ice water in her grip.

Ariel licked her lips, suddenly thirstier than she'd been in her life.

The water tasted off. Or maybe it was just her. She set it down, but the glass held a ring that seemed to shimmer. Like it was watching her too. She blinked, but the shimmer didn't fade. It sat there, still and gleaming in the ice. A quiet, frosty eye.

And then she saw it, the tiniest fleck of white on the surface of the water.

She turned to tell Shane. To say something was wrong. But in the window above the sink, her reflection swayed. Her mouth was moving. But not the way she thought it was. And the rushing in her ears was the only thing that proved she was still there.

"Tara . . ." she muttered, before the room went black.

Chapter Thirty-Six

Miranda

When Miranda introduced herself to society in New York City, her acquaintances had nicknamed her the Queen of Chaos. There was a reason for that. Every party she attended turned into something either catastrophic or legendary. She was the one they wanted at the party. Quite a bit different from high school, when invitations had been lacking and she was never the one people called when the party was over.

Tonight felt like a little bit of a mixture of both. One instant, everyone was dancing, vibing with the atmosphere that she'd created. And in the next, Ariel had disappeared. Shane was freaking out. Benjamin was shoving Brad in the shoulder. Shane was stepping between the two. Kennedy was slumped over on the couch. Samantha was marching back and forth on top of the counter, recounting tales of one of the most infamous Florida crimes—a murderer who had broken into a Florida State University sorority.

Lana Del Rey trilled through the speakers like the music hadn't noticed the room was on fire. And the breeze off Echo Lake filtered tranquilly through the slim opening of the windows, the calm of the salty water mixing with the sweat of desperation.

And Miranda had just sat back and watched it all happen right before her eyes. What had promised to be a legendary party was turning into complete chaos. Right on schedule. She felt a rush watching it all unfold, not unlike the adrenaline she used to get from tossing a match and walking away.

A slow smile spread on her face, power making her stand taller. Power wasn't taken. It was offered, and she collected. *My God, it feels good to be the Queen of Chaos.*

If only they realized just who they were partying with.

"Touch her again and I swear to God, I'll bury you," Benjamin growled at Brad, his finger landing hard against Brad's sternum. Miranda saw the way his hand clenched—not just with rage, but with panic.

Miranda cocked her head, setting down her glass, slick with condensation. Benjamin's jaw was tight. She watched her husband's nostrils flare—a look she hadn't seen since the Manhattan days when they'd played their wicked games.

"Or what?" Brad said between bared teeth, shoving Benjamin back by the shoulder.

Oh, Brad. Funny he picked this moment to have a backbone.

"Or else I'll ruin you."

A flicker in the chandelier lights made the whole room feel like it was glitching.

This wasn't the first time Benjamin had threatened to ruin someone. But it was the first time she wasn't sure if he meant it—and she kind of wanted him to.

Shane wedged himself between them, knocking into a barstool as he did so. "Jesus, save it for the parking lot, boys."

Nathaniel and Zachary joined the group in the kitchen, both of their chests puffed like if they needed to handle something they might.

Miranda bit the inside of her cheek at her husband's words. Back in New York City, Benjamin, who'd been a top-notch Wall Street guru, had been known to ruin a man or two. He'd traveled back and forth between Florida and the city while married, cheating on his ex every time he saw Miranda. Becoming the mayor in Crystal Harbor had always been about some sort of desire for wholesomeness, some sort of respect thing he wanted from the town he'd grown up in. Deranged, if you asked her. But as it turned out, you couldn't take the vengeful man out of Benjamin, even if you took the vengeful city out of his atmosphere.

"Benji, don't," Miranda said, trying to step between the two where Shane was holding them back, arms outstretched.

"Stand back, Miranda," Benjamin warned. "This man's about to get what he deserves."

"Oh, come on. We were just having a little bit of fun," Miranda said with a laugh. "Just like old times."

Benjamin swung his gaze in her direction, his eyes wild. "Old times?"

She saw it flicker in his eyes—doubt. And that was the most dangerous thing of all. Not rage. Doubt. She realized in that moment he wondered if she'd known Brad before. The truth might enrage him all the more.

Miranda let him stew for half a beat longer, then laughed. "Not like that, silly. Just like me and you back in the city. Old times."

Benjamin's shoulders relaxed at the reminder of their old life and how this wasn't new to either one of them—this sort of drug-induced haze. Bodies writhing. People hooking up who hadn't come together. People leaving with people they'd never met before.

"No, no, no, no, no." Brad's hands went up in front of him, shaking as if he were trying to emphasize the words. "I do *not* know your wife that way."

A spark of fury lanced through Miranda at how adamant he was. But she covered it up with a smirk, because it had been obvious for the entire evening and several engagements beforehand that he wanted to know her "that way." And she'd encouraged it.

Somewhere on the floor of the kitchen, Colleen moved, and Miranda followed the line of grout over to make sure her new tile wasn't being baptized in vomit. But, to her surprise, Colleen hopped up and sauntered over to the family room, where Kennedy lay on the couch with her leg draped over the armrest. Next thing, Colleen was embracing Kennedy on the couch. They broke away for a second as if to assess whether they would do it again. Kennedy's lipstick was smeared. Her smile was too wide.

Miranda couldn't look away. Because somewhere beneath the wild kiss was something close to freedom.

Miranda tried to stifle a laugh, but it came out like a squeak and her palm came up to cover her mouth. Everybody who was in the kitchen glanced over to where she was staring at the couch—two women, lip-locked, legs intertwined.

Miranda's skin flushed with excitement. For a moment, the room felt like it tilted—Brad yelling, Kennedy writhing, Samantha sauntering over to join them, her lips brushing Colleen's neck.

"What the hell." Brad jerked free from the two men holding him away from Benjamin as he marched over to the couch, where his wife was now straddling Samantha while Colleen watched.

"Sam?" Nathaniel seemed just as confused.

"Kennedy, get off of her." Brad sounded incredulous.

Kennedy glanced up, eyes bloodshot and glassy. "Don't be a party pooper, Brad. My new friend and I are just trying to have a little fun."

"Yeah, just a little fun," Samantha parroted, winking at her husband, who looked dumbfounded.

Kennedy shoved her hands in her hair, her head rolling back as she rocked over Samantha, clearly in a state of ecstasy that she hadn't felt in quite a long time.

Miranda stared at Brad, her curiosity piqued. Was it possible? The reason Brad seemed so unhappy in his marriage was because his wife wasn't into him? And she had a crush on Samantha this whole time?

If Kennedy was into women, did Brad know? Had he always known? Had they all been pretending? Liars never did change.

And what about Nathaniel? He looked like he'd just stopped breathing and left this earth completely.

When she decided to have this party, Miranda sure hadn't thought this was something that was going to come up. But it gave her a thrill of excitement all the same.

Kennedy's arm shot out to grab the front of Brad's shirt, tugging her husband close, her mouth clapping on his in a deep kiss. She grabbed Samantha's breast with her other hand.

"Oh shit," Shane said, his hand coming to his mouth just the same as Miranda's a moment ago.

"My girl knows how to throw a party," Benjamin said.

"This is what happens when you take the leash off, huh?" Brad seethed.

This wasn't just fun anymore. This was something breaking.

Something beautiful and brittle and ready to shatter, which only made it that much more dangerous. The danger itself heating Miranda's blood, fueling her need. She wasn't sure anymore if she was holding the match or just waiting for someone to beg her to drop it.

Miranda looked around at what she had created. Not just a party—but a fracture. A shift. Power bleeding from the cracks like champagne foam. And God, it felt good.

Something purred in her chest, satisfied. She tilted her head. Watched Brad's jaw clench. Benjamin's hands tighten. Shane's gaze slide to her lips.

Amid the mess, she could move unseen. That was the gift of well-timed chaos.

From the corner of her eye, she watched Brad watch Kennedy and Colleen walking into the spare room. Watched Nathaniel toss Samantha over his shoulder and twirl her around, dancing close enough to sizzle.

"I think this party just got a whole lot more interesting," Miranda said. She hopped up onto the counter and tugged Benjamin close, his body between her thighs, her arms around his shoulders. The marble was cool beneath her thighs, grounding her for one brief second before Benjamin's warmth pressed in. She kissed him like it still mattered. Like he was still hers. But her eyes stayed open.

This wasn't about Benjamin. Not really. She loved him the way a queen might love her kingdom: possessively, ruthlessly, with purpose. He was a means to her end, and sometimes pawns needed to be reminded who built the castle they lived in. Who could topple it if they wanted.

Power wasn't a crown she wore. It was a hunger. And tonight, they were all feeding it. Brad's touch. Shane's smolder. Benjamin's jealousy. Nathaniel's stunned silence. Even Kennedy's wild grin on the couch. They thought they were spinning out—but Miranda had her hand on the wheel.

And God help them when she let go.

From behind, Brad's hand slid down her back like he was claiming something. Silly man. No one could claim her without her permission. But she decided to let him play for a little longer, let him think he was in control.

She didn't pull away. Nor did she warn her husband when Brad's hand slipped down lower to grip her ass. A static charge sent a shock through her body, and she gasped, kissing Benjamin harder.

It wasn't about sex. It was about power. And she was tired of pretending she didn't want it back. They'd all just crossed a line they couldn't take back. She'd built the vibe. She could tear it down, too—and she would.

On a scale of chaos to legendary, Miranda was pretty certain she'd just hit a whole new level. Crystal Harbor was never going to be the same again.

And for one brief second, she wondered if she'd gone too far—or if this was just the beginning.

They never saw her coming.

Chapter Thirty-Seven

Jennifer

The Fifteen Commandments of a Tradwife

Eleven: Thou shalt welcome a new woman into the fold. Invite her for fresh-pressed juice, show her how to knead dough—just don't forget to note who she talks to.

At some point during the night, Jennifer must've lost interest in what was going on across the way and fallen asleep. She woke up to the echo of a shout, jolting upright and confused for a moment about where she was. She was surrounded by darkness, the couch beneath her on the back porch already growing damp from the humid spring night air. Without the sun to burn off the wetness, everything had turned sticky.

There was a shout again.

Shadow growled low under his breath.

"What was that, boy?" Jennifer rubbed her eyes then blinked, trying to focus, to see in the darkness. She wasn't exactly sure what words were being exchanged, but she was fairly certain she heard something like *That's my wife.*

Well, what she'd seen earlier, staring at the windows across the lake, would lend credence to those words. It looked like, before she fell asleep, there'd been a swinger party going on—which could only ever lead to trouble.

Jennifer tucked her hair behind her ears, leaning closer, hoping that would help her discern any further words. A gentle breeze blew off the brackish water. A sour, metallic tang drifted from the lake—algae, or something rotting beneath the dock. It made her stomach twist, even as she told herself it was nothing. There was more shouting—loud chatter from women, yelling from men. Maybe her imagination was running wild, but she thought she heard skin against skin. A punch? That would make sense, the shouting and the fighting escalating into a full-blown fistfight.

She pulled out her phone, slick from nighttime humidity, and tapped record, hoping that even at this distance she'd be able to pick up some of the sounds though she couldn't see anything.

Should she call 911?

Jennifer hesitated, recalling another time she'd wanted to call 911. The way she'd been discouraged. Told that speaking out would only get other people in trouble, when nothing could be done. There had been a time when she believed the right thing and the safe thing were the same. But over time, guilt had forced her to make better choices. She'd once called the police on a neighbor who left their dog locked in a car for twenty minutes—midday in July, windows cracked just an inch. The dog had been fine, but Jamie hadn't let her live it down. Said she'd embarrassed him. Said she was *always making a scene*. That she'd better not get any other ideas in her head.

She wanted to be the kind of woman who would march around the lake, flashlight in hand, and confront what was happening. But Jamie had trained that desire out of her—shame by shame, year by year.

Jennifer closed her eyes, letting the breeze from the lake slip across her face. It was cooler now, but the damp clung to her neck, her scalp, the backs of her knees. Somewhere in the dark, a frog croaked once, then fell silent. The silence pressed like a weight.

She rubbed her thumb against the edge of the phone, her finger hovering over the number pad. Just one call. She could call anonymously, but they'd still have her number, her identity in their system. But the image in her mind wasn't of help arriving—it was of sirens bouncing off the lake and neighbors peeking through their blinds. Of her name being dragged through another PTA meeting. Of Jamie hearing about it and finding a way to twist it all against her. Of the one truth she'd kept quiet about all these years getting out.

Another shout echoed across the water. Something sharp. A word she didn't catch. Maybe it had been her name. Maybe not.

The screen door creaked behind her, shifting in the wind. She glanced back at it, half expecting to see a figure in the shadows. But there was nothing—just the scent of damp mulch and something faintly sulfurous drifting off the shore, like the lake was letting out its breath.

She told herself it was nothing. Just noise. Just the night playing tricks on her.

Still, she didn't stop recording.

Jamie used to say she overreacted. Imagined things. Maybe he was right. Her hand hovered over the phone screen, fingers trembling, not from fear exactly—but from the weight of decision. Did someone call 911 for a fistfight when they couldn't even see it happening? Did you call 911 when a party was just getting out of hand?

If it weren't for her ex-husband threatening her lately—threatening to take away the children, threatening to dismantle the life that she had held together by only a thin thread—then she would have already dialed.

But what if it was just a little fight? A regular argument that got loud? Jennifer chewed on the tip of a fingernail, her mind warring with indecision. Jamie's taunts were playing overtime in her head.

Somewhere in the distance, a screen door slammed and bounced back open, creaking like a throat clearing in the dark.

Calling 911 was a whole lot more complicated than it needed to be.

Calling 911 could mean giving her name, if they decided not to accept her tip anonymously. Police officers possibly showing up at her house. Their lights strobing, their questions overwhelming. The attention too much. As if she didn't already have enough eyes on her. If the police showed up, there would be speculation. People wouldn't think she'd called in a party across the lake—they would think she had some sort of domestic issue herself. And then the rumors would be out of control once more, piling on top of everything that was already happening.

That was the last thing she wanted or needed.

So instead of calling 911, Jennifer listened. And she recorded.

Until there was silence from across the way.

Until the blackness enveloped her.

Until it was so quiet and so dark, she wasn't sure she'd heard anything at all. That maybe it had just been her imagination running wild. A dream that had awakened her, and now she was just sitting outside like the woman she swore she wouldn't be. Fear buckling her desire to be stronger.

Jennifer turned off the recording. She picked up her empty teacup and went inside, placing it in the sink. She stared at her phone, at the voice memo that read nine minutes and fifty-eight seconds.

And then she pressed play.

It was silent at first. But then she could hear the shouts. The thump came softly through the speaker, but it landed in her body like a punch. Then another shout. A man's voice, fractured.

Jennifer stood frozen, as if the floorboards might buckle beneath the weight of what she'd heard.

It hadn't been a dream.

What she'd heard—what she'd borne witness to with her ears—was, in fact, real. The question was: What was she going to do about it?

Jennifer plugged her phone into the outlet and set it down. She knew without a doubt that she wasn't going to do anything with it right now. And probably not ever. There was no grace for a mother who made the wrong call—not from the courts, not from her community, not from Jamie.

She'd told the kids once, back when they were little, that being brave meant doing the right thing even when it was scary. Now she wondered if that had ever been true—or just something she read in a picture book. Something she wished her children would do differently from her.

Pastor Joseph would be disappointed in her, she thought, as he'd always lamented the loss of the Good Samaritan spirit—the instinct to help others. But was she supposed to help others at the detriment to herself and her family? Hadn't self-preservation gotten her this far?

She half convinced herself that Pastor Joseph would think she was right to stay out of it.

Fog was starting to drift in off the lake, soft and low like something trying to hush her. A hawk's cry pierced the silence, a second warning, sharp and high, as if the town itself was watching—and waiting to pounce. Behind her, the screen door creaked again—just the wind, probably. Still, she didn't turn around.

Jennifer stood in the stillness, surrounded by fog and secrets. Even silence, it turned out, left a record.

And records could be played back.

Chapter Thirty-Eight

Tara

Summer 2013

A strange clicking pulls me out of a dream, faint at first, then sharp. It takes a second to realize it's my teeth, chattering. Purple haze spills over Echo Lake, the kind of dawn that should feel gentle. I'm freezing. Naked.

The night before floods back in jagged shards. How long have I been here?

Brad's awake, too, a towel wrapped around his waist, his gaze flicking away from me like I'm something dirty. Voices from the lakeside fire drift up the lakeshore beach—still partying, still laughing.

Brad's gaze returns, covers my boobs, my crotch, and he tosses me a damp hoodie.

"Thank you," I manage. My voice is cracked, my mouth cotton dry. "Can you help me?"

He snorts. "You think I want to help you after this?"

"What? I didn't—"

"Didn't you? You think I'd be your boyfriend? No." He shakes his head vehemently, anger coming off him in waves. "You were just an easy lay. I'd be embarrassed to be seen with you."

My breath snags in my chest. "What?"

And then there's clapping. Colleen steps out from behind a palm, the glow of her phone lighting her smirk. "Good job, Brad. Tell it like it is."

"What did I ever do—"

Colleen waves her cell phone in front of my face, and though my eyes are still a little blurry, I can see what she's showing me. My naked body. A picture she's shared hundreds of times by the looks of it.

"Delete it!" I shout.

Colleen laughs, a sound like glass breaking. "Not a chance, trash girl. That's who you are now. Just like your mother—trash, and a homewrecker."

The words land like a slap, burning through the cold already clinging to my skin. Brad had clearly lied to us both—but instead of turning her anger on him, Colleen had found comfort in sharpening it against me.

I lunge, fingers outstretched for her phone, desperate to erase the damage before it spreads. Colleen's eyes widen for a split second before she darts toward the pier, still tossing barbs over her shoulder.

I chase her, my pulse pounding, breath ragged. The weathered boards groan under our weight as I close the distance—close enough to grab the phone—when my toe catches on a warped plank. Pain shoots through my foot, my body pitching forward into hers.

Colleen shrieks, twisting away. Her shove comes hard and fast, and my skull cracks against the pier's support beam. Stars burst across my vision.

Then I'm falling.

The lake swallows me whole, the cold punching the air from my lungs. Pain radiates from my head as darkness presses in, pulling me under.

What a day to die—on the day I was born.

Today was supposed to be my birthday.

Part Three

Verities . . .

Chapter Thirty-Nine

There is a body on Crystal Harbor Beach.

Sand is crusted beneath the fingernails. A trickle of blood trails from the temple over a cheek. The mouth is flat. The eyes are open, staring toward the darkened night sky. Within the iris stars are reflected from overhead.

The body has lain here for hours. No one coming to find it. No one aware of its existence. Well, perhaps there is someone, or more than one someone, who's aware of it.

Soon the sun will rise, exposing the body to the elements, to the people who will walk past and wonder just what happened here. The clothes are torn, a rip from the shoulder down over an arm, exposing skin and sinew.

One shoe has fallen off, and one shoe is still half on, hanging by a toe, as if somehow that one digit might keep it in place.

There was a witness to the falling of this body. There was also a villain. The body's hair is tangled in knots. Fingers curled in a last-ditch effort to fend off death. Anguish in the curl of the neck. Soon the body will be rigid, and then it will go slack.

There's no coming back for this one. No coming back at all.

There will be rumors. People will connect the dots from one rumor to the next. They will make a list of suspects. They will believe things they hear simply because they sound plausible. They will say silly things that sound smart, like *there are three sides to every story: yours, mine and the truth*. But saying things like that is just an excuse for ignoring facts. A way of brushing things under the rug. A way of giving leeway to those who should be blamed.

They are excuses.

The body would not agree. The body—now lying stiffly without life on this beach—would say there's only one story that happened here. And it is a sad one. It is a tragedy that could have been avoided.

The soul who used to occupy this body could've stayed home, safely ensconced behind the walls, the door locked. Didn't have to go to the beach. Could have refused. But no.

And this makes it seem it is the victim's fault for having fallen. The victim's fault for having been attacked. And we know that's not fair, right?

Or is it? Maybe this body got what it deserved.

No, no, no. What could have truly stopped this was the one who put it to the test. The one responsible for taking the breath from the body. They alone are at fault. For luring the body out onto the beach. For attacking the body. For leaving it to be exposed.

The question is: Will they come forward and say what they have done?

Likely not.

Will the rumors and speculations lead back to them? Maybe.

It wasn't as if they did a lot to cover their trail.

In the distance, a cell phone rings. But there will be no answer. The ring will echo in the silent night. The caller will be worried, and then devastated.

The heavy breaths of the guilty will fade.

And the silence will be the loudest thing of all.

Chapter Forty

Ariel

5:27 a.m.

Pain seared through Ariel's forehead. She could hardly remember a thing from last night. A drink. The fuzziness after. At some point, she remembered drinking water to try to mitigate the oncoming headache and the wooziness Miranda's mock cocktail gave her.

Blinking against the light, she opened her eyes, expecting to find herself somewhere in Miranda's house—she didn't recall getting home—but there she was, ensconced in the butter-yellow walls of her bedroom. The house felt too still, the air too clean. Like whatever had happened had taken something with it—and left her behind.

The white down comforter was pulled up over her shoulders, the fan overhead shuttering wind against her cheeks. From somewhere in the house, her baby cried. Every cry from Tara was a cymbal crash against her spine.

From somewhere else, little footsteps bounced on the floors, running down the hall toward the sound of the crying child.

Beside her, the space Shane usually occupied was empty. He wasn't there. There was no dent in the pillow to signify that he'd ever been there. The bed on that side was still made, the comforter pulled up tight against the pillows. He'd never come to bed? Ariel sat up straight, her head splitting with pain.

The door to her bedroom burst open, tiny little faces appearing in the space. She held her hand up to her eyes as if to ward off the incoming sounds of her children in the morning. As if she didn't want to witness their morning joy.

"Mommy, Mommy, Mommy, Mommy!" They bounced around the room, calling her name, and each syllable struck a chord somewhere deep inside her brain. The pain ricocheted down her neck.

"Good morning, sweethearts," she said, rolling her legs over the side of the bed and forcing her feet to touch the floor. Her voice didn't sound like hers, but gravelly, as if she'd been screaming all night long.

Edith, her oldest daughter, grabbed her hand and jerked away. "Mommy, your hands are dirty."

Ariel stared down at her palms. The dirt was caked under her nails like dried blood. The same way it had been over a decade ago when she'd stepped into the water, searching, scraping against the bottom of the lake and coming up empty.

Had the sitter seen her like this? Did her kids peek down the stairs, watching her stagger in with dirt-streaked hands and wild eyes?

It looked like she'd been digging in the yard all night long—not unlike other things she'd done before. Sometimes, when sleep wouldn't come, she wandered the yard—checking on the chickens, mucking the stalls, dancing barefoot in the dark.

"That is gross. I'm so sorry," she said, trying to smile, but her kids looked at her, horrified, never having seen her climb out of bed looking as filthy as she was right now.

"You smell weird." Ada, her third, was sharp as a tack. Her nose wrinkled. Ariel forced a smile. What did fear smell like?

"Is Mommy sick?" asked her Arthur.

She closed her eyes and saw a flash—moonlight on water? A hand gripping her arm? The faint slosh of something deep. But it was gone before she could grab hold of it. She paused, a faint metallic scent catching in her nose—not dirt, not blood exactly, but something that didn't belong, something wrong that she couldn't name.

"How about this? You guys get Tara out of her crib and take her downstairs. Her bottle is in the fridge, you know how to put it in the warmer. I'll be down soon to help make breakfast."

Noah, her youngest son, tilted his head. "You look like a witch," he said, not unkindly. Just an innocent observation. But the words sank into her chest like stones.

Ariel reached out to tickle him, but he bounded away.

"Mommy, can we make you breakfast today?" Edith asked, diverting the conversation.

A smile tugged at her lips. Breakfast would no doubt be some strange concoction drummed up by her children's imaginations and the ingredients in the fridge.

"I would love that, my dears," she said.

As her children trundled out of her room, Ariel dragged herself into the bathroom and shut the door behind her. The mirror confirmed what she already feared—bruised hollows under her eyes, skin pale and streaked with dirt. Had she been sleepwalking through a storm? Or something worse?

The faucet squealed as it turned, water roaring hot within seconds, steam curling in ghostly tendrils. Oblivious to the burn, she shoved her hands under the stream, the skin flushing red. Brown runoff spiraled down the porcelain as she splashed her face, scrubbing at grime she couldn't explain.

Brushing a hand across her hip, her fingers snagged on something gritty—sand, clinging to the seam of her dress pocket. The lake? Had she gone there? Waded in? Fallen? Relived that night from the summer of 2013?

Nothing returned but a whisper of wind and a flash of cold.

Last night's dress clung to her skin—her pajamas never made it on. Just the same dress from the night before, hanging limp and heavy.

As she pulled the dress over her head, something small clattered to the tile. She flinched, heart racing, and looked down. A broken seashell lay at her feet, its pinkish curve dulled, one side jagged like it had been snapped clean in two. Bending down, she picked it up—the cool, briny surface oddly soothing in her palm. She didn't remember picking it up the night before. Didn't remember going anywhere near the water. And yet, somehow, it had come home with her—tucked into her pocket like a secret. She set it on the bathroom counter and stood there for a long moment, staring. The shell's pale curve caught the morning light. She didn't know where it came from. But somehow, it felt like a piece of her—dragged ashore and left to dry.

A jagged scrape ran down her forearm, thin and red, catching her glance as she reached for the towel. It wasn't from the coop—this looked newer. Like something had clawed back. The mark on her skin. The shell on the counter. Were they connected somehow?

The broken edge looked sharp enough to cut. Had she fallen? Grabbed for something in the dark? Or had she been holding on too tightly to something that didn't want to be held?

A scary thought chilled her to the bone . . . Had the stalker finally found her alone?

Her entire body looked like she'd rolled in the mud last night, and she needed to shower. But her kids were downstairs, running amok in the kitchen, which would end only in disaster, so she took a wet washcloth, wiped herself down and then pulled on a fresh pair of yoga pants and a T-shirt—not bothering with a bra or underwear.

Just as she suspected, her bedsheets were filthy. She stripped them off, dumped them in the laundry room and then headed toward the kitchen, where the sounds of dishes clinking echoed. One of the children had put the baby in her high chair.

The sunlit kitchen usually made her feel safe. Today, it made her skin itch.

"Where is Daddy?" she asked. Five tiny heads stared at her.

"Daddy's not here," Arthur said, looking at her strangely, as if she was the one who was supposed to know the answer to that.

Ariel said, "He must've gone out early to play golf." Her smile was brittle, because the lie was sour on her tongue. She had a very good idea of exactly where Shane was. If he hadn't come home with her last night, that meant he was still over there at Miranda and Benjamin's.

Slow-burning anger filled her chest at the idea that he'd let her go home without him. He hadn't even bothered to leave a message on her cell phone.

Except, she hadn't checked her cell phone.

Ariel went looking for her purse, finding it tossed on the floor by the front door. Her cell phone was thrown there, too, next to her keys, as if she had simply flung open the door and tossed her belongings inside. The door wasn't even locked.

Ariel lifted her phone. The battery was dead from not having charged it the night before. In the kitchen, she plugged in her phone, hoping this was the reason she hadn't gotten a message from Shane—because she hadn't heard the phone ring.

A few seconds later, the phone powered on. There were several messages. None of them from Shane.

One was from her babysitter, who asked how she was feeling this morning. Ariel's face caught with embarrassment. What state might she have been in last night when she relieved the babysitter?

The rest of the messages were from friends around town. She ignored them, not having any patience for that sort of thing right now, with her head splitting and her husband MIA.

She clicked again on her text messages, her finger hovering over Miranda's name, wanting to ask if Shane was there—but knowing she should probably text her husband first.

Shane's name glowed back at her. The last message? Yesterday morning to see if she needed him to pick up anything for the party. She hadn't answered the text because she'd already been at the store—where she'd told him she was going—and she was irritated by it.

Fingers hovered, then typed: Where are you?

She stared at the screen, willing it to come alive. Just a dot bubbling up to indicate a reply was forthcoming. A word. Something. But there was only silence.

She set the phone down with a thud. Whatever had happened last night—she was going to find out. Even if finding out the truth terrified her.

She swallowed the bile at the back of her throat and wiped her palms on her pants. Her fingers trembled, but she pressed them flat against the counter, grounding herself. This time, she wasn't going to let the truth stay in the dark.

Chapter Forty-One

Miranda

5:43 a.m.

Miranda always knew she'd had a good party when waking up the next morning was one of the hardest things to do. But this hadn't been just a good party. This was something else. She stretched luxuriously in her bed, feeling lighter than she had in months. Years.

The party had been a chaotic reckoning, and she had enjoyed *every* minute.

She clicked the remote to open her blinds, letting the sunrise in from over the beach at the front of her house. This was a view she'd like to wake up to every day for the rest of her life.

There was just the ever-so-slightest twinge of pain in her forehead, even though she hadn't drunk her special "mocktail." In fact, she'd been quite sober for a little while. But once things started to get crazy, Colleen dug out the bottle beneath the sink and offered Miranda a shot. She couldn't refuse and cause Colleen to question her.

They'd snuck into the bathroom, done one shot, and then another, eyes turning fuzzy with glee—and then Colleen had kissed her. Nothing too romantic, more like good friends getting excited at a party, flashing a pact. Innocence personified.

How ironic.

After that, however, the party had gotten louder, wilder—she could remember that—Brad and Benjamin constantly having a pissing contest. Shane trying to step in.

It was funny, because back in New York with Benjamin, before his divorce, before he brought her back to Crystal Harbor and they became these iconic leaders of the community, this had been one of their favorite games. Watching men hit on her. Seeing just who would take the bait. Whoever it was who fell for their little game, Benjamin would pick a fight with. But it had never been anything serious. She'd step in, tell him to calm down—knowing that when they got home, he was going to nail her to the bed, fuck the shit out of her.

She had hoped for that last night. Maybe there was some credence to that saying *Don't shit where you eat.* Oh well.

More than one of the partiers had gotten fucked last night—and not in the fun way. The tussling on the banks of the sandy lake, echoes of their shouts ripping across the water, no doubt, was not hot.

Miranda slowly climbed out of bed, body and head screaming for a big cup of dark coffee—the kind of sludge coffee she used to get at the diner near her apartment in New York City. The kind of coffee people said put hair on your chest.

She caught her reflection in the glass of her bedroom window. Hair wild. Lipstick smudged. Not glam—feral. Like she'd clawed her way out of something. Which she had, several times. Her contacts were out, revealing the deep mahogany of her eyes, instead of blue. She usually slept with them in so Ben wouldn't notice the change. But she hadn't needed to last night.

Miranda fixed her eyes, tossed her hair up into a messy bun.

The house was eerily quiet, and there was no sign of Ben, though his side of the bed was shuffled as if he'd slept there. If someone asked, she'd say, *Oh, he probably got up early to clean up.*

Then she'd laugh, because who was she kidding? Ben hadn't cleaned up a thing in his life. That man issued orders. She laughed just thinking about it. Wishful thinking, she supposed. Maybe it was better to assume he'd gone to pick up his dumb dog.

The kitchen still smelled like too many perfumes, too many bodies pressed together. And something sour beneath it all. The counters were still cluttered with cups and the snacks she'd made the night before, the cheese dry and crunchy on the edges, the strawberries practically melting into the plate.

She glanced at a wineglass in the sink. Stem snapped clean. Her mind flicked to a moment a few months ago she didn't want to remember. How one time with Ben he'd gotten so mad, he'd actually snapped the stem.

The fridge kicked on and she jumped. Stupid machine. Always so loud when she was alone. Miranda shook her head. She'd clean up later—right now she needed coffee, immediately.

Her gaze examined the damage. A lipstick kiss on the patio door in a shade she didn't own. A single heel by the fireplace that wasn't hers.

The floor was sticky beneath her bare feet as she walked to the cabinet to reveal the expensive coffee maker Ben had insisted on. The one he wanted to remain a secret, hence hiding it in the cabinet. The rest of this town might not drink coffee, but in this house, it was a daily ritual.

Had someone thrown up? Spilled something? She glanced down at the floor, annoyed at what she'd see, but it didn't appear covered in vomit, and that was a good sign.

Miranda had been in charge of plenty of messes last night and was glad not to see another one glaring at her feet.

She hovered over the coffeepot, pressing the appropriate buttons and grateful to her past self for presetting it the day before, knowing this morning was probably going to be a difficult one.

As the machine whirred and cranked, the scent of coffee filled the air, covering up the mess of party smells. She glanced around the kitchen. Benjamin's phone charger was still plugged in, cord snaking across the countertop like a breadcrumb trail.

The telltale sound of a dog's nails clicking across the floor alerted her to the mutt's presence. It yipped, sniffing the spot on the floor before shaking its head in disgust. Well, the excuse of Ben walking the dog wasn't going to work.

The sitter must have arranged with Ben to drop the fluffball off early.

She stood up from the island chair and padded toward their long-paneled window, staring out over the lanai, imagining Ben down on the pier. She paused, listening. Nothing. Then—maybe—the faintest echo of a voice. No. Just the wind through the screens. There was no sign of her husband—just the sandhill cranes doing their morning march in search of food.

Ben disappearing wasn't part of her plan.

Where was her phone?

She normally went to bed with it and didn't remember seeing it there on the nightstand. As the coffee continued to brew, she marched toward the front of the house and the basket where they kept their keys and last night—oh, yes—everybody's phones.

There was more than one inside, meaning they'd probably have a couple guests this morning coming to retrieve theirs. Hers was among them.

She picked it up, clicked on the messages to see if Ben had texted her. There were several texts. One of them from Brad, saying he was going to come by to pick up Kennedy's phone—which she would discover later had a photo of Miranda and Brad in a compromising position on it. She wished she could be there for that discovery, and to hear Brad's excuse since he likely had little memory of the encounter.

But there was nothing from Ben.

Though his messages, too, indicated he had a string of people looking for him. She clicked through his messages from work, seeing if there was anything he might've had an appointment for this morning that might explain where he was. Sometimes, as mayor, he had to work on the weekends. But it looked like they were looking for him, too.

There was a quick thought that a concerned wife might call her husband's ex to find out if she knew—but that would just be embarrassing, wouldn't it?

She could practically hear the woman now, talking in her ear about not knowing where Ben was. About how it had been her before Miranda had taken him away.

She tapped the screen with her nail, watching it dim. She knew how it would go—because it was a conversation they'd had before. Not because Ben was missing. Just a jealous rant from another woman. And really, she couldn't blame her.

It was true. Miranda had stolen him.

But to be fair, Benjamin had wanted to be stolen. He was bored in their stale marriage. His ex had no longer cared about the things he thought were important.

Sure, she cleaned the house, took care of the kids—but at some point, she'd stopped caring about herself. Refused to have fun.

Men liked a woman who took good care of herself—and even better care of him. And Benjamin deserved a woman who looked good on his arm, who was willing to play the games he liked.

The coffee maker beeped, momentarily halting her search on her husband's cell, the desire for coffee so sharp, it pulled her attention.

She took out her favorite coffee mug—the one that said *A Cup a Day Keeps the Darkness Away*. Miranda poured the black liquid into her cup, spilling several droplets on the counter. From reflex, she grabbed a paper towel to wipe up the mess. Though it was clean, she wiped the counter again, hard this time, noticing her hands were shaking.

Coffee. Stat. Her mouth watered, knowing that in just a few moments, the headache sitting on the surface of her skull would abate. All these bitches who refused a cup of java had no idea what they were missing.

She breathed in the rich, savory aroma—and then she took a sip. A long, slow, savoring type of sip. The first sip grounded her. The second made her stomach twist.

She was about halfway through the cup when she remembered Benjamin wasn't in the house and she still had no idea exactly where he was.

Maybe she'd never see him again.

A cool chill raced over her skin.

Her gaze strayed around the room, her mind replaying the events from the night before, trying to make sense of things, when her eyes fell toward the back sliding door where a pair of sandals sat discarded.

"Snow?" she asked. "Care for a walk on the beach?"

Chapter Forty-Two

Jennifer

The Fifteen Commandments of a Tradwife

Twelve: Thou shalt keep thy home a haven. A safe place for your family . . . and a stage for those who are watching.

8:13 a.m.

Rare was the morning that Jennifer had off work. And mostly, those days weren't off, because her kids were home and she had chores and caretaking to do. But today was different. Ever since she started working at the grocery store, her hours had been much more manageable than at the diner. And today she was off work—*and* had managed to arrange for her kids to attend an open-gym day at the local gymnastics club. So, she could do whatever she wanted and had given herself permission not to do a single chore. This was a morning solely for her.

She decided to take Shadow for a walk on the beach by the ocean, instead of lakeside. At this hour, she hoped the beach was still quiet and not littered with sunbathers on the sandy shores.

"Come on, tough guy," she said to her dog, beckoning him out of the car where they'd parked just over the dunes. "Let's go get some exercise."

Shadow barked as he hopped out of the minivan. There were only a few other cars in the parking lot, to her relief. Her patience was already rubbed raw from morning drop-off and the furtive whispers of the other mothers she was certain never to live past. Perhaps the most relieving part was knowing she likely wouldn't see anyone she knew. Confronted. Maligned for having spoken the truth online. The truth no one wanted to acknowledge. She hadn't used her name, or Jamie's name, but they still knew. After all, she'd stopped hiding her face.

They crossed over the short boardwalk that bridged the dunes to the beach on the other side. Waves crashed lightly against the shore. The sun had crested just above the horizon, and mist rose from the ocean's depths. Shadow went running down the beach, his feet kicking up sand. She'd brought a ball with her to throw—but he appeared more interested in chasing the birds wading at the shoreline, waiting for little creatures to pop up from the sand, and she rather liked watching him play with glee.

Despite the strangeness of the night before, she'd managed to get some good sleep before the alarm went off. Though when she'd woken, she'd wondered if she'd hallucinated the whole thing, and listened to the recording again. Definitely real.

Jennifer drew in a deep, cleansing breath. Listened to the sounds around her. The caws of gulls, the distant drone of a boat engine, the squelch of Shadow's paws in wet sand. The sun was warm on her skin, but with the gentle ocean breeze, the temperature was comfortable. The beach still smelled faintly of last night's bonfire. Charcoal and beer. Something burnt beneath it.

The combined scents mingled with memory made her nauseated.

Shadow took off at a run, blasting down the beach, and Jennifer laughed, feeling lighthearted in a way she hadn't in so long. It was almost like this wasn't real life. Almost as if she was in some sort of fictional tale, where something bad was about to happen, or all the bad things of the past would resurface. The peaceful calm before the storm.

My goodness, she was being dramatic.

She was thinking too much like her old friend Samantha, whom she used to have breakfast with on Monday mornings after drop-off before her divorce. Samantha would regale her with endless crime show stories she'd binged over the weekend. The woman was obsessed. But after the big D, Samantha had canceled breakfast one week, and then the next, until Jennifer stopped asking.

Jennifer had never been into crime shows. She didn't want to know about other people's misery, other people's deaths. That only made her depressed. Made her think more about her own life. The past she'd buried. And how could Samantha? She was there that night too. Samantha had joked that she went to sleep each night watching a different crime show, finding the terrifying stories relaxing. Samantha was a little off that way—but then again, she had known plenty of people who did the same thing, so who was Jennifer to judge?

Shadow's bark echoed down the beach. He stood over something—

probably a horseshoe crab. She hated the smell of rotting ones, always worse in the sun. She picked up her pace, hurrying down the beach, not wanting him to dig into whatever feast he'd found and turn her relaxing trip into a cleanup job.

When she reached Shadow, all she saw was a pair of sandals.

"Just someone's sandals. What's the big deal?" she muttered. Discarded sandals on the beach. So what? It wasn't like her dog was going to answer, but sometimes she felt like he would, if he just had the ability.

They were familiar. Leather thongs. Flip-flops, really—though the fancy people around here didn't call them that. It was a man's pair. Large. Maybe a size 12 or 13. Hard to tell; not like she was a shoe salesperson. But something about them pinged her gut.

They looked almost like Jamie's.

The ones he'd kick off when he got home from wherever he'd been that day. Even the toe indents worn down into the leather were in the right spot—the longer second toe, just like his.

She held her breath. A cold sweat prickled the back of her neck. She didn't want to pick them up. Didn't want to confirm. Lots of people had a second toe longer than a first.

Jennifer stared down at the sandals, then followed the line of footprints that led into the dunes. Instinct told her to follow. But the twist in her stomach made her want to turn around, pretend she never saw the sandals. What good could come from this? If he was over in the dunes, it's not like she wanted to see him.

She told herself she was being ridiculous. People kicked off their sandals at the beach all the time. That's what you did. Only she was the weirdo who walked the beach in sneakers because she hated the feel of sand between her toes. And after years of sweeping sand out of the house, who could blame her?

Still, her feet carried her toward the dunes.

Curiosity weighed heavier than her desire to flee confrontation. The dry dune grass scratched at her calves. A stick snapped beneath her shoe.

Shadow rushed ahead, crashing through the brush, but Jennifer wasn't that brave. She climbed onto the small boardwalk that led through the dunes to another parking lot. She peered through the brush, hoping she wasn't about to stumble across two lovers in an embrace. That would be embarrassing.

The dog barked. She held her breath. The wind slowed. Shadow froze.

And then—Soft. Hushed. Like wind curling through tall grass: "Shhh."

Her chest went tight. Not just from fear but recognition—like the sound had been meant for her.

Shadow came bounding out of the brush, tongue flopping, looking pleased with himself.

And that's when she saw it.

One foot stuck out at a strange angle. Pale. Still.

A body.

Lying prone in the dunes. Unmoving. There was something . . . off. Not quite right. Not quite dead.

Jennifer's stomach pitched at the thought, like she'd just missed a step, except she was still standing in the same place.

She called out.

No answer. No movement.

But hadn't someone just shushed the dog?

"Hey, please—answer me! Do you need help?" Jennifer called. "Do you need me to call 911?" Her voice cracked. "I'm talking to you in the dunes! Please answer me!"

Silence.

Jennifer felt in her pockets, ready to dial—but they were empty. She'd left her phone in the car.

"Shit," she whispered.

"Come on," she said, patting her thigh to get the dog to follow. She returned to the beach, sprinting down it, sand kicking up on the backs of her calves, past two men setting up their fishing poles in the sand, back to the car. Grabbed her phone. Dialed 911 as she ran back toward the dunes.

"911, what's your emergency?"

Jennifer sucked in a breath, her lungs shouting for reprieve. "Yes, there's someone lying down. I don't think they're breathing. I can't really see them clearly—"

"Ma'am, please calm down. I need you to tell me exactly where you are."

Jennifer inhaled, eyes fixed on the foot still poking out of the brush. Still unmoving.

"Yes—Crystal Harbor Beach. Someone's in the dunes. I don't know if they're breathing—hello?"

Shadow took off down the beach, barking at a bird and knocking over a toddler who was searching for seashells.

"Sorry!" she yelled to the mother, who—miraculously—was gracious.

Torn between the body and Shadow's antics, she rushed toward her dog, who was eagerly digging in the sand beside the toddler as if to help in the quest for shells. Apologizing again, Jennifer clipped on his leash and rushed back to the dunes.

But when she returned—

The foot was gone.

For a moment, she thought she'd imagined the whole thing.

Just like last night. Just like the voices she wasn't supposed to hear.

"Ma'am? Ma'am? Are you still on the phone?"

Jennifer blinked. Was it a prank? Had someone been watching her? How the hell . . . ?

"Yes . . . they're gone."

"Who's gone, ma'am?"

Shadow whined softly beside her.

"The body," she whispered. "The one I saw. The one in the dunes. It's gone."

Chapter Forty-Three

Ariel

8:55 a.m.

Ariel's teeth were chattering, but not from the chill. In fact, it was from fright. The children's private dance instructor had come by at the scheduled time, and she'd been able to call on a babysitter to come watch the younger children, who weren't ready for lessons, so that she could sit and think—think about why Shane wasn't home yet. And where he was.

She hadn't realized he was gone until this morning.

Hours. Hours of him possibly in trouble.

When she woke up, it was with her heart pounding and dirt under her fingernails. She was still in yesterday's clothes—rumpled, sand-streaked—and had no memory of how she'd gotten home. No memory of Shane at all. Just flashes: a bonfire. Laughter. Music that was too loud. A sharp cry.

The silence of the house this morning had been louder than any of it—no heavy footsteps on the stairs, no Shane humming to himself in the shower. Just *nothing.*

His side of the bed hadn't even been touched. And that's when she knew—he'd never come home at all.

But that had been three hours ago, and since then she'd received a strange text from Samantha. The words of the text replayed in her mind over and over again: They found a body on the beach.

Ariel had started to type back to ask *who was it?* But she didn't want to know. Didn't want to know if it was a man or a woman, afraid that it would only solidify what she already believed. That something had happened to Shane. And unlike his twin, Tara, they would find his body crumpled by the water.

Her thumb brushed the bandage on her arm. The shell had sliced deep. But the deeper wound? That hadn't surfaced yet.

Her calves were scratched, too—thin red lines she hadn't noticed until she changed clothes. Her head throbbed behind her eyes, a dull pressure that didn't feel like a hangover but something else, something toxic and strange. Like something had been poured into her and stirred around. She didn't drink. Not like that. Not ever.

Something had happened last night. Shane was missing, her fingers had been caked in mud, and now there was a body on the beach. It was easy to draw the lines from one to another. She'd seen enough thrillers and been in enough shows to know exactly how this script was going to play out.

A fight between two men. A wife waking up with a hangover—when she doesn't drink at all. A wife suspecting she was drugged at a party. An out-of-control, inappropriate party. The kind of party that doesn't happen in this town. The kind of party hosted by a woman who Ariel had suspected wasn't right from day one.

Flashbacks of water. A cut from a shell.

Every possible explanation ran through her mind, each one worse than the last. A fall. A fight. A disappearance. A death. Her pulse raced faster with each possibility, like her body was speeding toward the truth her brain refused to name.

The past and the present collided, and the faces of the people from the party last night melted into the faces of those from the party over a decade ago.

Miranda's smirk played out in her mind. The same one last night as from the bake sale when the little boy had eaten the glass-filled brownie. The same smirk she'd seen Miranda wear in the grocery store. Or when they'd gone for aguas frescas and she was watching Colleen, thinking she was unobserved.

Did Miranda have something to do with Shane's disappearance?

Instead of texting Samantha back, she texted Miranda: Where is my husband?

Three little dots bubbled underneath her message, indicating that not only had Miranda read what she'd written but she was planning to write her back. And then—the bubbles stopped. The silence of an unwritten message echoed in the empty kitchen.

Well, she had a babysitter here, and her other children were with the tutor. There was nothing to stop her from actually going over to Miranda and Benjamin's house to see if Shane was there.

But when she stood, her legs shook. Her stomach pinched. She'd barely been able to eat a piece of toast this morning. She'd eaten out of obligation, not hunger. Her babies had made it, and she'd tried to smile, even as acid churned in her belly. But carbs couldn't soak up dread.

She kept seeing a hand gripping someone's wrist—Not Shane's.

Not hers. Someone else's. But when she tried to place it, it flickered away like a mirage, morphing into a shove on a pier, and Tara falling into the water.

And then she remembered . . . The last thing she'd seen before falling asleep last night had been Tara's face. Not her baby, but Shane's sister . . . They'd never found her body. Was she . . .

If fiction were about to become reality—or rather, if a crime show were being played out before her eyes—then Ariel was about to find out that Shane was the body on the beach. And Benjamin the villain. Or rather, Miranda the one who'd orchestrated it all.

And Miranda must know exactly what had happened. That was why she wasn't writing her back. It was easy to pretend you didn't know something if you ignored it.

Ariel typed again: I know you saw my message. Answer me. Where is my husband?

Three dots. Then nothing. Again. Like Miranda wanted her to know she was reading—but not replying. Like she wanted Ariel to squirm.

The kettle on the stove began to whistle though she hadn't even turned it on. Or had she? The scream of steam sent her fingers scrambling over her phone.

Ariel frantically typed: You think this is a game? If something happened to him . . .

This time the text said *delivered* but did not say *read*, and the little bubbles never appeared.

She pressed the phone onto the counter a little too hard, the crack against marble making her jump. She picked it up to check the screen, relieved that it wasn't broken.

Well, she couldn't just sit here. Miranda might not have wanted to write her back, but she was going to answer the door or Ariel was going to break it down. She was going to find out exactly what had happened to Shane.

Ariel hurried upstairs, threw her hair into a ponytail, pulled on a bra and underwear and slipped her feet into flip-flops. She never left the house without her hair and makeup done, and for a split second, she worried that people wouldn't recognize her.

But maybe that was to her benefit.

She grabbed her keys and her phone, let the babysitter know that she was leaving and asked if she wouldn't mind getting the kids lunch when they got out of tutoring, in case she wasn't back.

She paused at the door, watching the sitter laugh with the kids. She shouldn't leave. She knew that. But how could she stay? What kind of mother would she be if something had happened to Shane and she'd done nothing?

Then she went into the garage.

Her breath stilled as she saw that Shane's silver Mercedes was there, parked beside her white Escalade. It hadn't been moved. But a faint smear of sand streaked the windshield, and the keys weren't on the hook by the door.

Ariel blinked, her brain trying to figure out just how her husband's car could be here and he not. How his keys could be missing.

How had she gotten home? Had he driven her and then walked back to the party?

The cars sat side by side like nothing had happened. But something had. And Ariel felt it in her bones—whatever it was, it had left a mark.

What if this was her fault? What if she said something, did something . . . worse?

She opened his car, hoping for a clue, something. In the passenger cup holder was the other half of the broken seashell she didn't remember taking. Its pale curve caught the light—dragged ashore.

She was going to leave the sanctuary of her beach house and go back to Miranda's—and this time, there'd be no silence.

Chapter Forty-Four

Miranda

9:28 a.m.

Miranda might've hated cleaning, but cleaning up messes, as it turned out, happened to be one of her specialties, even if she loathed it. And this party was no different. She turned her phone on Do Not Disturb and set it back on the counter after reading Ariel's messages. She had almost written her back to let her know that Shane had left with her the night before, but clearly Ariel knew something was going on. The woman might've been tranquilized most of the time, but she wasn't stupid.

And Miranda hadn't been the only one who'd heard her whisper *Tara*.

Shane had mumbled that she must be worried about their baby, but Miranda wondered.

She went to her computer, logged into their surveillance cameras' cloud and viewed all of the footage from the night before—some of it damning, some of it innocuous. Didn't matter. She deleted it all from the cloud but saved some of the juicier bits to a thumb drive. Of course, if the cops came looking, the neighbors had cameras, too, but hopefully their houses were distant enough that they wouldn't have noticed a thing. Just people walking toward her house, people leaving. Maybe they'd been smart enough to count just how many people had left—and maybe they hadn't. All she knew was that she wasn't about to get into trouble.

That wasn't part of the plan.

All she'd done was open the door. If people destroyed themselves, that was on them.

All she'd done was host a party. Had a little fun. Encouraged others to have a little fun.

Besides, she was the mayor's wife. An upstanding citizen of Crystal Harbor. If anything bad were to have happened, maybe she was a victim too.

After deleting the camera footage, she hurried back into the kitchen, working double time to clean up the mess of the party—to straighten the pillows, sweep and mop the floor. Discard the heel by the fireplace. Clean up the broken glass. The sticky stuff on the floor. The kiss on the patio door.

The house must look like nothing had happened. Because after seeing the footage from last night, especially from the camera out back, anyone watching would know exactly what went down. And she was pretty certain that the evidence would be damning.

She scrubbed away the mess, the faint scent of perfume that wasn't hers. The citrus tang of disinfectant couldn't quite mask the undertone of sweat, sex and something sour that clung to the drapes. Something like panic.

She flushed the things that made the Miranda Special so special.

After making sure her house was picture-perfect, Miranda went upstairs to do her hair and makeup. She was going to look like the picture-perfect wife, waiting for her husband. She had just finished putting on her mascara when the doorbell rang, causing her to poke herself in the eye.

Fuck.

Her mind flashed to the texts from Ariel, and she had a good feeling that woman was the one hammering away on her door right now. If she didn't stop, her knuckles would start bleeding.

Miranda groaned, put her mascara back into her makeup bag and, taking the stairs slowly, marched down.

Through the glass and sunshine, Miranda watched Ariel fidget on her front porch, tucking her hair behind her ear, smoothing her . . . ohmygod, were those yoga pants? The woman was glancing from side to side as if she expected someone to jump out at her.

Miranda drew a breath, pulling from somewhere deep in her center the woman who remembered just who she was—the strong one, the one capable of lying easily. The one all of these motherfuckers owed. She opened the door with a confident smile.

"Oh my goodness, Ariel, what a surprise. I was just about to stop by to chat with you. Didn't expect you'd be making house calls." Miranda kept her voice sweet as singed sugar on a crème brûlée.

"Cut the crap. Where is Shane?" Ariel's voice was not so sweet but crunchy, like burnt toast.

A flicker of panic slithered beneath Miranda's skin, but she strangled it with a smile. She'd survived much worse than an angry housewife on her porch. *Much* worse. "You must be confused, sweetie, he left with you last night. Remember?" Miranda offered an expression that conveyed *oh, you poor thing, bless your heart*, all the while trying to rein in her irritation at Ariel showing up unannounced.

Despite the redness in her eyes, Ariel's gaze was sharp, unflinching. "Don't try to gaslight me, Miranda. He never came home." Ariel's voice was hard, brutal. The way she was dressed was quite the opposite of the woman Miranda had met in the grocery store. That wilting woman had vanished. In her place stood a woman with teeth. "Stop playing games. You're not fooling me."

A spasm flicked in Miranda's cheek. She stilled it with a breath. Miranda forced her shoulders down, schooling her features into serene indifference. Hysteria was contagious—and she didn't want to catch it.

Ariel crossed her arms over her chest, tapping her foot in rhythmic movement on the porch. Then, she must have thought better of it and pushed her way inside.

Ariel's eyes swept the foyer, pausing a beat too long on the staircase. Miranda felt suddenly, irrationally exposed—as if the other woman could see the memory of last night still smeared on the tile floor.

As if Ariel had peeled back all the layers that made Miranda, Miranda, and could see the real girl underneath.

Miranda backed up, unsure what to think of Ariel's sudden show of guts, but still kept her face neutral.

"I don't know what you were up to last night," Ariel said, "but I'm going to get to the bottom of it."

"I don't know what you mean." Miranda guessed Ariel didn't remember much of the party—a small mercy. "I was just being a host. We had a great party. Everyone seemed to have a good time—including you." She shrugged. "You're clearly upset. Maybe take a moment before throwing accusations around."

A cloud fell over Ariel's features, masking the sharp irritation from before. A flash of fear cut through Miranda's spine and made her shiver.

"They found a body on the beach." Ariel whispered as if she didn't want their reflections in the foyer mirror to hear it. "Did you know that?"

Miranda blinked just once. A muscle at the corner of her eye twitched, barely visible. She had not known they'd found a body. Heat surged from her chest up her neck, making the back of her scalp tickle. Though her palms grew slick, she didn't move, just kept her smile painted in place, like a pageant queen seconds before the crown slipped.

"A body?" Her voice was light, too light, floating just above the crack forming underneath her composed expression. Shane wasn't supposed to be that body. "That's . . . news to me."

But the rock slamming against her ribs knocked loose the fear she'd swallowed whole and buried deep. For a split second, Miranda felt like she was being dragged underwater—kicking, breathless, helpless.

Stoically, Miranda straightened her shoulders. Fine. Let her ask. Let her push. Better to give Ariel just enough rope to wrap around her own neck than to implicate Miranda. She caught her reflection in the foyer mirror. Immaculate. Smiling. Lethal. She was exactly who she needed to be.

"Do they know who it is?" Miranda asked.

"If they had said who it was, don't you think I would've mentioned that?" Ariel snapped, sounding extremely annoyed.

"It sounds like you think I had something to do with it, from the way you just came over here, barging into my house." Her voice sugar-dipped and arsenic-laced. Miranda was getting increasingly irritated. How dare she come into her house making accusations?

"Where is your husband?" Ariel said, looking around the house and walking into the kitchen. Her eyes scanned every surface as if she might have missed something.

Miranda was glad she hadn't fucked around with the cleaning.

Then she realized there was the basket by the front door, two sets of phones and keys left. Was Shane's one of the ones in there? Brad had already come by for Kennedy's phone—barely met her eye, said he "wasn't feeling great" and didn't ask a single question. There was something about the way he clutched the phone like it held all his secrets. Something about how fast he walked away.

Of the two phones left, she had no idea whose they were. One had a black lock screen, no background image, and the other had an image of the beach. When she'd tried to open it, the phone had died.

"Listen, I need to go into town, so I'm going to have to ask you to leave." Miranda pointed toward the front door as elegantly as she could. "I need to run by the mayor's office to speak with Benjamin."

"Benjamin is at work?" Ariel looked at her skeptically.

Miranda decided to lie. "Of course he's at the office. He's the mayor. They don't take off on weekends. He picked up the dog and then went." She hooked her thumb over her shoulder toward the ratty thing, who sat accusingly in the foyer.

Ariel looked like the wind had been knocked out of her sails. As if she had come in here hoping to find information and received nothing.

Miranda couldn't blame her. Shane should have been at home.

Miranda's heart hammered behind her ribs. She needed to confirm for herself who the body was.

Ariel looked distracted—glancing to her phone, then back to Miranda—her lips pinched. Had she been viewing a headline? A photo? Whatever it was, it had pulled her focus. "I have to go," she said.

"Yes, you do," Miranda said, without questioning what she had seen on her phone. If it had been something about *her*, then she would've said something. Miranda was certain.

Ariel stormed out the door, marching down to her fancy oversize SUV as quickly as she had stormed in moments ago.

As soon as the door was shut, Miranda locked it. She went to the basket, staring down at the phones, trying to figure out just who had left theirs behind. Just who else she might expect to knock on her door.

Then she picked up the basket and hurled it at the wall.

Shane was not part of the plan.

Just as she turned to leave the room, an annoying chime rang from one of the phones now scattered on the floor. Miranda froze. One still had battery. One was still alive.

The chime was the distinct screech of the Find My Phone feature. The fucking thing might as well have been shouting: *Guilty, guilty, lying bitch.*

Miranda marched over to the belting cell and crushed it with her heel, silencing it forever, just like she wanted to silence everything, and everyone, else.

Chapter Forty-Five

Jennifer

The Fifteen Commandments of a Tradwife

> **Thirteen:** Thou shalt cultivate skills worth passing on. Recipes, quilting patterns, the right way to fold a napkin—and the unspoken rules of survival.

9:29 a.m.

Jennifer had never been in trouble with the law before. And even though she wasn't in trouble right now, she felt as if she were. Blue and red lights flashed from the parking lot over the dunes, quiet now when they had drilled into her ears moments before.

People had started to gather around to see what was happening. Four police officers stood in a half circle in front of her, notepads out, eyes staring. One of them had his thumb hooked lazily in his belt, like this was a coffee break, not someone's worst day.

Exactly the same as in 2013, except this time she'd seen the body afterward.

She told them about the foot she'd seen in the bushes, and she was pretty certain that no one believed her—their eyes squinting at the edges and their mouths flat. They encouraged her to keep talking.

The wind slapped strands of hair into her mouth as she tried to answer. Sand stung the backs of her calves. Shadow let out a soft growl, his body rigid against her leg. Her ponytail had come loose, strands clinging to the sweat on her neck. The cuffs of her sleeves were damp where she'd wrung them with her hands. She'd meant to look composed, but she probably looked deranged—like someone who'd just stumbled out of a storm.

She explained to them how she'd come to the beach three times now. How Shadow had raced toward a pair of abandoned sandals she'd believed to be Jamie's, which they'd collected as evidence. And then she'd chased after her dog and seen the body. After she'd gone back for her phone to call 911 and returned to the dunes, the body had disappeared.

"Are you sure it wasn't just driftwood, ma'am? People panic when they're out here alone."

Jennifer shook her head slowly. Maybe she hadn't seen what she thought she saw. Maybe it wasn't a foot. Maybe it was a trick of the shadows. But no—no. She'd seen toes. Pale. Human. Real. "No, it was definitely a foot." She wasn't making it up. She had seen it. She knew she had.

But the problem now was that they had found another body, down the beach. Not in the dunes.

And the surf kept rolling in like nothing had happened, dragging secrets out to sea.

Jennifer's entire insides were shaking. She couldn't seem to stand still. And she felt like throwing up. Shadow was getting antsy, too, and tugged on his leash as he paced back and forth, wanting to disappear from this place just as much as she did.

"Ma'am, when was the last time you saw your husband?"

"I'm not married."

She'd watched enough crime shows to know that you didn't say anything you didn't have to. Stick to the facts. For some reason, they were trying to nail a crime on her that she hadn't committed.

The cop who asked her the question glared at her as if she'd done something insubordinate—which she had not. It was true. She wasn't married. She didn't have a husband. He had not asked her about her ex-husband.

"Ma'am, when was the last time you saw your ex-husband?"

Well. Now to at least impart something that seemed like she was cooperating.

"Maybe last week? We split custody, but most of the time we do drop-offs and pickups at school. There's really no occasion for us to see each other."

The cops stared at her as if they'd never heard of such a thing. Even though she knew this was completely normal. Was it cordial? No. But many people who couldn't stand the sight of each other didn't want to force that sort of awkward situation on their children.

"Okay. So you say you haven't seen him in the last week. When was the last time you spoke to him?"

What was the last thing Jamie said to her? Did he threaten her, mock her, mention the beach?

"I'm sorry, what does Jamie have to do with this?" she asked. "Shouldn't you be searching for someone who could be hurt or possibly stumbling down the beach?"

Oh God, had the person been alive when she saw them? And then stumbled away and died down the beach? Could she have helped them?

What she really wanted to ask was why she was being treated like a criminal here. She wanted to scream that she'd called them. That she was the one who'd found the damn missing body. They seemed to have forgotten that. But she knew how that would look—loud, emotional. Hysterical. Like someone trying to shift blame.

"Let's focus on the situation here, ma'am."

Jennifer bit the tip of her tongue to keep from snapping that was exactly what she was trying to do—and *he* was not.

Instead, she nodded.

"I'll ask again, ma'am. When was the last time you spoke to your husband?"

Jennifer bristled, not sure if the cop had done it on purpose, calling him her husband. She'd said "ex-husband." But she didn't correct him this time, not wanting him to see her agitation.

"Maybe a week ago?"

"What did you speak about?"

"The kids. Pickup, that sort of thing." Really, it wasn't any of their business what she and Jamie had talked about. And she definitely wasn't going to tell them about how he'd threatened her—that would just make her look guiltier.

The officer kept looking at her sneakers. It took her a second to realize she was shifting from foot to foot, like a kid caught lying.

The question was why she was being questioned about Jamie at all. And why was she feeling so guilty about it? Ever since she was a child, she'd had that weird guilty feeling about things even when she hadn't done anything wrong. Mostly because she was often blamed for things. And seemed to have a guilty face.

She could almost hear her mother's voice from childhood—*Don't argue, you'll only make it worse*—right before she felt the switch on her bare bum.

Jennifer again shifted on her feet. Her toes were going numb. Suddenly, her sneakers felt as if they were tied too tight. She just wanted to go home. What was supposed to be a day of relaxation, of giving to herself by walking on the beach with her dog, had turned into something awful.

"Did something happen to Jamie?" Her blood ran cold at their dark expressions as they stared at her.

It was the way they stopped writing when she said Jamie's name. Pens paused. Eyes narrowed. A shared glance between the two of them. Suddenly, it didn't feel like they were listening—it felt like they were collecting.

One officer shifted slightly, hand brushing near his holster. That was when her body caught up to her mind. She wasn't here to help. She was here because they thought she might know something. Or had done something. "We're not at liberty to say."

That was answer enough for Jennifer, and she felt her knees buckle. One of the cops reached out, grabbing her elbow and helping her to stand. Shadow didn't like that and started to bark. Jennifer shushed him, soothing his ire by patting him on the head.

"If we're all done here, I think I need to get this guy home. He's stressed." She squeezed the handle of the leash, trying to quell the trembling in her hands.

The cop in charge nodded and flipped closed his notebook. "We see a lot of concerned moms around here. Sometimes the imagination runs a little wild, especially after a divorce."

Jennifer's mouth fell open. A woman alone. A beach. A body that disappeared. No witnesses. No photos. Just a frazzled mom with a barking dog and a voice shaking too hard to be convincing. But before she could even think of a way to respond, the other officer said, "We may have more questions, ma'am."

Jennifer wanted to say *And I have need of answers, clearly, because* you *haven't answered any of my questions and nothing has been done pertaining to my call about someone lying in the bushes.*

But she didn't say anything like that, not wanting them to hold her further. She just wanted to get away from here.

So she nodded and said, "Yes, sir," and then, tugging on her dog's leash, headed back toward the parking lot, toward the flashing lights.

When she got there, she noted the ambulance—and getting into the ambulance were several paramedics pulling a gurney. On the gurney was a body, wrapped in a black body bag, zipped tight. They *had* found a body on the beach. She wasn't delusional. But was it the one she'd seen? Or were there two?

The way they surrounded it, she couldn't get a good look at the size. Man or woman. The blackness of it, the lumpiness of it, screamed *anonymous*. The bag sagged with the unmistakable heaviness of someone who wouldn't get up again.

Where had the person in the bushes gone? Had they been alive one second and dead the next? Perhaps if she hadn't gone for her phone, but taken the risk and stayed, she might've been able to help save them.

She was riddled with guilt at not having tried harder.

It was only when she got behind the wheel, Shadow panting

behind her, and was driving out of the parking lot that she saw Jamie's car. The color was right. The tiny scratch on the bumper where Craig hit it with his bike last week. The sea turtle sunshade still in the window. It was his. Had to be. Her chest squeezed tight, her body suddenly too small to contain her lungs.

Maybe he was, in fact, the one they found on the beach.

Maybe the body in the bag was Jamie.

She made it half a mile before pulling over. Then the truth hit her like a wave—and she emptied her stomach into the sand.

Her mind flashed back to a drop-off a few weeks ago. The way Jamie had lingered by the car, said something low—*You always did like to play the victim*—before driving off. At the time, she'd rolled her eyes. Now it felt like a curse.

She wiped her mouth, stared at the surf. If it was Jamie, she hadn't just found a body. She'd lost the one person who still had the power to destroy her.

When she glanced up, an officer had pulled over and was cautiously approaching her.

Chapter Forty-Six

Ariel

10:05 a.m.

Ariel's hands gripped the steering wheel so hard she was sure her palms would be bruised by tomorrow. She'd been driving around town, pulling into every place Shane normally went, looking for him. The visit to Miranda's had done little good. Shane was still not picking up his phone. In fact, it had stopped ringing and gone straight to voicemail—as if the battery was dead or he'd turned it off. But why would he turn it off? And where the fuck was he?

She pulled into his men's golf clubhouse, marching inside like a woman deranged past the plumes of cigar smoke. The employee looked at her, concerned, as they scrolled down the list of men checked in to play. Her husband's name was not on the list. They quickly shooed her out of the building. It was no place for a woman—especially one who looked as mad as she did.

She drove to coffee shops, gas stations, even the hospital, and asked if anyone had seen or heard from Shane, showing his picture.

The woman at the hospital's front desk had just shaken her head and looked at her with pity.

There were a dozen police officers at the beach, and she pulled over to find out what was happening. Skin instantly slick, either from the humidity or nerves. They just shook their heads and said they couldn't confirm any details. But a bystander nearby said they'd seen a gurney with a body bag earlier.

Ariel pulled out her phone, flicked to a picture of Shane and showed it to a few of the cops, asking if they'd seen him, hoping for even a flicker of recognition. All of the cops shook their heads firmly.

"No, ma'am."

Ariel numbly got back into her car, gripping the wheel, and drove straight home.

Upon Ariel entering the house, the babysitter looked at her with concern. The babysitter's perfume—vanilla and nerves—hovered in the air as Ariel walked by. She passed the bowls of macaroni and cheese still in the sink from lunch. The normalcy of it mocked her.

Ariel just smiled as pleasantly as she could and marched upstairs to the bathroom, where she threw up the meager bits of toast she'd eaten.

If Shane had been the body on the beach, when she showed the police his picture, they would have asked her at least to come to the station. She didn't know whether to be relieved or more scared. If he wasn't the body on the beach—then where the hell was he?

The lining of her stomach felt like it was being eaten away by acid. A second later, she heard the squeals of her children, shouting, "Daddy! Daddy's home!"

Shane? Ariel stood up from the toilet. The room tilted slightly. Sweat pooled under her arms, her bra sticking like duct tape to her skin. She splashed water on her face and walked into the bedroom, her limbs still shaking with adrenaline and fury.

Shane stumbled into their bedroom a second later, his clothes filthy, vegetation in his hair, scratches and bruises all over his face and arms. His left sleeve was torn off. He smelled like the beach and campfire. His feet were bare, sand crusted between his toes and dotted along his heels.

"Oh my God. What happened?" she asked, staring. It was obvious he'd been in some sort of fight or accident. "Where are your sandals?"

"No idea," he said. "Woke up in a bush. I don't even know how the hell I got there." He rubbed his hand over his face, and she couldn't tell if it was because he was trying to hide the fact he was lying—or because he was genuinely confused.

He stared at the photo on the nightstand—Ariel with the kids at the beach—as if he didn't recognize it. Beside it was a photo of Tara. Then his gaze shifted to the broken halves of the shells beside the frame, where she'd placed them side by side an hour ago. Did he recognize them?

His eyes flicked away too fast. *He knows something.* Ariel's mouth went dry.

Ariel stepped in front of her husband, forcing him to look at her. "What happened last night? I woke up this morning and you weren't here, but your car was. How did you get home?"

Shane frowned, staring a beat. "Uber. I just said—I have no idea what happened. I woke up in a *bush.* Are you even listening to me, Ariel?"

The disdain in his voice cut deep. He'd woken up in a bush, had no memory of the night before, looked like he'd been in a fight—and he was angry at *her*?

"I think you need to direct your anger somewhere else," Ariel said. Her voice was steady now. The trembling had stopped. She directed her anger at her husband. "Whatever situation you got yourself into—that's on you." Her voice was tight. "Besides," she added, "someone's dead."

Shane frowned, but there was something behind that frown that deeply disturbed her. Something that looked like knowing.

"Who's dead?" he asked. His voice was soft, hesitant, as if he didn't want the answer.

And she didn't blame him. She didn't want to know either. She was glad, for now, that she didn't.

Ariel shook her head. "I have no idea. Nobody knows. There's a long line of group texts going out. I even stopped by the beach and saw the police when I was looking for you."

Shane straightened, his body going stiff as he glowered at her. "You went to the beach?"

The way he said it—it was like she'd done something horrible. Like she'd emptied their bank account or poisoned their neighbor's dog.

"I was *looking for you.* You weren't answering your phone. You didn't sleep here. You weren't at Miranda and Ben's house. *Of course* I went looking for you." She shook her head. "What wife wouldn't?"

"I think I lost something important last night," he muttered, patting his pockets.

Ariel froze. What did he mean? His wallet? Phone? A ring? Or something worse—something he couldn't say aloud?

Frowning, Shane let out a groan, his hand raking through his hair—coming away with blood on his fingers.

"Oh my God. You're hurt," she said. "Let me look."

She stepped toward him, but he held a hand out, warning her off. And a flash of another memory came back to her. She remembered Shane helping her into the car, but not where they were. Just the briny scent of seaweed, the pulse of bass from the party still echoing in her bones and a raw ache blooming near her elbow. A laugh. His hand on her leg. Then nothing.

"Did you know that . . ." He trailed off, shaking his head, then, "I'll be fine," before marching into the bathroom and shutting the door—leaving a trail of sandy footprints in his wake.

Ariel stared at the sand on their hardwood floor. Sand. Beach. Her mind drifted to the broken shells she'd found. Her husband, bruised and filthy. His anger at her for going to the beach. For talking to the police. For asking questions.

Ariel turned to the bathroom door, hearing the shower run, hearing his movement behind it. Maybe he really didn't remember. Or maybe he was hoping she wouldn't ask the right questions.

Oh, Shane. What have you done?

Ariel pressed her hand to the bathroom door. A chill racing up her spine told her something inside Shane had gone cold.

Either he was lying or he truly didn't remember. And Ariel didn't know which was worse.

And what had he been about to ask her?

Her mind whirled back to him staring at the picture of Tara. Of how there was another body on a beach, only this time, it wasn't his sister.

Chapter Forty-Seven

Miranda

11:49 a.m.

"Pick up," Miranda screamed into the phone, swiping her coffee mug into the sink, where it shattered.

The line went straight to voicemail. *Again.*

Miranda's long fingernails tapped nervously on the counter. She had called Ben's ex-wife at least three times now with no answer. Why wouldn't she pick up?

The dishwasher popped open with a musical note. The audacity of the machine telling her it was time to empty it, as if she didn't have more pressing matters.

That didn't stop her from calling again, over and over. She wasn't going to stop until the bitch picked up. She needed to make an effort to locate her husband, and the fact that his ex-wife wasn't answering the phone was fucking irritating.

Miranda had never really thought of herself as a jealous person. She, in fact, liked sharing quite often. But there was something about his ex—the shared history, the life they built together that she couldn't emulate—that made her angry.

On the ninth try, the bitch picked up.

"Where is Ben?" Miranda ground out.

There was silence on the other end of the phone. But she knew she was there.

"Answer me! Is he there with you?"

There was a heavy sigh on the other end of the phone, as if Jennifer just couldn't handle the drama of Miranda's call. What an annoying little bitch. No wonder Ben had been thinking about asking for full custody of their kids. He didn't want to have to deal with her nasty attitude. Just like Miranda was right now. What she wouldn't do to have this woman out of their life forever.

"You sound upset," Jennifer said, her voice syrupy and smooth. The implication being: Miranda never could handle anything on her own. "Jamie's not here, Miranda."

Jamie. God, why did she insist on calling him by his childhood nickname? The way Jennifer spoke—like Miranda was a child who had done something stupid, that she was a child calling to see if Benny could come out and play, mocking her through her tone—made Miranda grip the counter so hard she snapped a nail. She let out a little cry of pain as her nail cracked down to the nail bed.

"What's going on?" Jennifer had the audacity to ask. "Seemed like quite a party last night."

Miranda stuck her bloody finger into her mouth, sucking away the rustic, metallic taste.

"Hello? Miranda? What's going on? Where is he?"

"If I knew where he was, do you think I would've called *you*?" Miranda seethed into the phone. "You're the last person I've ever wanted to call."

There was that sigh again—the one that made Miranda feel like a toddler having a tantrum, and the almighty ex was summoning all the patience in her body just to deal with her.

"Well, I have no idea where he is, Miranda. But if I were you, I would check his office."

"Do you think I haven't already done that? As I said, you're the very last person I would want to call. He's not anywhere."

There was silence again on the line. A heavy silence that seemed to permeate every pore in Miranda's body.

"I'm not sure what you want me to say," Jennifer said. There was sadness in her voice now. "I'm not his keeper, Miranda. That's your job."

Anger boiled in Miranda's chest, a red-hot flame. She wasn't anyone's keeper—and certainly not her husband's. Their marriage wasn't like that. Maybe it had been with his ex—keeping tabs on each other—but Miranda and Ben had never done such a thing. She wasn't about to start now.

She regretted calling this woman. Regretted the censure and judgment she could feel through the phone. She could practically see her face—plain, sad, bitter—as she nodded at the phone, feeling superior to Miranda.

"Forget I called," Miranda said. "He's probably just out for a run."

"He always runs when things get hard," Jennifer said with a superiority that made Miranda see red. "Some things never change."

Then the line went dead.

She knew what Jennifer was saying was ridiculous, just as much as she knew his ex on the other end of the line would think the same thing of Miranda. There was no reason for Miranda to have ever called, unless there was some sort of emergency. And Ben's disappearance—his not answering the phone, his absence from anywhere familiar—did not bode well. They both knew it.

Miranda threw her phone across the room and screamed.

She felt the sting behind her eyes and blinked hard. Not today. Weakness was a luxury for other wives. Her gaze caught on a photo of her and Ben from a New Year's party. She flipped it over, unable to stand looking at their smiling faces.

Her phone lay across the kitchen tiles, screen splintered. Let it stay there.

Frustration inside her cut so deep she thought her body might split in half. And she couldn't just stay here. It wasn't like Ben was going to come marching through the door with lattes. It had been hours since she'd woken up, and already Ariel had stopped by looking for her husband too. The fact that both men were missing made her blood run cold. Shane wasn't supposed to be missing. Ben, well, that could go either way.

Of course, Shane and Ben had fought about something on the shores of the lake the night before, but it had all been resolved after that. Hadn't it? Especially after the accident . . .

Even though the videos had been erased from the cloud, and her mind was a little fuzzy from shots, she could still see them. A blur of bodies. A scream. Her own face, twisted into something she didn't recognize. Things had not ended well, as she'd known this morning.

Maybe she should call Brad. She'd already texted Samantha and Colleen, but neither of them had answered. Not surprising.

Outside, a lawn mower roared to life. Miranda flinched. The world dared to go on like nothing had happened.

Miranda went to the bathroom to check herself. A little bit of mascara lingered at the corners of her eyes. She scrubbed at the mascara, but a faint gray shadow clung beneath her lashes. Of course it did. Even her makeup refused to behave.

She touched up her lipstick and wiped it from where it had smeared on her teeth. She swiped the lipstick from her teeth with the precision of a surgeon. Red always made her feel powerful—except now it reminded her of something else. That flash of someone shouting. A slap. The taste of something metallic on her tongue. No, that couldn't be right.

Her cheeks flushed with unease. Everything had gone according to plan, until it hadn't. And then she'd improvised. But still, if she were to look back, she'd say she got what she came for. So why was she unraveling?

She stared hard in the mirror. And then she pointed a finger at herself.

You're Miranda fucking Peterson. You don't fall apart. You make people wish they had.

There is a simple explanation to this. And the Miranda that we have embodied is going to walk out that door, get into a car and find our husband. We are not going to break. We are not going back.

Miranda straightened, holding her head high, and nodded at herself in agreement. Then she marched out to her BMW, climbed inside, the seat farther back than where she usually positioned it. Miranda adjusted the seat and grabbed the wheel—something tacky. She pulled her hand away, with what looked like flakes of dried blood now staining it.

Her breath hitched. It wasn't hers. She had no cuts. Just the weird bruise on her shoulder.

She wiped the blood against her dress and scanned the car.

Wedged between the seat and the console, she spotted a watch. She picked it up like it might burn her, the second hand still ticking. She turned it over with shaking fingers to read the inscription she'd had put there: *You know what time it is.*

Not Ben's. But it was familiar. What the fuck was it doing in her car?

She backed out of the driveway, unsure where she was going.

The sun outside mocked her with its cheerfulness, laughing at her world unraveling.

She didn't know what she'd find. But she knew how far she'd go to find it.

She'd made a vow to herself, and she wasn't going back. The only kinds of games Miranda liked were the ones where she made the rules. And if someone broke them last night—she'd rewrite them in blood and sign it *Miranda fucking Peterson.*

Chapter Forty-Eight

Jennifer

The Fifteen Commandments of a Tradwife

Fourteen: Thou shalt honor family traditions. Every blessing rehearsed, every rule obeyed, every role fulfilled in perfect order.

12:20 p.m.

The tea in Jennifer's cup was cold enough that she might have taken it from the fridge—except an hour ago, it had been steaming hot. The mug's rim left a faint circle on the counter, and her fingertips kept returning to it—as if touching that ring might summon a version of her life before all this.

Several hours had passed since she'd walked back up the dunes and climbed into her car, sand still clinging to her calves, but it felt like another lifetime. The smell of salt still clung to her clothes, to her skin, as if the shore was refusing to let her go.

After she'd thrown up, the police officer had given her a bottle of water and asked if she was okay to drive. Jennifer couldn't get out of there fast enough.

Next to the teacup was her phone. The phone she had hoped would ring with news of Jamie's appearance.

Her blood ran cold, chilling her to the core, because the only call she'd gotten so far had sucked the marrow from her bones. She had never spoken to Jamie's new wife on the phone before. She didn't even know Miranda had her number. But when the caller ID had popped up and she hadn't recognized the number, she refused to answer—watching as the person called her over and over again.

On the ninth ring, she finally answered. Miranda's voice had been angry. Accusatory. As if Jamie would've ever stepped foot in her house again in any sort of romantic fashion—or whatever it was Miranda thought was going on.

Jamie had rebranded himself using his full name, Benjamin, when he had returned from the city with a new wife. He had metamorphosized into Benjamin the mayor after dumping her, and now he was clearly missing. And the questions she'd had at the beach, the accusatory glances of the police officers and now this phone call led Jennifer to one conclusion: It had to be Jamie's body on that beach. Miranda's husband. Jennifer's ex-husband. The father of her children.

And so, her tea sat cold—as cold as the blood running in her veins—as her mind whirled, trying to stitch together a night and morning already unraveling in her head. Was it fate that she'd been called to the beach that morning by some strange desire to listen to the sounds of the surf, to feel the sun on her face? Was she meant to discover Jamie's body? Except it wasn't Jamie whom she'd seen in the bushes. That was clear. Whoever had been hiding in the bushes must be the one responsible for his disappearance. Possibly his death.

The sneakers she'd worn on the beach sat by the front door, sand spilling onto the floor she'd cleaned the day before.

Her finger played over the keys of her phone, and she nearly called Miranda back sixteen different times before exiting out of the phone app. She didn't want to speak to that woman. Miranda had only ever been unkind to her, for some strange reason. Whatever Jamie—now Benjamin—had told her about their marriage. Or maybe it was that he wanted to keep Miranda in the dark. Didn't want Miranda to find out what marriage with Ben—or Jamie—was really like. Except with his new wife, he seemed like a changed man.

She'd seen Miranda marching around the grocery store, having tea in town, walking or running around the lake; she embodied everything that Jamie had ever wanted in a wife. Beautiful. In shape. The best hostess. The best baker of bread. A woman he could have on his arm. Who made him feel powerful and special. After four kids, those were some of the things that Jennifer just couldn't supply him with anymore. And it didn't matter how much he tried to punish her for it—she just didn't have the energy to pull forth.

The town still called Jennifer "the mayor's ex" like it was a job title. No one mentioned the years she'd held everything together. One of the tradwives had once handed her a fruit spritzer in a wineglass at a PTA gala and called her "the practice wife" under her breath. That was the last gala Jennifer went to.

Yet she felt freer without Jamie than she had with him, even if she was struggling to make ends meet.

If it really was Jamie who'd been found on the beach, her whole life—and her children's lives—was about to change. She didn't know what it meant. The new uncertainty layered over the last like bruises that never faded. Her heart pounded against her ribs, her palms were damp with sweat and her breathing grew labored. This was a panic attack. She was fairly certain. She'd had many of them after the divorce, when she hadn't known how the hell she was going to survive.

Her vision pinholed, and she pressed her hands to the coolness of the counter, hoping to ground herself in real time. Bile rose up the back of her throat, sharp and acrid. She swallowed it down, forcing herself to breathe in through her nose and out of her mouth.

Perhaps worst of all was what she would tell her children when the news broke. They would be devastated. And she would be devastated for them. Athena had once slept in her closet for a week after Jamie moved out, convinced her stuffed animals couldn't breathe without him there. Jamie might have been a terrible husband, but he cared about his kids. And his kids loved him. And their whole lives had already been upended with the split. With his new marriage. Two houses.

She should spend this time trying to figure out if it was him—calling the hospital to see if his body had been brought in. But after talking to Miranda on the phone, there was every chance that his wife was going to be the one who did that. And it really wasn't Jennifer's place anymore. She just had to sit tight and wait. But how do you wait when your body is bracing for a verdict?

The only thing scarier in this life than Jamie having breath was the idea that the police were blaming her for his lack of it. They clearly thought she was a suspect. She'd been on the beach at the same time a body was found. She'd called, saying she'd found a body, and it wasn't in the same place. Would they think that had been some sort of distraction she was trying to concoct?

What if she was being framed somehow? Her fingerprints found on evidence she had no idea was planted? Maybe she was meant to find the body. But who would have known she was going to the beach this morning? She hadn't told a soul.

Maybe she needed a lawyer. Or maybe the body on the gurney wasn't Jamie at all. Maybe, in fact, it was someone else altogether, and all of this was just some big mystery that would be easily solved very soon.

Her mind flashed to that body bag being lifted into the ambulance. The lumps beneath the black fabric. From where she'd been standing, it was hard to tell if it was Jamie's shape. And perhaps the fact that she hadn't immediately known it was the shape of Jamie—a body she'd lain next to for over a decade—was a good sign.

Or maybe she was just delusional.

Then she remembered the argument she'd heard the night before across Echo Lake. The party at Jamie and Miranda's house. The recording on her phone.

And she was glad she hadn't deleted it.

This time, she wasn't going to stay quiet.

Chapter Forty-Nine

Ariel

12:43 p.m.

Ariel was in the barn, mucking cow stalls, when Shane walked in. He'd been avoiding her since he'd gotten home. Or maybe it was the other way around. And actually, it was quite fitting that she was cleaning up shit given what he was about to tell her. She could tell by the look on his face—anguish pulling at his eyes and a downturn of his lips—the one that said *brace yourself.*

"What is it?"

"I've done something." He used to sneak in behind her just to kiss her neck, once spinning her in circles in this very stall.

Now she flinched when his shadow crossed the stall.

Ariel wasn't certain that she wanted to hear whatever it was he had to say. There'd been so much shit going on in town lately. The way he'd come home. A body discovered on the beach. People missing. She pressed the brush into the cement. This was the worst part of the day. The stink. The weight. The scraping. And now Shane had brought more of it, just in a different form.

Another pile she'd have to bury. Another stink she'd never get out from under her nails.

"I'm not sure I want to hear it," she said. She was honest in her words, probably for the first time in forever. If he didn't say what it was he needed to confess, then did it happen? If she didn't know, then she couldn't say. She couldn't think about it. She couldn't be questioned about it. She wouldn't feel the guilt for years to come of knowing something terrible and remaining silent, unlike she had for Tara.

Shane ran his hands through his hair and stared at her, his eyes bloodshot.

"Ariel, please. I need to say it." One of the cows snorted behind her.

"You might need to say it," she said, "but I don't think I need to hear it. I know what you're going to say, and I'd rather not be involved."

He stepped closer to her, his hand wrapping around hers on the handle of the mucker. She stilled the scraping of the muck to stare up at him. She'd never challenged him before, always agreeing to everything he said. But in this moment, she felt the need to protect herself. To protect what she knew. To protect her children. Life was so much simpler when she was shoveling actual crap, and not just metaphorically.

A rustling in the rafters, a bird swooping down to peck at something on the barn floor.

"Ariel, I did something, and you need to know."

The way he stared at her, she was fairly certain she was not going to escape without hearing his confession. She let go of the mucker and took a deep breath, backing away from Shane to sit down on a hay bale.

"What is it, then?"

She was simultaneously disappointed in herself and resigned to his demands.

"I hurt someone."

"I figured as much." Her voice was flat when she said it, and she avoided eye contact, instead focusing on the center of his forehead, on the freckle that seemed to be a target. Now would be a good time to tell him the truth about herself too.

He crouched in front of her, his elbows resting on his knees, hands folded, his eyes on hers. The pale skin of his bare wrist visible without his watch. She remembered that watch sitting on the counter this morning. Or had that been yesterday? She wasn't sure anymore. Time had been leaking ever since.

"It's Ben."

Ariel nodded, feeling like she might throw up. Her stomach squeezed and squeezed, bile rising up her throat. Yep, she was going to lose it. She shoved Shane, who fell back in the muck as she ran outside to throw up next to the barn.

At the rate she was going, she'd be lucky if she kept anything down for the next year. She was wiping away the bile from her lips with the back of her sleeve when Shane came out of the barn.

"We got into a fight," he said. "He told me something . . . about Tara."

What did Ben tell him? Did he say anything about how Ariel had been there?

Ariel knew they shouldn't have gone to the party. The moment she'd felt weird, they should've just gone home. Now this was what happened. If he had just listened to her—

"What . . . did you do?" Her voice came out sounding a little choked.

Shane just looked at her as if she already knew what he was going to say. And what had he done? Killed Ben for retribution? Two wrongs didn't make a right.

Would he make her keep this quiet? He was the man of the house. The leader of their family. The patriarch. And she was simply to fall in line. Not to ever voice her own desires or expect anything from what she wanted.

"Ariel," he said, drawing out her name.

"No," she said, shaking her head. "I can't. I told you I didn't want to hear this. And you forced the issue on me anyway. I'm going inside."

She pushed past him toward the house, wanting the safety of her children around her, the lightness, the buttery yellow of her kitchen. Sunlight would streak across the white cabinets, casting long, accusatory shadows.

If he'd been willing to kill Ben for his part in Tara's death, then what would he do to her?

The scent of fresh-baked bread would cocoon her inside the house. As if somehow baking was going to save her from this moment. Her husband had murdered someone. At least, that's what it felt like. And now the floor of her life was beginning to tilt. Their lives as they knew it were over. And all because of a stupid fucking party.

She could hardly breathe as she stepped into the facade of safety—the safety of her foyer. She wasn't sure what she was thinking. Her fingers gripped the doorknob, numb. It felt like she was watching someone else lock the door. She used to call him in for supper with the same hand that turned the lock against him now.

She watched Shane's advance, knowing that any second, he was going to bang on the door for admittance. Now that he'd confessed to her, did that mean that he was going to kill her too?

She backed away from the door, watching Shane's approach. He pressed his hand to the glass of the door but didn't bang on it like she'd expected. She'd once trusted the shape of his shadow in the dark. Now it moved like a stranger.

"I don't want to hear it—"

"Ariel, what do you think I did?"

She shook her head, not wanting to put voice to the words. As if saying them aloud would make them real. And how could they be? Shane was not a violent man. He was blind sometimes, stubborn, but never cruel . . . And yet, people snapped all the time. And Tara had been his twin. Whether spoken aloud or internally, the word still meant the same thing. *Murder.* Her husband was a murderer.

"You need to go to the police," she said through the glass, feeling the presence of her children in the house. She couldn't risk their safety. "You can't come inside."

Shane did slap the door then. His palm slid down the glass like he was smearing her version of events away.

"This is my house," he said, the threat evident in his voice. "You will open the door, and you will let me inside."

"You killed someone," she whispered. The words weren't loud enough for Shane to have heard, but he clearly recognized the shape of her mouth through the glass.

"Killed someone? I didn't kill anyone, Ariel. But I know who did." Was he talking about Tara or the body found this morning?

For half a second, she wanted to believe him. And that half second made her sick.

She thought of his bare wrist. The watch left behind. Given to him by his sister for his birthday before she died. The tick of what was missing—and what couldn't be undone.

Ariel shook her head. She couldn't let him in. She didn't know if she could believe him, or if she should call the police. If he hit the door a second time she'd call 911.

She heard the soft slap of bare feet before she heard the voice. "Mommy? Why is Daddy outside?"

She turned slowly, pinning a smile in place that didn't reach her eyes.

Protect. Protect.

Behind her, her child.

In front of her, the man who might tear their world apart.

"You were there, Ariel. Now let me in."

And she did.

Later that night, Ariel sat on the edge of her bathtub, staring at the gash along her forearm.

Shane's voice echoed again in her head: *You tried to help. You screamed. You were there.* Her memories from last night and from thirteen years ago blurred—splashes, shouting, the sound of Colleen's voice . . .

The pier. The lake. The beach.

Miranda's trunk. Open. A rolled-up towel soaked with red. The weight of someone being lifted.

Ariel's own hands trembling, dirty, useless.

She didn't remember the whole story. Only the bits and pieces Shane had told her. And that made her complicit. Guilty.

Again.

Chapter Fifty

Miranda

2:56 p.m.

Miranda jumped when her cell phone buzzed beside her on the counter. The caller ID made her blood run cold.

Crystal Harbor Police Department.

There were only two reasons that they'd be calling. One: they had found Ben dead. Two: they had found Ben alive.

Either way, he wasn't coming home.

She should have gone with them to make sure everything went as planned.

She blew out a shaky breath and pressed the green button to answer, putting it on speaker, since she didn't trust her hands to hold the phone against her head.

"Hello?"

"Mrs. Peterson?"

"This is she." Miranda was unable to keep the slight tremble from her voice. Things were either going according to plan or not.

Well, according to Plan B. This was not how last night was supposed to end. But she supposed the tremble on this call, which was probably being recorded, would be good for future reference in her defense.

"Mrs. Peterson, we've got your husband here at the station."

Not dead. "Oh my goodness, is he okay? Was he in an accident?"

"He's perfectly healthy," the deputy said. "He's phoned a lawyer and asked that you come to the station."

Miranda frowned. "Requested a lawyer? For what?"

"It would be best if you came down here to discuss that with him."

Miranda's insides bristled. She didn't want to go down to the station. "Of course. Does he need me to bring anything?"

"Not sure what you mean, ma'am."

"Right." Miranda nodded. Because a man behind bars couldn't accept anything.

Miranda hung up the phone and stared down at the little pooch. Was that a mocking joy in the dog's eyes? "Shall I drop you at the pound on the way?"

Snow took off running toward Ben's home office.

"You can run but you can't hide," Miranda muttered. She fixed herself up and then forced herself to get in the car.

It took a lot to shock Miranda. After the life she'd lived, the things she'd seen. But today she was genuinely shocked at her revenge coming together so beautifully. And the shock of what she saw before her was stunning.

She was at the police station, sitting behind a pane of glass, Benjamin on the other side. The station smelled like bleach and betrayal, like someone trying to scrub the truth out of tile grout.

The air-conditioning blasted like punishment, humming over the fluorescent lights. Even the chairs looked guilty.

She hadn't yet picked up the telephone to speak to her husband on the other side of the glass. She wasn't sure she wanted to. When she got the call to come to the station—that Ben was alive—she'd been filled with relief. Until the cops had questioned her for over an hour. But Miranda had played dumb, batted her eyes, and left the police with nothing but garbage to scribble on their notepads.

There'd been a few seconds before the officer told her Ben was alive when she was pretty sure Shane had killed him. After all, the argument on the surveillance cameras at the back of their house had been loud and clear.

Ben telling Shane he knew what happened to Tara. Describing in detail what happened that summer.

She was only glad Ben was alive because his death wasn't part of the plan, and she didn't want Shane to be in trouble. Ben had been arrested. For murder. The word was sweet on her tongue.

Even if Ben hadn't killed Colleen, he had been part of the reason Tara was dead. Didn't try to save her. Might as well burn.

Sitting here under annoying fluorescent lights, she was surprised at the twist in her stomach filled with hunger for food and freedom. Not even an ounce of guilt. The idea that she could start over . . . It wasn't comforting. It was thrilling. And that, maybe, was the real sin.

For anyone else, this would be a nightmare. But for her, revenge tasted like freedom, like champagne. Finally, no more pretending.

Ben indicated for her to pick up the phone, his face pleading. And for a second, she was reminded of how much fun she'd had pretending to be his wife and taking down the assholes of the town.

The hands he used to cup her face with now rested limp and cuffed in his lap. Good. He deserved it. She rubbed at the bruise on her shoulder, a silent reminder to him of his transgressions.

The phone was slick in her hand, the mouthpiece still warm from the last desperate caller. Across the glass, Ben's prison shirt was wrinkled, sweat-dark under the arms. The smell of him—cedarwood and salt—rose unbidden in her memory and made her stomach twist further. His breath on the other end sent warmth through her that she fought against.

Then she sat, holding her breath, feeling herself crack down the middle. *Hold it together. Just a little longer.*

"Miranda, I'm so sorry." He shook his head. There was such thick emotion in his voice, he sounded as if he were being strangled by the telephone cord itself. "I never meant for this to happen," he said. "It was just a party."

Miranda knew it was never *just* a party. And she didn't feel the least bit of remorse at having been the one to set it up. To put all the players into motion. She didn't make Ben confess to Shane, although that had been delicious icing on the cake, to watch Shane deck him. And now Ben had a black eye for his follies. Soon he'd have more. From what Miranda had learned, men who picked on women were often on the receiving end in lockup.

Colleen had been found on the beach, where Miranda had instructed Ben and Shane and Ariel to put her. Her body near the waves. A watery grave, just like Tara's. Lake or ocean, didn't matter. Water was water. Colleen's legs would have been wet from the tide, as if the ocean had tried to take her back. Her hair, perhaps, full of sand and secrets. Secrets that she'd keep forever in her watery grave.

Ben's sandals, with a little bit of Colleen's blood on them, would have been found, too, putting him at the scene.

Colleen's head showed signs of blunt force trauma, bone protruding through her split skin from where she'd fallen getting in the middle of Shane and Ben's fight. They would think they killed her. But the thing was, she was already dead. Miranda had taken care of that. If the medical examiner looked close enough, he'd see the tiniest pinprick in Colleen's neck. A deadly dose of fentanyl on a toxicology screen, which with Colleen's background of abuse they'd assume she'd self-administered.

Ariel had been screaming the whole time, just like she had the night Tara died.

"Miranda, talk to me," Ben said.

She wanted to ask him what happened, to see how much he remembered. But there were too many people listening right now. Miranda cocked her head, watching him. She wanted to tell him to stop calling her that. To use her real name. But she needed to play Miranda for a little while longer. "I don't know what to say. I don't know what possessed you."

Possessed him. Possession—that was what it was always about, wasn't it? No one was ever in their right mind. Especially when they were all hyped up.

"Say you forgive me," Ben said.

Miranda scoffed. "Forgive you? For what? For taking someone's life? Or for ruining *ours*?" The bitterness in her tone was etched on his face. The stupid idiot was actually buying her act.

"All of it." He shook his head, tears gathering in his eyes, and wiped his hand over his face. "Was Shane arrested too?"

"I don't know. They just called me down here to talk to you. I didn't even know you had been arrested." She made a show of sadly shaking her head, as if she were so disappointed.

"I'm innocent."

The way Ben said it—the way he looked at her—she knew he was lying. He actually believed he'd killed Colleen. And he was starting the precedent now. If he could lie to her and she could believe him, then maybe he could get a jury to see past the truth as well.

Except for the evidence she'd planted that put him solidly at the crime scene.

Miranda rolled her eyes. "Don't try to play mind games with me, Ben. Don't you remember? *I'm* the master. I hope you rot in hell. Or just here."

She stood and hung up.

It was time for her to start a new life, she supposed. There really wasn't an option to go back to who she used to be. The survivor. The queen with bloodless hands. They would start to dig into her past. She had enough buried secrets and skeletons in her closet that didn't need to be set free.

The first thing she was going to do was to drop his silly dog off at the pound. Maybe. The little rat was kind of growing on her.

On her way out of the police station, she saw Shane and Ariel sitting in the waiting area. Ariel looked as though she'd been crying. The poor girl always looked better with a little mascara smudged. Tragedy suited her. Miranda almost pitied her. Almost.

Ariel might have shouted for help, but in the end, she didn't go get it.

Shane looked a bit worse for wear. Not as solid and stoic as she remembered. When Ariel looked at her, she gave her such a glare—such a look of blame. She'd always known Ariel didn't have the stomach for this town. Miranda's gaze slid to a jagged, fresh cut on Ariel's arm, which Ariel moved quickly to cover, tugging at her sleeve that had ridden up. She'd fallen on the beach last night, when she'd tried to revive Colleen.

Miranda walked up to them, eyes on Shane, and pulled his watch from her purse. "You left this behind."

Shane glanced up at her, a flicker of recognition in his eyes. "My sister gave me that watch."

"Tara, right?" Miranda said.

Shane swallowed, squinting his eyes up at her. "Yeah."

"Ben's going down for Colleen. And Colleen, well, I heard she's the one who pushed Tara in the water." Miranda shrugged. "Karma's a bitch."

Shane glanced at his wife, who nodded.

"See you two around."

Freedom was almost hers. All Miranda had to do was walk out the double doors and feel the sunshine on her face.

The house. The bank account—all of it was going to be hers, thanks to Ben's ironclad prenup. That little coffee meeting she'd had with Beth had been enlightening.

She could almost laugh at how Ben thought he had the upper hand with the whole baby thing. That the prenup was meant to protect him. And all he had to do was not commit a crime. And why would he? He was the mayor.

She caught her reflection in the glass as she pushed open the door: unbothered, impeccable. The Queen of Chaos, still standing. If the news cameras showed up, she already had a statement rehearsed. But the parking lot was surprisingly empty.

Miranda drew in a deep breath through her nose, letting her face tilt up toward the sun. Breathing in the scent of jasmine from the row of bushes at odds with the stark stucco building.

When she'd been a girl, she'd always known she was meant for greatness. Until the night her life had almost been ripped away.

And now, it would appear, she finally had what she needed.

Freedom. Money. A passport. If she wanted to travel the world when this was over, she could. If she wanted to go back to New York, she could.

But there was just something about this Florida sun that made her want to stay right here in Crystal Harbor, the place where she'd been born. The place where she'd been Tara.

Chapter Fifty-One

Jennifer

The Fifteen Commandments of a Tradwife

> **Fifteen:** Thou shalt love thy husband and children fiercely. Stand by them, protect them—and guard them from truths they may never need to know. Unless your husband is a murderer.

Three months later . . .

Jennifer sat down heavily on her couch, her dog beside her, staring down at the threadbare rug over the foot-worn wood of her floor. The couch cushions sighed beneath her like an exhausted ally. A candle burned on the end table, a defiant attempt to claim serenity. The candle smelled like vanilla and forgiveness—the latter of which was hard to offer.

After finding out from Miranda, of all people, what had happened to Jamie—and Colleen—she'd turned her TikTok back on full force. Jennifer wasn't going to hold back from sharing her message. People needed to know what happened when wives followed rules that were stifling and archaic. And Jamie couldn't stop her now.

And she was glad she did. One woman in Tennessee stitched her latest video with tears in her eyes. *This saved me*, she said.

Her following had grown exponentially over the last few months, and she posted daily messages, encompassing the good and the bad. Her phone still trembled from the last live video she'd done—comments flying up the screen faster than her heart could follow. She wasn't there to harp on women who chose a certain way of life. She was only there to share a message—a warning to women who didn't protect themselves.

She stared at the cell phone in her hand, replaying in her mind the phone call she'd just had. An editor from a publishing house. They wanted her to write a book.

They were willing to pay her a lot of money for it too. An exorbitant amount. Not that she necessarily needed it. After Ben's arrest, Miranda had called her to let her know what she'd written into the prenup. Apparently, if Ben had committed a crime, Miranda got everything. But there was a provision for the children. If his estate ever went into some sort of criminal escrow—or whatever it was, Jennifer wasn't exactly sure; she wasn't a lawyer, after all—the assets would be frozen, but the money Ben had put into a trust for the kids was safe.

Jennifer had tried to ask Miranda exactly what happened that night, but Miranda had lied through her teeth, saying, "I was *asleep*, Jennifer. Can you imagine waking up to that kind of betrayal in your own home? I've done everything I can for that man. If he did something terrible, I'm as much a victim as anyone. What matters is that Ben is where he belongs, darling. Let's not dig up the past—it's so terribly unflattering, don't you think?"

And so, even though she knew it for a lie since she had heard Miranda that night, Jennifer had let the matter drop. Especially because Miranda had figured out a way to give her Ben's money up front. And maybe it had something to do with the little flash drive Jennifer had given to Miranda. Maybe not. With him behind bars, she had no use for the information—though Miranda would never know she'd made a copy to keep just for insurance.

Jennifer hadn't even known Ben had so much money, though she suspected as much. During the divorce, he'd hired a slick lawyer who basically gave her pennies on the dollar each month for child support. It was highway robbery. But now she had a fat bank account for her children, which she, in turn, had also used to set up trust funds for their college.

She stared down at the Post-it where she'd jotted down a note during the phone call. The tackiness of the back of the sticky note stuck to her finger.

She stared at the paper like it might detonate. Seven figures. For her story. It was more money than she'd ever had. More than she ever thought she was allowed to imagine.

Ben's money had given her the confidence to speak out. When another mother scolded her daughter on the playground, Jennifer swooped in fast—eyes blazing, voice like a whip. "We don't talk to girls like that," she said, shielding her child with her whole body.

She joked once on a live video that she was going to write a book. The comments had lit up. Now there was no more joke. She was going to write a book that would expose tradwives and the circles they lived in. Stress the importance of breaking free, of speaking out when something bad happened.

Jennifer had gotten off the phone with the editor in New York after telling her she needed to think about it. But even as her finger had hovered over the red end-call button, she'd already made up her mind.

She was going to write this book. She was going to share her story, the stories of the other wives. Let it be a warning to women who thought they were being cared for by their husbands. Let it be a warning to women who believed their subservience would get them closer to heaven.

Closer to safety.

To security.

When, in fact, it was doing the opposite.

A notification popped up in her messages. A memorial for Colleen. Jennifer wasn't going to go. She'd not spoken to Colleen since that awkward conversation in the parking lot. And it was Colleen's son Scotty who'd told Craig Jennifer was a bitch.

Besides, Jennifer couldn't decide if it was a fitting end or not. Colleen, after all, wasn't innocent. Then again, neither was Jennifer.

There had been some initial skepticism about the cause of death. Blunt force trauma to the head, surprisingly, not drowning. Toxicology reports showed there were drugs in Colleen's system too. But ultimately, Jamie's shoes at the scene solidified what had happened. Not to mention Shane and Ariel had come forward as witnesses. That they'd tried to stop it. That they had little memory of anything else from the night except Jamie shouting, Colleen screaming.

So, no one would ever really know what had happened on that beach. They would only know the end result. That a woman had lost her life.

That a man was behind bars.

That the entire town had changed.

Children had lost their mother.

People had lost their friends.

There was speculation, however. Samantha, who was a crime fanatic, had been giving every crime podcast on earth an interview, until an anonymous caller phoned into one of the live tapings to ask what Samantha knew about Tara Olsen's death in 2013. Weird.

The current theory on Colleen's death perpetuated by amateur sleuths was that a fight broke out on the shore of Echo Lake. Colleen had tried to intervene, at which point Jamie had hit her—hard. Apparently, she'd gone down, face first, in the lake and drowned. By the time the two men stopped fighting and realized what had happened, it was too late. Except there was no water in her lungs.

Ariel had watched it all unfold, and hadn't tried to stop them, which was odd but explained away by a strong interaction of her medications with alcohol, which everyone professed not to have imbibed.

Later, the three of them—Jamie, Shane and Ariel—had put Colleen into Miranda's trunk and driven across the inlet road to the oceanside beach to stage Colleen's death. Ariel, cutting her arm on a broken shell, had gone home, distraught. It sounded like a soapy crime show—but maybe that was because soapy crime shows sell. And also, because sometimes the truth does.

After staging the drowning, Jamie, freaked out, had hopped into Miranda's car and gone home. Shane, hyped up on something, had hidden in the bushes. At some point in the early morning hours, Jamie was certain he'd be arrested and had left his house only to be picked up by police in the next town over.

No one mentioned Colleen's part in Tara's death, perhaps thinking the truth was better left where it had buried them both.

Jennifer wasn't sure if she believed any of it. Seemed too clean-cut and weird. And so many details were missing. She didn't know if the theory was true, not really. But it was the one that made the most sense. And maybe the scariest part was how plausible it sounded. Like it could've happened to anyone.

At the trial, Jennifer saw Miranda at the courthouse. Not in designer heels this time, but flats. Her hair pulled tight. Looking very demure. A victim of her husband, like poor Colleen. No one had dared speak to her. And she hadn't looked at anyone either. No one had seen her since. Jennifer had kept watch on Jamie's lake house. There was the occasional flicker of a shadow, but for now it appeared the queen had no kingdom.

Miranda had vanished from public view—but not from the story. Her fingerprints were still everywhere, like smudges on glass. Just subtle enough to miss, just sharp enough to cut.

Shane and Ariel were also quiet. Both of them having taken a plea deal in exchange for a confession. There was still so much speculation. But Jennifer had read the police report. Shane had finally told them everything about that night. That he'd been part of the fight. That Colleen had tried to pull Jamie off him. That Jamie had shoved her, and she went down. That Shane froze. That Ariel had seen what happened, too, and tried to help Colleen. Her voice cracked when she spoke to the detective, Jennifer had been told. But she told the truth. And that truth—two messy, shattered versions of it—was enough to put Jamie away.

And now she'd never have him threaten her again. Never have to hear him tell her to be quiet. So yes, she was going to take the book deal. For the women who couldn't—or wouldn't—stand up for themselves. For their daughters, who might grow up to be just like them. For the women who wanted out.

When Jamie had first told her he wanted a divorce, she'd thought her entire life was over. At the time, she'd been completely devastated. And she still was sometimes.

Mostly for her children.

But now, she realized what a gift it had been. The freedom to choose a different path. The freedom to help save other women.

And she wasn't an advocate for divorce—unless it was necessary. She still wanted to find love. To marry a man who respected her as an equal partner. Did a man like that exist?

She liked to think so.

Love was unconditional. Love was kind. Love was sharing and taking care of one another.

These were the things she wanted for herself. For her daughters. For her sons.

"Mommy, what's fu—"

Jennifer glanced up to see Dominic standing behind Craig, his hand over his mouth and a grimace on his face. *This is what safety feels like. Not marble countertops or curated marriages. But my children. Moments like this.*

"Don't say it," Dominic said.

"Oh boy. Did we learn another word at school today?"

Craig nodded behind his brother's hold.

"Scotty?"

Dominic and Craig both nodded at this. Jennifer opened her arms, and the boys came running, tossing themselves against her, all pointy elbows and knees.

Yes. Love was unconditional. And some part of her would always love Jamie for giving her the only thing he ever did right. The rest she was happy to leave behind.

And if telling the truth meant never being invited to another bake sale again, so be it.

She knew exactly what the title of her book would be. *Tradwife.* And she would write it without apology. If just one more woman left before it was too late, then maybe—just maybe—it would be worth it.

Chapter Fifty-Two

Tara

One year later . . .

The same moon as last year hung over Echo Lake, cold and complicit. I liked that it was midnight, exactly one year later. Death deserved precision.

I poured a crisp glass of pinot grigio and carried it to the couch. The automatic shades had sealed off every inch of glass. I'd been waiting all year for this.

With the flat of my palm, I patted the cushion beside me. Snow leapt up and curled into my lap, trembling slightly as if she, too, could sense the shift in the air. I almost laughed. After all those years of despising the dog, here I was, grateful for the company. The skittish little twat made a decent companion. Better yet, she alerted me to every sound, a built-in alarm system with soft ears and sharp instincts.

In the silence of my home, where I lived alone with the dog and my ghosts, no one judged the wine in my hand. Being a dog-mom was so much better than being a tradwife.

No one clutched pearls or froze behind painted, lip-filler smiles when I reached for the remote.

And pressed play.

The video.

The surveillance footage.

The truth.

I took a long, slow sip as the black-and-white figures flickered onto the screen.

The angle captured the bottom of the steps leading from the back garden to the sandy shore of Echo Lake, bathed in the hazy glow of motion lights. Shane and Ben were already at it—arguing, volatile. Me, Ariel, Colleen—each trying, failing, to keep the peace. Shane shoved Ben. Ben raised a fist. At the same moment Ariel stumbled forward, delirious, colliding with me, who, shoved against Colleen, took the opportunity to stick her with a needle I'd had in my pocket all night.

Colleen staggered directly into Ben's swinging fist. She crumpled to the ground with a sickening grunt, her head cracking on a rock. Ariel cried out, sinking to her knees, and I slinked away.

The men kept fighting. As if Colleen weren't motionless on the ground with Ariel trying to revive her.

An eye for an eye, bitch. Colleen killed me, and I killed her back.

I hadn't planned for anyone to be there when I jabbed her, but it actually worked out better that way. Who knew?

On-screen, I'd slipped back inside and watched the rest from the window.

The scene outside shifted. The men, breathless, wide-eyed. Ariel wailing that Colleen was dead—that Ben had done it.

Then, confusion. Quiet panic. The three of them whispering, frantic, as they lifted Colleen's limp body.

The video cut to the garage, missing the part where I gave them directions on how to dispose of Colleen away from the house. Ben pried open my car's trunk. Shane hauled the corpse inside. Ariel trembled, watching it all with her fist pressed to her mouth.

Static. Then: the driveway. My car pulled away, Ben behind the wheel. Shane beside him. Ariel in her own vehicle, trailing behind.

I tsked softly, watching the figures on-screen flee the scene, half dazed and wholly stupid. I took another long sip of my wine. Snow licked the condensation from the side of the glass, eager to join the ritual.

Another cut. My car returned—Ben alone at the wheel. Then Ben running, from the truth or himself. Who gave a fuck? Certainly not I.

I'd saved myself. Again.

I smiled, slow and sharp, and poured another glass of wine. Snow shivered again, as if she knew the house remembered too. I'd had a lot of fun here. Stealing Jennifer's husband and framing him for murder, tormenting Ariel into thinking she had a stalker, ruining Samantha with that anonymous call to the podcast when she thought she was so special, and Brad, well, he'd never lived down that photo; Kennedy divorced him.

It was a beautiful thing, I thought, to be so very clever—and walk away clean. No wonder they had all done the same thing after they watched me die.

Chapter Fifty-Three

Body on the Beach

Summer 2013 . . .

I wake on the lakeshore beach, coughing water so hard I think my insides will come out. Everything hurts.

The sun is rising. But the moon is still out. The tide is gentle. The silence isn't.

I lie there, letting the water lap at my bare feet, up my bare legs. The sand clings to my skin, and a thatch of lake weed tangles around my calf. The cold sinks deep into my spine.

I feel like I'm dead. But I'm not.

I expect to hear sirens. An ambulance called to fetch me. But all is quiet, as if the lake has swallowed me and spit me out in a different dimension. An upside-down world.

My forehead throbs, and I reach to touch the spot, feeling where my skin has split deep. My fingers come away bloody.

How long have I been in the water? How did I not drown?

Maybe the better question is, why hasn't anyone called for help?

I roll over, my lungs still burning from sucking in lake water, and stare at the sky. Colleen tried to kill me. There are witnesses, I can still see them. Brad, Samantha, Jennifer, Jamie and Ariel. But the pier is empty. No one even standing on the shore. No voices calling for me. No one came to my rescue. No one called 911?

I close my eyes to the morning sky, trying to remember everything that happened. The pictures. Colleen's vicious taunts. I can go to the police. But they will just say I was drunk or high, or just another girl who asked for it.

I don't care so much what people say about me, but Shane will be ashamed. He'll never live it down. All the careful plans he's made for himself will be destroyed because of me. I can't let that happen.

Tara needs to stay dead.

I reach for the necklace at my throat, the one Shane gave me for my birthday, and I rip it off, throwing it as far as I can into the lake, watching the ripples swallow it whole.

I stand on shaky legs, staring down the lake toward the pier, imagining I can see Colleen standing there, surrounded by her asshole friends. This isn't the end, but a beginning. Colleen will pay. They all will.

I'll make sure of it—but not as Tara. Tara is gone.

Someone else has risen in her place.

Acknowledgments

Writing a book is never a solitary effort, and without the support and assistance of many wonderful people, *Tradwife* would not be the book that it is today!

I am endlessly grateful to my superhuman agent, Kevan Lyon. Thank you so much for all of your support and encouragement. I don't know how I'd do this without you!

Thank you so much to my marvelous editor, Tessa Woodward, and her assistant editor, Madelyn Blaney, at HarperCollins, for your enthusiasm and expert advice. Thank you to my fabulous copyeditor, Karen Richardson, and equally fabulous production editor, Hope Breeman. Your catches and suggestions were spot on! To all of the amazing people at HarperCollins, thank you for your support and hard work to make this book available to readers.

Thank you to my family for eating all the sourdough I made—although, really, I should say you're welcome! *winks* Just kidding. I love you guys!

Hugs and heartfelt thanks to my wonderful eldest daughter, Ashleigh Inglesby, for reading and rereading drafts of this book and being willing to brainstorm with me over and over and over and over and over again! You have such a vibrant and brilliant mind! I love you!

My thanks to my writer pal Heather Webb, who read an early draft and helped me plot where the story needed shoring up and who joined me on a writer's retreat alongside Kris Waldherr, E. Elizabeth Watson and Madeline Martin—this time at a retreat deep in the woods. These women poured me wine, offered wisdom, and gave me the push I needed to get to the end when I needed it most. Thankfully, the only drama came from the page and not the bear that was lurking nearby!

Many thanks to all of my writing buddies and agency sisters who listened to me talk about this book nonstop over glasses of wine. This wonderful community makes this job even better!

Last, but never least, my deepest thanks to you, dear readers, for reading my books. You all make a writer's world go round.

About the Author

Michelle Brandon is a pseudonym for Eliza Knight, an award-winning and *USA Today* bestselling author. A travel junkie and fan of wine, when she's not writing, she can be found lounging on the beach with a delicious book or taking a long restorative walk. Surrounded by palm trees and wild animals, she lives in the Sunshine State with her husband, daughters, one slobbery doggy, a hermit crab and a turtle named Fish.

Read more from

MICHELLE BRANDON

An irresistible, juicy contemporary novel based on the TikTok phenomenon #BamaRushTok—about four sorority sisters brought back to the top-tier house they ruled at the University of Alabama, when secrets they'd thought long buried threaten to resurface.

"Catty deliciousness—with a foundation of strong, true friendship. If reality TV did a show about sororities, Hollywood wishes it'd be this good!"

—Christi Barth,
USA Today bestselling author of *Will You (Pretend) Marry Me*